"You're a most unusual woman, Briana O'Neil," Keane said.

"I've never known a highborn woman who mingled with the servants."

"Highborn." She gave a snort of derision.

"You have to admit that the O'Neil family is far from poor."

"Aye. But it's none of my doing. We have no say over where we'll be born or how we'll be taught. What we can choose is how we'll live our lives once the decisions are in our own hands."

"And so you choose to live without boundaries."

Briana thought about it a moment. "If you mean without boundaries of wealth or poverty, aye. It isn't the coin in a man's pocket that makes him hero or knave. It's what's in his heart. His soul."

"And which do you suppose I am? Hero or knave?"

"That isn't for me to judge. You know what's in your own heart...."

Dear Reader,

Autumn is such a romantic season—fall colors, rustling leaves, big sweaters and, for many of you, the kids are back in school! So, as the leaves fall, snuggle up in a cozy chair and let us sweep you away to the romantic past!

With over thirty books to her name, bestselling author Ruth Langan knows how to bring the fantasy of falling in love to life. *Briana,* set in England and Ireland, is the final book of THE O'NEIL SAGA. It's the love story of a feisty Irish noblewoman and the lonely, tormented landowner who first saves her life—and then succumbs to her charms!

In *The Doctor's Wife,* by the popular Cheryl St.John, scandalous secrets are revealed but love triumphs when a waitress "from the other side of the tracks" marries a young doctor in need of a mother for his baby girl. *Branded Hearts* by Diana Hall is an intriguing Western about a young cowgirl bent on revenge who must fight her feelings for her boss, an enigmatic cattle rancher. Jacqueline Navin's evocative story, *Strathmere's Bride,* features a duke who suddenly finds himself the single father of his two orphaned nieces, and in dire need of a wife! But who will he choose—the proper lady or the girls' very *improper* governess?

Enjoy. And come back again next month for four more choices of the best in historical romance.

Sincerely,

Tracy Farrell
Senior Editor

P.S. We'd love to hear what you think about Harlequin Historicals! Drop us a line at:

Harlequin Historicals
300 E. 42nd Street, 6th Floor
New York, NY 10017

RUTH LANGAN

BRIANA

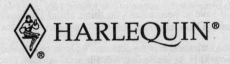

HARLEQUIN®

TORONTO • NEW YORK • LONDON
AMSTERDAM • PARIS • SYDNEY • HAMBURG
STOCKHOLM • ATHENS • TOKYO • MILAN • MADRID
PRAGUE • WARSAW • BUDAPEST • AUCKLAND

ISBN 0-373-29080-2

BRIANA

Copyright © 1999 by Ruth Ryan Langan

Books by Ruth Langan

RUTH LANGAN

traces her ancestry to Scotland and Ireland. It is no surprise, then, that she feels a kinship with the characters in her historical novels.

Married to her childhood sweetheart, she has raised five children and lives in Michigan, the state where she was born and raised.

For Nicole Brooke Langan,
the newest link in our chain of love
And for her big brother, Patrick, and her proud parents,
Pat and Randi

And for Tom, who truly founded a dynasty

Prologue

Ireland 1653

"My lord O'Neil. You must come quickly." The servant paused in the doorway of the private chambers of the lord and lady of Ballinarin. She clutched the door and choked in several deep breaths before she could find her voice to continue. "It's Briana."

At her obvious distress, Gavin O'Neil looked up in alarm. "What is it, Adina?"

"She's been wounded, my lord."

"Wounded?" Gavin's wife, Moira, was already on her feet, clutching a hand to her throat.

"Aye, mistress. At the hands of an English sword, I'm told." The servant's eyes were round with fear. "A runner came ahead with the news. Some lads from the village are carrying her across the fields."

Gavin was already strapping on his sword and striding across the room. At the door he turned and exchanged a look with his wife before taking his leave.

Moira raced after him, calling orders to the servant as she did. "We'll need hot water, Adina. And clean linens. Tell Cook to prepare an opiate for pain. And send someone to fetch my sons and their wives.''

She had to run now to keep up with her husband's impatient steps.

There was a murderous look in his eyes as he tore open the massive door leading to the courtyard. ''If those English bastards have touched one hair on her head, I'll kill every one myself.'' He had already pulled himself onto the back of a waiting horse when he spotted the procession of villagers walking slowly across the sloping lawns of Ballinarin. At the front of the line was a muscular lad carrying the motionless figure of his youngest child.

His heart nearly stopped.

''Dear God in heaven.'' He slid from the horse and crossed the distance at a run.

Seeing the lord of the manor, the villagers paused in their march, whipping the hats from their heads in respect.

''Ah. Briana. Briana.'' With a sob catching in his throat he took the limp, bloody form from the lad's hands and gathered her against his chest.

By the time Moira reached them, he was kneeling in the damp grass, rocking his child the way he had when she was a wee babe.

Rory and his wife, AnnaClaire, came racing from their rooms, with their adopted son, Innis, leading the way. Behind them came Conor and his wife, Emma. All came to a sudden halt at the sight that greeted them.

''Who did this thing?'' Gavin's voice was choked with tears, his face filled with unbelievable anguish.

''That can wait, Gavin.'' Moira touched a hand to her daughter's throat, then gave a sigh of relief. The heartbeat was strong and steady. However much blood had been spilled—for the lass's gown was soaked with it—the wounds were far from fatal. "We must get her inside."

Gavin felt as if he'd taken a knife in his chest, making his breathing labored and painful. Nothing in the world mattered to him as much as his children. And this one, his youngest, his only daughter, his beloved Briana, owned his heart as no other.

As tenderly as if she were still that tiny bundle he had first seen ten and five years ago, he cradled her against his chest and made his way inside the keep, with his wife and family and the parade of villagers trailing somberly behind.

In the great hall the servants had gathered in silence.

"Adina." Moira's voice was stronger now, relieved that there was work to be done. "You will help me tend Briana's wounds."

"Oh, aye, mistress." The smile returned to the servant's eyes, for fiery little Briana was a favorite among all of them. Life was never dull, the chores never mundane, when Briana was near.

"Come." Moira indicated the fur throw in front of the fire. "Lay her here, Gavin, and I'll see to her shoulder, which seems to be the source of that blood."

As she and the servant began to cut away the blood-soaked sleeve and wash the wound, she said softly, "Despite appearances, it is but a small wound."

Gavin watched in silence. Now that the first wrenching wave of fear had swept away, a newer, stronger emotion was beginning to emerge. He turned to the villagers, his blood hot for vengeance. "Now you will tell me everything. Who did this thing?"

"A group of English soldiers, my lord." One tall

lad answered for the others. "They were coming out of the tavern."

"How many were there?" Gavin knew he fed the flames of anger, allowing the hatred to grow before he knew the facts. But he couldn't help himself. He had spent a lifetime hating the English soldiers who moved in small bands across Ireland, defiling, not only the land, but innocent women and children in their path.

"At least a score, my lord."

"So many?" Moira made a sound of surprise.

Gavin interrupted with a hiss of impatience. "Which way were they headed?"

"The last I saw, they were heading toward the forest, my lord."

Moira looked up from her work. "But why did they attack our daughter?"

The lad stared hard at the floor.

Gavin's voice was a growl of command. "Why did they single out Briana, lad?"

"She…" He swallowed, and shot a glance at the others. "She attacked them, my lord."

Gavin's brow furrowed. "Briana attacked them?"

The villagers nodded, dreading what was to come. Gavin O'Neil's temper was a frightening thing to see. It was already there, growing with each moment, darkening his eyes, flaring his nostrils.

"Are you saying the English did nothing to provoke the attack?"

The lad stared at his fingers as they played with the ragged edge of his hat. "The English didn't even see her until she charged into their midst with her sword aloft."

"Her sword?" Gavin spun around, glancing upward, seeing the empty space over the mantel where his father's sword always hung. "What did they do then, lad?"

Briana pushed aside the servant's hand and sat up, brushing tumbled red locks out of her eyes. Her voice, a husky mix of breathlessness and energy, deepened her brogue. "They laughed at me."

Everyone turned to stare at her. But the only one she saw was her father. His face, looking tight and angry. His eyes, staring at her with a look of puzzlement. It wasn't the proud, joyful expression she'd been anticipating.

Hoping to put the light of pride back in his eyes she hurried on in a rush of words. "At first they managed to evade my blows. But when the leader ordered me to throw down my weapon, and I refused, the English dogs were forced to defend themselves."

"Aye, my lord. 'Tis true." The lad nodded. "One of them struck her with the flat of his blade, knocking her from her horse. When she fell to the ground, she seemed stunned, but she's a true O'Neil. She managed to get up and attack again." There was admiration in his tone. And a sense of awe, that one small female could take such blows and keep her senses about her.

Briana O'Neil was a constant source of amazement among the villagers, for, despite her life of luxury as daughter to the lord of Ballinarin, she was a wild thing, always plowing headlong into danger. There were those who said she was in a race with her warrior brothers, to see who was the fiercest. There were others who said she was merely trying to please a harsh, demanding father. Whatever demon drove her, Briana O'Neil was surely the fiercest female in their midst.

"That's when the leader pinned her with his sword, drawing blood. He ordered his men to mount and ride.

And when they were safely away, he followed, my lord.''

Gavin spoke to the lad, but kept his gaze fixed on his daughter. "Did the soldier say anything?"

"Only that he had no desire to have the lass's blood on his hands."

Gavin's eyes had narrowed with each word until they were tiny slits. Now he swung the full weight of his fury on his daughter. "You little fool. Is it death you desire?"

"Nay, Father." She struggled to her feet, determined not to let him see any weakness in her. "I desire the same as you."

"Do you now? And what might that be?"

"I've heard it since I was a wee lass." With her hands on her hips she flounced closer. "Freedom from tyranny. And death to the bloody English."

Gavin's voice rose, a sure sign that his tightly-held control was slipping. "And you thought you'd see to it all by yourself, did you? You're an even bigger fool than I thought. It's lucky you are that the leader of that band had the sense to only wound you. He'd have been within his rights to kill you."

Crushed by his words, Briana exerted no such control over her own temper. With eyes blazing she shouted, "You call me a fool? If I had been Rory or Conor, or even young Innis, you'd have had nothing but praise for my courage. I've watched you, Father, sitting around the fire at night, boasting of your sons' courage. But never once do you recognize that I have the same blood flowing through my veins. The same courage. And the same need for vengeance. Why can't you see it? Why can't you see me?"

He caught her arm and pulled her close until his

breath seared her skin. His voice trembled with emotion. "Oh, I see you. And do you know what I see? A foolish, headstrong lass who hasn't one shred of sense in that empty little brain. Don't you understand that those soldiers could have taken you with them for their sport?"

If he'd expected to shock or frighten her, he was mistaken.

"I wish they had tried." She tossed her head. "They'd have found my knife planted in their black English hearts."

It was, for Gavin O'Neil, the final straw. He looked, for a full minute, as though he might strike her. Instead he flung her from him and looked toward his wife. "You were charged with teaching your daughter the ways of a woman."

Moira stood a little straighter, aware that half the village was witnessing this scene, and the other half would hear every word of it repeated before nightfall. "And so I shall. But you must be patient, Gavin."

"Patient? Patient?" He slammed a fist down on the mantel, sending candles toppling.

Nervous servants hastened to upright them before they began to smolder.

"I've been patient long enough." He pinned his wife with a look that had long struck fear into seasoned warriors. Moira knew that he had now crossed the line from anger to full-blown rage. There would be no stopping him until the storm had run its course. "Now I'll take matters into my own hands."

Moira braced herself for what was to come. Beside her, her daughter watched with wary eyes.

"This very day Briana will go to the Abbey of St. Claire."

"A cloister? Nay, Gavin. You can't mean this."

"You know me better than that, woman. I do mean it."

Her voice quavered. "I beg you, Gavin, don't do this thing."

"It is the only way to assure she will live to womanhood."

Briana's eyes had gone wide with shock and fear. "You wouldn't send me away. I couldn't live without you and Mother. Without Rory and Conor and Innis. I'd rather die, Father, than leave Ballinarin."

"You should have thought about that before you took up the ways of a warrior. Now you must pay for your foolishness. In the convent, you'll learn a woman's ways."

"A woman?" Her voice rang with scorn. "What care I about such things?"

"You'll learn to care. A woman is what you are. What you cannot deny. You'll learn how to pray and weave. How to be humble and docile and respectful. In the silence of the cloister you'll learn how to hold that tongue of yours. In the cloister you'll have time to contemplate your foolish, impulsive behavior."

"I have no desire to learn a woman's ways."

"I care not what you desire. I care only what is good for you. If, after a year, I receive a good report from the mother superior, I'll consider allowing you to return to Ballinarin."

"A year. Gavin, consider what you're saying." Moira stepped closer to her daughter, while fear began growing in the pit of her stomach. She could see the darkness in his eyes; could hear it in his voice. This time it was more than anger; it was desperation. This time he meant it. He would do whatever it took to

keep his beloved Briana safe. Even if it meant breaking her spirit. And her heart. All their hearts. ''They'll
dress her in coarse robes, and force her to sleep on the
floor. And her hair, Gavin. They'll cut it all off.''

He couldn't bear to look at the mass of red tangles
that spilled around a deceptively angelic face. It had
always secretly pleased him that his only daughter had
inherited his mother's lush, coppery hair.

Because they lacked conviction, his words were
hurled like daggers. ''All the better. 'Twill be good
for her humility.''

Briana's eyes filled with tears, but she blinked them
back furiously. She'd rather die than let the village
lads see her cry.

Gavin saw the way his daughter was struggling for
control and turned away abruptly. He had crossed a
line. There would be no turning back now. By evening, all in the surrounding villages would know that
Gavin O'Neil had banished his only daughter to the
Abbey of St. Claire, to turn her into a lady.

Because I love her, he told himself. *Because I would
do anything to keep her safe. Even turn her out of her
beloved home, and deny her mother and me the pleasure of her company.*

''I'll have a messenger ride ahead to the cloister.
Pack her bags and bid your daughter Godspeed, Moira.
Briana leaves on the morrow.''

Chapter One

The Abbey of St. Claire 1656

"**B**riana." The voice of tall, stern Sister Immaculata came from just outside the doorway. "You must wake, child."

"Not yet." The figure huddled deeper into the nest of coarse blankets, wanting to return to her dream. It had been such a sweet dream. She'd been riding her favorite steed across the lush green hills of Ballinarin, in the shadow of towering Croagh Patrick. Her best friend, Innis, and her brothers, Rory and Conor, had been with her, laughing and teasing. She'd been free. Gloriously free of the odious rules that now governed her life. Prayers before dawn, followed by a meal of tasteless gruel, and then work in the fields until noon, when the Angelus was prayed and they were allowed a meal of meat and cheese before retiring to their cells to pray and rest. The afternoon was the same. Endless work, followed by bread and soup, and then evening vespers. Even sleep was regulated, broken at midnight and again at three o'clock in the morning for common prayer in the chapel.

Out of consideration for their age, the older nuns were given duties inside the convent, scrubbing floors, washing linens, cleaning the chapel. The younger ones, students and postulants alike, worked the fields and tended the herds.

"Briana, you must get up now." The voice was beside her. A hand touched her shoulder. That, in itself, had her coming fully awake, for there was no touching allowed in the convent. There were no hugs. No squeezing of hands. Even the brush of one shoulder by another caused both parties to stiffen and turn away.

She opened her eyes. The blaze from the candle held in the nun's hand made her squint. "I've only just fallen asleep, Sister. It can't be time to pray yet."

"I haven't wakened you for prayer, child. Mother Superior awaits you in the refectory."

"The refectory? She's eating?"

"Nay. She is seeing to a meal for the lads who have come to escort you home."

Home. Briana blinked, unable to say the word aloud. Her banishment of one year had grown to two, and then to three, as she had railed against the injustice of the rules, managing to break every one of them. For each rule she broke, the prospect of ever seeing Ballinarin again had become so remote, she had feared it would never happen. And now, without notice, she was being given a reprieve. Still, though there was the slightest flicker of hope, she held back, refusing to allow it to burst into flame for fear it would be snuffed, as it had so often in the past. "But why now?"

"I don't know, child. Mother Superior will explain

it to you. Now hurry and dress.'' Satisfied that her young charge was not going to fall back asleep, the old nun took her leave as silently as she had come.

Briana slipped off the coarse nightshift and crossed to a basin of cold water, washing quickly. Then she dressed in a shapeless brown garment and scuffed boots, before folding up her pallet and setting it in a corner of the room. A quick glance around assured her that the cell was as clean and as bare as when she had arrived, three years earlier.

Despite the time she had spent here, there was nothing of Briana in this simple cell. No mementoes of home and family. No small comforts. The sleeping pallet consisted of a rough blanket on the floor. On a plain table rested a basin and pitcher, which bore no adornments. There was no mirror. For that, Briana was grateful. She had no desire to see how she must look now, with her hair shorn, her hands, rough and callused, the nails torn and ragged from her hours spent tending the crops and flocks in the fields. Even her body had changed. Gone were the soft, round curves of younger womanhood. Over the years she had grown taller and reed slender, with the merest slope of hips, and breasts so small and firm, they were easily concealed beneath the robes of a peasant.

She stepped from the cell and pulled the door closed behind her, moving soundlessly along the darkened corridor.

When she entered the refectory, Mother Superior hurried over.

''These lads have come to fetch you home.''

Briana glanced at the lads who were seated at a long wooden table, eating a hastily prepared meal of meat and cheese and crusty bread. With a sinking heart she realized that they were the faces of strangers. The lads she'd known in her girlhood had probably moved on with their lives, no doubt with wives and children of their own.

"Why am I being summoned home?"

Mother Superior motioned for her to sit. At once Sister Ascension, the cook, waddled over to place a platter of meat and cheese in front of her.

While Briana dutifully ate, Mother Superior explained. "Your father was recently wounded."

"Wounded? What…?" Her words trailed off at the look on the nun's face.

Mother Superior gave a sigh of dismay. Even after three years of training, the lass still hadn't learned to hold her tongue. But at least she had remained seated. The firebrand who had first come to the convent would have leapt to her feet and demanded all the details immediately.

"The wounds are not serious. But your mother desires your assistance in caring for The O'Neil. She feels that the challenge is too great for her to carry alone."

Briana's smile was quick. "Aye. My father healthy is challenge enough. My father wounded would be unbearable. Especially once he started to mend."

Then another thought intruded. It was her mother who had sent for her, not her father. Did that mean that he had still not forgiven her? She felt the pain, sharp and quick, then quickly dismissed it. It no longer mattered. Once Gavin O'Neil saw her, he would realize that she had changed. She would win his love. She had to. It had been the one thing that had always driven her.

She suddenly found that she had lost her appetite.

The thought that she was really going home had her nerves jumping. Because she had often been lectured on the sinfulness of wasting food, she gathered the rest of her meal and placed it in a pocket of her robe, before getting to her feet. Across the room, the lads pulled on their cloaks and headed toward the door. Briana and Mother Superior followed.

In the courtyard, the horses were saddled and ready. Mother Superior handed Briana a coarse, hooded traveling robe. "The ermine-lined cloak which you wore here was given to the poor. As was the purse of gold which your father sent. But though this is a humble replacement, it will serve its purpose, Briana, and keep you warm throughout your long journey."

"I care not for clothes, Reverend Mother."

"I know that, child." It was one of Briana's most endearing qualities. The lass had no artifice. And though she was an incorrigible rascal, she was much loved by all at the convent.

It had been plain, from her first day, that she would never fit in to the life of a humble sister. But it was also plain that she was kind, and dear, and with her impulsive behavior and irrepressible humor, the most impossible challenge of Mother Superior's life. As she looked at Briana now, she wondered just how she would fit into that other world beyond the convent walls. She'd had no time to flirt, to dance, to experience the things of young womanhood. By now, the women Briana's age would be wives and mothers. And though this sweet lass would be treated like a woman by those who met her, she was still, in her heart, that naive girl of ten and five who had burst upon their silence and order, bringing with her chaos and passion.

The older woman lifted a hand and Briana bowed her head. "Until we meet again, child, may God hold you safely in His hands."

"And you, Reverend Mother." Briana turned away and was assisted onto her mount.

With a clatter of hooves, the horses moved out.

Briana turned for a last glimpse of the Abbey of St. Claire. Mother Superior stood, her hands folded as always inside the sleeves of her robes. Behind her the roof of the building, and the cross that rose from the highest peak, were still cloaked in darkness.

Briana turned her head and stared straight ahead. Toward the sunrise, just beginning to tint the sky. There lay Ballinarin. Her heart fluttered with unrestrained happiness. At long last, she was going home.

"What is it? Why are we stopping here?" When the leader of their little group signalled a halt, Briana urged her mount forward.

"A village, my lady." From his position at the top of a small green hill, the lad pointed. In the distance could be seen the thatched roofs of sod huts, and the smoke from turf fires, and beyond them, the towers and turrets of the distant keep. "We'd be wise to seek shelter before it grows dark."

"I'm not yet weary. I could continue for a few more hours." For every hour would bring her closer to home.

"You have been away now for several years, my lady." He kept his tone respectful, but Briana felt the sting of censure. "There are many more English soldiers in our land now. And no one, man or woman, is safe after dark."

It was on the tip of Briana's tongue to remind the

lad that she was an O'Neil, and that the decision should be hers and hers alone. But though it stung, she knew he was right. She had been sheltered so long, she had no way of making a proper judgment. The lad was only looking out for her safety.

Reluctantly she nodded. "Aye. We'll seek the shelter of a tavern then, and be on our way again in the morning."

Below them lay a field of green. Peasants from a nearby village could be seen tending their flocks. It was a pleasant, peaceful scene that brought a smile to Briana's lips as she and her escorts urged their horses down the hill. This was what she had missed. Laughter, as clear and tinkling as a bell, carried on the breeze. The sound of voices raised in easy conversation. How long had it been since she had heard such things? Even in the fields, the sisters and novices never broke their vow of silence.

As her horse moved in a slow, loping gait between the furrows, she lifted a hand and waved, and the men and women straightened and returned her salute.

She was halfway across the field when she heard the thunder of hooves. For a moment she didn't know what to make of it. Then, seeing the lad in front of her turn and mutter an oath as he unsheathed his sword, she followed his gaze.

An army of English soldiers, perhaps fifty or more, was heading directly toward them from a nearby forest.

With a feeling of dread Briana looked around. They were caught in the open. Trapped. There was nowhere to run. Nowhere to seek shelter from the trained warriors bearing down on them.

The leader of her escorts, a fierce, muscular lad of

perhaps ten and six, shouted orders. "The village. At once. It is our only hope."

As they urged their horses into a run, Briana glanced over her shoulder. The peasants, caught off-guard, were being cut down by the invading soldiers' swords. In the blink of an eye, five, then ten, then more, were seen falling to the ground, screaming in anguish.

The air was filled with the sound of voices shouting, swearing. Women weeping. The sharp clang of metal on metal as those few peasants who were armed strove to defend themselves. Horses whinnied in pain as they died, crushing their riders. That only made the soldiers more determined to retaliate against those peasants who dared to fight back.

The once tidy rows of grain were now slashed and torn, the earth red with blood as the mounted soldiers overtook the fleeing peasants and, in a frenzy of killing, left not a single one standing.

When they had finished with the peasants, the soldiers turned their attention on the five horsemen, fleeing across the fields. Within minutes they fanned out, determined to cut off any chance of escape.

Seeing that there was no hope of making it to the safety of the village, the leader of Briana's escorts signalled for the others to form a circle around her. "Come lads. We must defend the lady Briana with our lives."

"Give me a sword," she shouted.

But her voice was drowned out by the thunder of hooves and the shouts and jeers of the approaching army. As soon as Briana and her escorts slid from their saddles, their terrified horses took off at a run. The lads formed a ring around her, swords at the ready, determined to defend her to their last breath, as the soldiers bore down on them.

"Halsey." A soldier's shout had the leader of the army turning in the saddle. "Look at this. These lads are spoiling for a fight."

"Then, let's give them what they want." The one called Halsey threw back his head and roared. It was obvious that he was enjoying the killing. "I'll do the honors myself. The rest of you can see that the sniveling cowards don't escape."

His soldiers held back, allowing him to lead the charge. He singled out the leader of the band of defenders, plunging his sword through the lad's heart with a single swipe.

His voice rang with disdain as the lad fell to the ground, writhing in pain. "Embrace death, Irishman. And may your sons and their sons join you in it."

At his words the other soldiers began to laugh. When the remaining lads formed a tighter circle around Briana, several of the soldiers slid to the ground and drew their swords.

"Jamie," Halsey called to a comrade. "Throw me your weapon. Mine's buried too deeply in the Irishman."

The soldier tossed his sword, and Halsey easily caught it before engaging a second lad in battle.

Briana watched with sinking heart as the lad fought bravely. But each time he managed to dodge a thrust from Halsey's sword, the soldiers behind him would strike him about the head and chest with their weapons, leaving him dazed and bloody. Soon, seeing that the lad was too weary to defend himself, Halsey gave a final death thrust with his sword, sending the lad to the ground, where he gasped his last.

"That leaves only three," Halsey said with an evil grin. "Who would care to test his skill next?"

The last of Briana's defenders stood back to back, keeping her between them. With drawn swords, they fought with courage and skill, though they knew they had no chance to win. Even if they were to best the one called Halsey, his soldiers outnumbered them by fifty or more. His death would make their own that much more painful. Still, they had sworn to see the lady Briana safely to her home. No matter what the odds, they would fight to the death to keep their word to the lord of the manor.

"Do you think two Irishmen can outfight one English soldier?" Halsey's voice rang with contempt. "Not even a dozen could best me."

As if to prove his boast, he cut down the first lad with a single thrust, then turned his attention to the second. Though the lad was clumsy, he was tall and strapping, with muscular forearms. His first blow with the blade caught Halsey by surprise, and the soldier had to leap aside quickly to avoid being wounded.

Annoyed that his soldiers' taunts had gone suddenly silent, he slashed out, catching the lad's arm, laying it open. With blood streaming down his arm, the lad fought back, but was quickly slashed a second time, and then a third, until his tunic and breeches were stained with his own blood.

"Come, Irishman. Is this the best you can do?" Halsey leapt forward, causing the lad to back up too quickly.

He tripped and landed on his back. Like a feral dog, Halsey stood over him, the tip of his sword at the lad's throat.

"You'd best pray that the God you worship is merciful, Irishman. For you're about to meet Him.'' With a laugh he plunged his sword through the lad's throat. Then, for good measure, he pulled the blade free and thrust it again, directly through the lad's heart.

His men sent up a cheer as he turned toward Briana, who stood alone.

If her years in the convent had taught her anything, it was that death was not to be feared, but rather to be embraced. She took a deep breath and lifted her head, prepared for what was to come.

"So, lad." Halsey glanced around at his men, clearly enjoying his role as fearless enforcer. "I see you're too young to be entrusted with a sword. Is this why the others were protecting you?"

Briana blinked. It took her several moments to realize that this man and the others mistook her for a lad. No wonder. In the coarse robes of a peasant, with her hair shorn, she would never be mistaken for a noblewoman.

"It's too bad." Halsey took a step closer, his sword raised for the kill. "I would have enjoyed a bit of a challenge before retiring for the night with my men. Ah well. I suppose it was too much to hope for."

As he stepped over the body of his last victim, Briana took that moment of distraction to bend toward the lad lying at her feet. In one swift motion she pulled the sword from his chest.

She cursed the fact that it had been too many years since she'd handled a weapon. She was surprised at how heavy it felt. It took both hands just to hold it aloft.

Halsey looked up, his eyes narrowing. Then, seeing how she struggled with the heavy weapon, his lips split into a grin.

"That's my sword you're holding, lad. I'd wager it doesn't like being held by Irish hands. Be careful the hilt doesn't burn your flesh."

The others roared with laughter.

"Maybe you're the one who should be careful." Briana slowly lowered one hand, flexing her fingers. Though she hadn't held a sword these last three years, she had held her share of plowshares and scythes. Her work with the flocks and in the fields may have whittled her weight, making her lean, but it had also made her strong. She tightened her grip on the hilt of the sword and tested its strength.

Halsey's smile grew. "You Irish always have so much to say until you taste an English sword. Then your babbling turns to the bleating of lambs at slaughter. Prepare yourself, lad. You're about to face your own slaughter."

He stepped forward, giving a deft jab with his sword tip. To his surprise his opponent danced to one side and caught his arm with a sharp slice. The yelp that bubbled to his lips was quickly turned into a string of oaths, in order to save face in front of his watching men.

"The Irishman must pay for that, Halsey," one of his soldiers called.

"Aye." Gritting his teeth, Halsey charged forward, determined to inflict pain.

Instead, his opponent once more managed to avoid his sword and swung out, catching his shoulder with a sword tip.

As blood spilled down the front of his tunic, his eyes narrowed to tiny slits. Gone was the sly smile of a moment ago. Now, this was no longer sport. It had become deadly serious.

"I tire of this game, Irishman." He signalled to two of his soldiers. "Hold the lad while I teach him a lesson."

Briana turned to face the two men who advanced. Wielding the sword like a club, she swung out viciously, and had the satisfaction of seeing them back away rather than face her weapon. But, with her back to Halsey, she was defenseless. She felt the white-hot thrust of a sword as it pierced her shoulder. The weapon dropped from her fingers and fell to the ground.

Stunned and reeling, she turned to face her attacker. His smile was back. His eyes were glazed with a lust for blood.

Up close she could see that his face bore the scars of many battles. His nose had been broken. His left ear had been cut away, leaving only a raw, puckered scar.

"Now will you know death, Irishman." His voice was a low taunt. "Not only your own, but the death of this land, as well. For all of it, and all who live in it, will answer to an English sword."

"Hold him," he shouted to his soldiers. "And this time, see that he doesn't break free."

With one soldier on either side of her, holding firmly to her arms, Briana was unable to move. She kept her eyes open as the one called Halsey drew back his hand and brought the sword forward with one powerful thrust. When the blade entered her chest she felt nothing at first, as her legs failed her and sent her crashing to the ground. And then there was pain, hotter than any fire, burning her flesh, melting her bones. Pain that seemed to go on and on until she could no longer bear it.

A loud roaring, like thunder, filled her head.

Then, from far away, came the sound of laughter. And Halsey's voice, that seemed to rise and fall. "Come. Let's find a tavern, and wash away the taste of these filthy Irish."

And then, mercifully, there was only numbness. And a deep black hole that swirled and swirled, stealing her sight, her mind, enveloping her in total darkness, as it slowly closed around her and took her down to the depths of hell.

Chapter Two

"Bloody barbarians." The old man from the nearby village knelt beside the body of his brother, cradling the familiar head in his lap.

"Aye." His son nodded toward the lord of the manor, who had brought a wagonload of servants to survey the carnage. "And there's another one of them."

"Aye. Bloody Englishman. A pity, what he's become. I knew his grandfather. Now there was a true and loyal son of Ireland."

"You can't say the same for his father."

"Nay. A wastrel, true enough. And now his son has returned as a titled gentleman. The only reason he came home was to claim his inheritance. With his father dead, he'll take the fruits of our labors back to England, to live as his father before him, like royalty."

"The bloody English will soon enough own all the land and everyone on it."

Though Keane O'Mara couldn't help but overhear the mutterings of the villagers, he gave no indication as he moved among the dead. On his face was a look of complete disdain. It was the only expression the villagers had seen since his recent return to his child-hood home.

When he came upon a body that had not been claimed, he paused.

"How many, Vinson?" he asked his servant.

The old man hobbled closer. "I've counted a score and ten, my lord."

Keane struggled to show no emotion. Thirty men, women, even a few children. All caught by surprise, apparently, while tending the fields. With nothing more than a handful of weapons among them with which to defend themselves.

He'd come upon this sort of thing so many times lately, he'd begun to lose count of the bodies. The bloody scenes of carnage had begun to blur together in his mind, so that they all seemed one and the same. And yet, each was different. Each time, he was re-minded of the families who would grieve. The widows who would never again see their husbands. The or-phans who would grow up without knowing their par-ents. He winced. The parents who would carry the loss of their children in their hearts forever.

"Has Father Murphy finished the last rites?"

The old man nodded.

"Order the servants to begin loading them into wag-ons for burial."

"Aye, my lord." Vinson shuffled off, and soon a staff of servants began the terrible task of lifting the bloody, bloated bodies onto carts and wagons for burial in the field behind the chapel, on the grounds of the family keep.

Many of the villagers had brought their own carts, and they now trailed behind in silence, unable to give voice to their grief. Only the anguish in their eyes spoke of their pain and sorrow.

As Keane approached yet another bloody section of field, his servant looked up. "These five were not of the village, my lord."

"You're certain?"

"Aye, my lord. Neither the priest nor the villagers has ever seen them before. They must have been strangers, who were just passing through."

"A pity they chose this time." Keane turned away. "Before you bury them, examine their cloaks and weapons. Perhaps you'll find a missive or a crest that will tell us the name of their village."

He hadn't take more than a dozen steps when the elderly servant called excitedly, "One of these lads is alive, my lord."

Keane returned and stared down at the figure, crusted with mud and dried blood, the face half hidden in the folds of a twisted hood.

"You're certain?"

"Aye, my lord." Vinson leaned close, feeling the merest puff of warmth from between lips that were parched and bloody. "There's breath in him yet."

"From the looks of him, he put up a bit of a fight. Take him to my keep and see to him, Vinson."

"Aye, my lord." The old man got to his feet. "Though his heartbeat's so feeble, he might not survive the trek."

Keane gave a sigh of disgust. So many wasted young lives. "All we can do is try. And hope he survives."

A servant approached, leading the lord's stallion. Keane pulled himself into the saddle and began the long sad journey to the chapel, where he would try to give what comfort he could to the grieving villagers. If he were his grandfather the villagers would accept what he offered. But because he was viewed as an outsider, his attempts would be rebuffed.

All along the way he prepared himself for the storm of anger and grief and bitterness that would be expressed. There was a groundswell of hatred festering, and for good reason. There would come a time, he knew, when it would spill over into war. And when it did, there would be even more death and destruction. For the English would never give up their hold on this land and its people. And though he understood the need for vengeance, he also knew the futility of it. Despite the growing tide of sentiment against the English, this small, poor land was no match for England's armies.

Hadn't he learned the lesson well enough? And hadn't he already paid the supreme sacrifice for his devotion to the wrong cause?

The thought of his loss brought an ache so deep, so painful, it nearly cut off his breath.

Aye. He'd paid. And he'd learned. But that didn't mean he'd given up hope. It just meant he'd mastered the art of patience. For a while longer he would bide his time and get his father's affairs in order. And then he would leave this sad land, with its sad memories, and try to make a life somewhere. Anywhere. As long as he would no longer have to remember the past with all its bitterness.

"Good even, my lord. Mistress Malloy has kept a meal on the fire for you."

Keane shrugged out of his heavy cloak and shook the rain from his hair. "I've no appetite, Vinson. Bring me a tankard.'' He started toward the stairs, favoring his left leg. He only gave in to the pain when he was too tired to fight it. At the moment, he was on the verge of exhaustion. ''I'll be in my chambers.''

''Aye, my lord.'' The old servant cleared his throat and Keane paused, knowing there was something important Vinson needed to say. It was always the same. When the old man needed to speak, he first had to clear his throat and prepare himself for the task.

''Perhaps, my lord, you could step into the chambers next to yours on your way.''

Keane gave a sigh of impatience. The events of the day had dragged him to the depths, and all he wanted was to wash away the bitter taste with ale. ''I'm sure there's a good reason?''

''Aye, my lord.'' The old man carefully hung the damp cloak on a hook, then picked up a tray on which rested a decanter and a silver tankard. He climbed the stairs behind his master.

At the upper hallway Keane gave a fleeting glance at the door to his chambers, then resolutely moved past it to tear open a second door. Inside a serving wench looked up from the figure in the bed, then stepped aside to make room for the master.

''Ah. The lad.'' Keane walked to the bedside. ''With all that transpired this day, I'd nearly forgotten about him. I see he survived, Vinson.''

''Aye, my lord. But...'' Vinson cleared his throat again.

Keane waited, a little less patiently.

''The lad isn't. A lad, I mean. He's a...lass, my lord.''

Keanc turned. The old man was actually blushing. Carrick House had been, after all, a male bastion for a quarter of a century. Except for the serving wenches, and a housekeeper who had been in residence since Keane's father was a lad, there had been no females under this roof.

"I'd managed to wash away most of the mud and blood from his...her face. But when I cut away his...her cloak, I..." Vinson swallowed. "I summoned young Cora to see to her."

Keane took a closer look at the figure in the bed. Several thicknesses of bed linens hid the shape of her body, but he could recall no hint of womanly curves beneath the shapeless robes she'd been wearing on the field of battle. Now that the face was washed, it was obvious that the features were decidedly feminine. A small, upturned nose. High cheekbones. Perfectly sculpted lips. The hair had been cut so close to the head, it was little more than a cap of tight red curls.

"A natural enough mistake. What do you make of it, Vinson?"

"Cora found this around the lass's neck." The old man held up a small cross, tied to a simple cord. "A nun, I'd say."

Keane nodded as understanding flooded his tired mind. "Aye. Of course. That would explain the simple garb and shorn hair. But what of the lads with her?"

The old servant shrugged. "I haven't fathomed that, my lord. We can only hope that the lass will live long enough to tell us."

"How does she fare?"

The old man and the young servant exchanged glances. "The wounds are extreme. The one to the shoulder is festering. The one to the chest left her barely clinging to life. The sword passed clear through, missing her heart. She hovers between this world and the next. If her heart and her will to live are strong enough…'' The old man shrugged. ''The next day or two will tell the tale.''

Keane nodded, then turned toward the door. ''You'll wake me if she grows weaker.''

''Aye, my lord.'' The serving wench returned to her bedside vigil, while Keane and Vinson took their leave.

In his chambers, Keane strode to the fireplace and stared into the flames.

Vinson filled a tankard and handed it to him. ''Will I fetch you some food now, my lord?''

Keane shook his head. ''Nay. The morrow will be soon enough. Take your rest, Vinson.''

''Aye, my lord.'' The old man seemed eager to escape to his bed. Nearly disrobing a young female had left him badly shaken.

When he was gone, Keane drained the tankard in one long swallow. Then, after prying off his boots and removing his tunic, he refilled the tankard and drank more slowly, all the while staring into the flames.

He thought about the lass in the next room, hovering between life and death. She'd barely had time to live. If Vinson was correct, what few years she'd had were lived in the shelter of a cloister. No time to laugh, to play. He frowned. No time to know the love of a good man, nor the joy of children.

A pretty enough face. No visible scars, though heaven knew, most scars were carefully hidden. Weren't his own? Still, he wondered what it was that drove young women to seek the seclusion of an abbey. Were they really there to serve God? Or were they hiding from the world?

No matter. This one appeared young and innocent.

Why was it always the innocent who must pay for the sins of arrogance committed by those in power?

He walked to the bedside table and picked up the framed miniature, studying once again the face of the one who held his heart. There were times, like this moment, when the pain was too deep, the sense of loss too painful to bear. But he had done the right thing. The only thing. Yet, if that be true, why did he feel like such a failure?

Suddenly overwhelmed by sadness and frustration, he hurled the tankard against the wall. With a string of oaths he dropped onto his back on his bed and passed a hand over his eyes.

Would there ever be an end to the misery? Or would he be forced to watch helplessly as all those he loved were forced to pay for his mistakes?

Dear God, he was weary. So weary. He prayed sleep would visit him. Else, he would be forced to fight his demons until dawn chased the darkness away.

"My lord."

Keane awoke instantly and found himself bathed in sweat. The demons, it would seem, were especially vile this night.

"Aye, Vinson. What is it?"

The old man stood beside the bed, holding aloft a candle. His robe had been hastily tossed over a nightshirt, his silver hair sticking out at odd angles. "The wench, Cora, summoned me. She feels the lass is at death's door."

Keane sprang from his bed. Without taking time for a tunic or boots he led the way to the room next door. The young servant straightened when the lord en-

tered the room. In her hand was a square of linen,
which she had been wringing out in a basin of water.

"Oh, my lord," she whispered. "The lass is slipping away."

Keane touched a hand to the lass's forehead and
pulled it away with a jerk. "Her flesh is on fire."

"Aye. I can no longer bring down the fever, my
lord."

He studied the still, pale figure in the bed, seeing
another's face in his mind. How tragic that so many
innocents were lost in battles not of their making.

"I've done all I can, my lord. But I fear we've lost
her."

Perhaps it was the finality of the servant's words.
Or the futility of his own nightly battles with his demons. Whatever the reason, Keane became infused
with a new sense of purpose, a fresh burst of energy.
This was one battle he wouldn't lose without at least
putting up a fight.

"Wake Mistress Malloy. Tell her to prepare a
bath."

"A…bath, my lord?"

"Aye." He took the linen from her hand and dipped
it into the basin. "A cold bath, Cora."

As Vinson watched, Keane placed the cool cloth on
the lass's forehead, then moved it across her cheeks,
her mouth, her throat. As quickly as the cloth touched
her fevered flesh, it became warm to the touch. Keane
then dipped it into the basin once more, wrung it out
and repeated the process.

Holding the candle aloft, the old man watched the
lass's face for any reaction. There was none. No sign
of relief from the fever that burned. Not even a flicker
of movement from lids that remained closed.

"My lord. I fear the lass is beyond help."

Keane didn't even look up. "Go to bed, Vinson."

"My lord…"

"If you cannot help, leave me."

The old man recognized that tone of voice. It had been the same for the young lord's father and his father before him. With a sigh of resignation he placed the candle on the bedside table and shuffled across the room, taking up a second cloth. The two men worked in silence, taking turns bathing the lass's face and neck.

Minutes later the housekeeper bustled in, trailed by half a dozen serving wenches, carrying a tub and buckets of water.

"You ordered a bath, my lord?"

"Aye, Mistress Malloy." Keane wrung out the cloth, and placed it over the lass's forehead, while Vinson dipped his in the basin.

The housekeeper watched for several seconds, then motioned for the servants to begin filling the tub. When that was done they waited for further instructions.

They were shocked to see the lord of the manor pull back the bed linens and lift the lass from bed. With no thought to her modesty, he carried her to the tub, where he plunged her, nightshift and all, into the cold water.

"My lord," the housekeeper cried, "on top of a fever, the cold water will cause her to take a fit."

"Perhaps, Mistress Malloy. But since she's near death, it's a risk I'll have to take. Fetch some dry blankets, please. And clean linens to dress her wounds."

While the servants scurried after fresh bed linens,

Keane gently cradled the lass's head against his chest
and splashed water over her face. Within minutes he
could feel her body temperature begin to cool.

He glanced at his butler, who had knelt beside the
tub. "She weighs almost nothing, Vinson."

"Aye, my lord. I thought that same thing when I
carried her up the stairs. Though at the time, I thought
her a young lad."

When the housekeeper and her servants returned
with blankets, Keane lifted the lass from the bath, drip-
ping water across the floor as he carried her to the
bed.

"You're not going to return her to her bed in that
soaked nightshift, my lord."

At the housekeeper's outraged tone, he shook his
head. "I thought I'd remove it first."

He glanced down. Now that her gown was plastered
to her body, the decidedly feminine outline was plain
to see. Small, firm breasts, a tiny waist, softly rounded
hips.

"I'll do that." The housekeeper's tone was brisk
and left no room for argument.

Keane stepped back while Mistress Malloy and her
servants removed the lass's wet garments and wrapped
her in fresh blankets, after first dressing the wounds
to her chest and shoulder.

"Now what, my lord?" Mistress Malloy asked.

"You may all return to your beds." He turned.
"And you, as well, Cora."

"But what about the lass?"

"I'll sit with her. I've no more need for sleep."

When his elderly butler made ready to pull a second
chair beside the bed, Keane shook his head. "Nay,
Vinson. You require your sleep for the day to come."

While the others eagerly sought their beds, Vinson remained a moment longer.

He cleared his throat. His voice was low, so that a passing servant wouldn't overhear. "I know the battles you fight each night, my lord. And why you have decided to fight for the lass. But this one is futile. You can see that she is at death's door."

Keane met the old man's look. "You know me well, old man. It's true. I have no desire to face my demons again tonight." He shook his head and crossed his arms over his chest, in exactly the same way his father used to. "But this is one battle I don't intend to lose. Now go. Leave me."

When the old man shuffled out, closing the door silently, Keane turned to study the lass. Her breathing was ragged, her lips moving in silent protest. Or perhaps prayer.

"Go ahead, little nun. Pray. But I hope you know how to fight as well." Aye, he could see that she did. By the jut of her chin. By the clench of her fist. The lass was a scrapper.

He sat back, his eyes narrowed in thought. Vinson was right, as always. This was, he realized, the perfect excuse to avoid returning to his own bed. But he had meant what he'd said. This was one battle he intended to win.

Chapter Three

Briana lay perfectly still, wondering where she had finally surfaced. Earlier she had visited the fires of hell. She knew it was hell, because she'd felt her flesh burning away from her bones, and her entire body melting. But then, just as she'd resigned herself to that fate, a fate she surely deserved for all the grief she'd given her family, she had found herself thrust into the icy waters of the River Shannon. She'd heard voices coming from somewhere along the shore, but she'd been too weary to open her eyes. And so she had slept and drifted in the calm, soothing waters.

Now she was awake and determined to see where she had landed. Wherever it was, she must have been tossed onto the rocks on shore, for her body felt bruised and battered beyond repair.

Her lids flickered, and light stabbed so painfully she squeezed her eyes tightly shut. Gathering her strength, she tried again. Her eyes were gritty, as though she'd been buried in sand. Her throat, too, was dry as dust, and her lips so parched she couldn't pry them apart with her tongue.

''So, lass. You're awake.''

At the unexpected sound of a man's deep voice, she blinked and turned her head to stare at the sight that greeted her. And what a sight. A man, naked to the waist, was seated beside the bed. He leaned close and touched a hand to her brow. Just a touch, but she could feel the strength in his fingers, and could see the ripple of muscle in his arm and shoulder.

"I see the fever has left you." He could see so much more. Up close, her eyes were gold, with little flecks of green. Cat's eyes, he thought. Wary. Watchful. And her skin was unlike any he'd ever seen. Not the porcelain skin he was accustomed to. Hers was burnished from the sun. But it was as soft as a newborn's.

That one small touch had caused the strangest sensation. A tingling that started in his fingertips and shot through his system with the speed of a wildfire.

It was the lack of sleep, he told himself. He was beginning to see things that weren't there. To fancy things that weren't even possible. The lass in the bed was a nun. Only a fool or a lecher would permit such feelings toward an innocent maiden who'd promised her life in service to God.

"For a while this night, I thought the fever would claim you."

Briana couldn't help staring at him. His voice was cultured, with just a trace of brogue. But not Irish. English, she thought, like the soldiers who had attacked. She cringed from his touch.

Seeing her reaction, he felt a quick wave of annoyance. "I'll not harm you, lass. Not after what I've gone through this night to save you."

"Save..." The single word caused such pain, she swallowed and gave up the effort to speak.

"Aye." To avoid touching her again he leaned back in his chair and stretched out his long legs. All the tension of the night was beginning to ease. He had fought the battle, and won. The lass had passed through the crisis. At least, the first crisis. He hoped there wouldn't be many more.

"Earlier, I thought you were ready to leave this life."

She studied him while he spoke. His face could have belonged to an angel. A dark angel. Aye, Satan, she thought. Thick black hair was mussed, as though he'd run his hands through it in frustration. A sign of temper, she'd wager. His eyes, the color of smoke, were fixed on her with such intensity, she found she couldn't look away. His dark brows were lifted in curiosity, or perhaps, disdain. His nose was patrician, his full lips just slightly curved, as though he were the keeper of a secret.

"Where...?" She struggled with the word and closed her eyes against the knife-blade of pain that sliced down her throat.

"Where are you?" He crossed his arms over his chest. "You're in my home. Carrick House. I had you brought here after you were found in the fields not far from here. There was a battle. Do you recall it?"

She nodded. How could she forget? It had seemed like a nightmare of horrors. One that never ended. Even now she could hear the cries of the wounded, and feel the thundering of horses' hooves as if in her own chest. Worse, she could still smell the stench of death all around her. That had been the worst. To surface occasionally, only to realize that all around her were dead.

"...others?" It was all she could manage.

He shook his head. "You were the only one who survived."

She felt a wave of such sadness, she had to close her eyes to hold back the tears. Four lads, with so much to live for. But instead of the promising future they should have enjoyed, they had given it all up. For her. She was unworthy of such a sacrifice.

"Here, lass. Drink this."

She opened her eyes to find him sitting beside her on the edge of the bed, holding a tumbler of water. With unexpected tenderness he lifted her head and held the glass to her lips.

Again Keane felt the heat and wondered what was happening to him. He must be more weary than he'd thought. That had to be the reason. It couldn't be this plain little nun in his arms.

She sipped, then nearly gagged.

"Forgive me, lass. I should have mentioned that I had my housekeeper prepare an opiate for your pain. Drink it down. It'll help."

Though it burned a pathway down her throat, she did as she was told.

He laid her gently back on the pillow, then set the glass on the bedside table and bent to smooth the covers. As he did, he realized she was watching him with the wariness of a wild creature caught in a trap.

He picked up something that he thought might soothe her, and held it up. "My servant found this around your neck."

She stared at the simple cross, then reached for it, before her hand fell limply against the bedcovers. When he placed it in her hand, their fingers brushed. At once she pulled her hand away, and shrank from him until he took a step back.

His frown returned, furrowing his dark brows. It was obvious that she disliked being touched by him. It was probably the way of holy women. "I'll leave you to rest now. My servant will be in shortly to look after you. Let her know if you need anything."

She nodded and watched until he walked away. By the time the door closed, sleep had claimed her. And the dreams that haunted her were dark. Dark angels. And a chilling laugh from a soldier whose name she couldn't recall, but whose face tormented her. A soldier who enjoyed killing.

"How is the lass?" Keane stepped quietly into the sleeping chambers and paused beside the bed. In the hush of evening his voice was little more than a whisper.

He had spent nearly the entire week in and out of these chambers, bullying the servants, seeing that the wounds were carefully dressed, to avoid more infection. Through it all, the lass had surfaced only briefly, before drifting in a haze of delirium and opiates.

He'd sensed that his presence made her uneasy. And the truth was, she affected him the same way, though he knew not why. Still, he couldn't stay away. She had become his cause. His fierce obsession. Behind his back, the servants whispered about it. And wondered what drove Lord Alcott to fight so desperately for this stranger.

"Her sleep is still broken by pain, my lord." Cora looked up from her chair beside the bed.

"Has she eaten anything?"

"Not a thing. And she, so thin and pale. Mistress Malloy sent up a tray, but the lass hasn't had the heart to even try."

"And you, Cora?" Keane glanced at the servant, whose head had been bobbing when he'd first entered.

"Mistress Malloy will have something for me later."

"Go below stairs now." He motioned toward the door. "Go. I'll sit with the lass awhile."

The little serving wench needed no coaxing. The long hours spent watching the sleeping lass had made her yearn for her own bed. But though she gave up many of her daylight hours to the care of their patient, the nighttime hours belonged to the lord. He would dismiss the other servants and sit by the lass's bedside, ever vigilant for any sign that she might be failing.

When Cora was gone, Keane pressed his hands to the small of his back and leaned his head back, stretching his cramped muscles. Agitated, he began to prowl the room, pausing occasionally to glance out the window as darkness began to swallow the land.

When he wasn't in there, hovering by the bedside, he was in the library, poring over his father's ledgers, or huddled in meetings with his solicitors. From the looks of things, Kieran O'Mara, the late Lord Alcott, had long ago lost all interest in his homeland and holdings. Several buildings were in need of repair. The land, though lush and green, had been badly mismanaged for years, yielding only meager crops. Carrick House, it would seem, needed not only an infusion of cash, but an infusion of lifeblood as well.

Not his problem, Keane mused as he stared at the rolling fields outside the window. He would soon enough be gone from this miserable place, with its unhappy memories.

It wasn't so much a sound from the bed, as a feeling, that had him turning around. The lass, with those strange yellow eyes, wide and unblinking, was staring at him.

"Ah. You're awake."

She'd been awake for several minutes. And had been studying him while he paced and prowled. Like a caged animal, she thought. Aye. A sleek, dark panther. All muscle and sinew and fierce energy.

He drew up the chair beside the bed and bent to her, touching a hand to her forehead. It took all her willpower not to pull away. Still, she couldn't help cringing as his hand came in contact with her skin.

He was aware of her reaction. He was aware of something else, as well, and struggled to ignore the strange tingling that occurred whenever he was near this female.

After so many nights watching her, he had begun to feel he knew her. He'd felt every ragged breath of hers in his own chest. Had marvelled at the quiet strength that kept her fighting when others would have given up. Had felt encouraged with every little sign of improvement.

"Do you remember where you are?"

She nodded, struggling to fit the pieces of her memory back into place. "Carrick House, I believe you called it."

She was pleased that she'd been able to manage the words without feeling a stab of pain. Her throat, it would seem, was healing, though the rest of her body was still on fire. "I thought I'd dreamed you."

He found her voice a pleasant change from the shrill voices of the serving wenches. It was low, cultured, breathless. But he couldn't be certain if it was her natural voice, or the result of her injuries. At any rate, he was anxious to hear her speak again. "And why did you think that?"

She shook her head. "I know not. The fever, I suppose. I began to think of you as my dark angel."

"Perhaps I am." His features remained solemn, with no hint of laughter in his voice. "My name is Keane. Keane O'Mara. Carrick House is my ancestral home."

He offered his hand and she had no choice but to accept. Would she ever get used to touching again? "My name is Briana O'Neil."

The moment was awkward and uncomfortable. As soon as their hands touched, they felt the rush of heat. At once they each pulled away.

"O'Neil? Where is your home?"

"Ballinarin."

He arched a brow. "I know of it. You're a long way from home."

The mere thought of it had her aching for that dear place. "Aye."

He heard the loneliness in that single word, spoken like a sigh. "Have you been gone a long time?"

"Three years."

His glance fell on the cross, lying on the bed linen beside her hand.

Seeing the direction of his gaze, her fingers closed around it, finding comfort in something so familiar. "I've been at the Abbey of St. Claire."

He nodded. "I know of it, as well. At least a day's ride from here. What brought you to our village?"

"I was passing through." She sighed, thinking of the eagerness with which she'd taken her leave of the convent. "We'd gone only a day's ride when the soldiers attacked."

"Who were the lads accompanying you?"

"Lads from our village. Sent by my family to escort me." She looked away. "How odd, that I should be the one to live. They will never see their families again."

He could hear the break in her voice and knew that she was close to tears. "I'll see that a lad from the village is dispatched at once to your home with the news that you are alive and will be returned as soon as your health permits."

"That's most kind of you."

He pushed back his chair and crossed to the side table. "My housekeeper sent up a tray. Could you manage a little broth?"

"Nay." She shook her head.

"Nonsense." Ignoring her protest, he filled a cup with broth and set it beside the bed. Then, without waiting for her permission, he reached down and lifted her to a sitting position, plumping pillows behind her.

He had thought, now that she had confirmed his suspicions that she was truly a nun, that the touch of her would no longer affect him. He'd been wrong. He couldn't help but notice the thin, angular body beneath the prim nightshift. And the soft swell of breasts that were pressed against his chest, causing a rush of heat that left him shaken.

It had been a long time since he'd known such feelings. Feelings he'd buried, in the hope they would never surface again. Now that he was touching her, there was nothing to do but finish the task at hand. Then, hopefully, he could put some distance between himself and this woman.

For Briana it was even more disturbing. The mere touch of him had her nerves jumping. But it wasn't this man, she told herself. It was the fact that she had been isolated for too long. Anyone's touch would have had the same effect.

He picked up the cup. "Can you manage yourself? Or would you like some help?"

Her tone was sharper than she intended, to hide her discomfort. "I thank you, but I can feed myself."

When she reached out to accept the cup, she was shocked to feel pain, hot and sharp, shooting along her arm. A cry escaped her lips before she could stop it.

"Careful." His tone was deliberately soft, to soothe the nerves she couldn't hide. "You sustained quite a wound in that shoulder. Another, more serious, in the chest. Had the blade found your heart, you would have never survived."

Before she could reach out again, he sat on the edge of the bed and held the cup to her lips. It was an oddly intimate gesture that let him study her carefully as she sipped, swallowed. He could see her watching him from beneath lowered lashes.

To steady her nerves, and his own, he engaged her in conversation.

"Do you recall anything of the battle?"

"I see it constantly in my dreams. But when I'm awake it's gone, like wisps of smoke caught by the wind."

"Do you recall how many soldiers there were?"

She avoided his eyes. They were too dark, too intense. "I don't recall."

"It would have been a fearsome sight, especially for one who has been so sheltered." He understood how the mind could reject such horrors.

She shivered. "What I do recall was the sight of so many helpless people cut down without a chance to defend themselves. There were but a few knives and swords among them.''

"The people are ill-prepared for English soldiers.'' A fact he bitterly resented, for it had been his own father's doing. Still, there was nothing to be done about it now. "But it would seem that you put up quite a fight.''

For the first time she smiled, and he realized how truly lovely those full, pouty lips were when they curved upward. "I didn't always live in a convent. I know how to wield a sword with as much skill as my brothers. In fact, if I were still living at Ballinarin, I'd probably be able to best them by now.''

He tipped the cup to her lips again. "Then perhaps it's fortunate that you went to live with the good sisters. I'm not sure Ireland is ready to be led into battle by a lass.''

"Spoken like a man.'' His words reminded her of her father's cruel, hateful words hurled in anger so long ago. She pushed his hand away, refusing any more broth.

He glanced down at the cup. "Have you had enough?''

"Aye. Thank you.'' And enough of him, sitting too close, causing her heart to do all manner of strange things.

"How did you come by a weapon with which to defend yourself?''

"I pulled it from the heart of a lad who had died defending me.''

He studied her a moment, hearing not just the words, but the underlying fierceness in her tone. What an odd little female. He'd always thought nuns would be more concerned with peace than war.

He stood and returned the cup to the tray. But when he glanced at the figure in the bed, he could see her rubbing her shoulder. The look in her eyes told him she was struggling for composure. Aye, a most peculiar little creature who was trying desperately to be strong despite overwhelming odds.

"There's an opiate here for pain. I think you ought to take it now."

"Aye." She nodded, and was grateful when he offered her the tumbler of liquid.

When she had drained it he set the empty tumbler aside and helped her to settle into a more comfortable position. It was shocking to feel his arms around her as he lifted her slightly, removing the pillows from behind her back. Then he swept aside the bed linens and laid her down, before returning the covers. As he smoothed them over her, his hands stilled their movements.

"You're so thin. Didn't they feed you in the convent?"

Her face flamed. "They fed us. Though no amount of food would be enough, considering the work we were expected to do."

"Work?"

She had forgotten how to speak to others. After the silence of these last years, the art of conversation was new to her. She struggled to put her thoughts into words. "There were classes, of course. History, literature, biology. And the teachings of the Church fathers. But we also were expected to plant and harvest, and tend the flocks."

"Like peasants?" His tone was one of amazement.

"Aye. Like the peasants we serve." Her tone softened as she remembered the lecture by Mother Superior, delivered nightly in their common prayer. "Because much has been given us, much is expected. And though we are educated, we are expected to serve all God's people. By punishing the body, we nourish the soul."

He was so moved by her words, he caught both her hands in his. "I didn't know there were such unselfish souls left in this world. Bless you." He turned her hands palm up. Seeing the calluses, he muttered an oath and, without thinking, lifted them to his lips.

Dear heaven. What had possessed him? He hadn't intended such a thing. And yet, seeing the ravages of such hard work on those small, delicate hands, he had reacted instinctively. Now there was nothing to do but cover his error with as much dignity as he could manage. Still, though he knew he had overstepped his bounds, he couldn't seem to stop. He kept her small hands in his and pressed a second kiss, before lifting his head.

At the shocking feel of his mouth against her flesh Briana gasped and struggled to pull her hands away. But it was too late. The damage had been done. She could feel the heat. It danced along her flesh and seared the blood flowing through her veins before settling deep inside her. A heat that had her cheeks stained with color. Her eyes went wide with shock. And though no words came out, her mouth opened, then snapped shut.

She looked up to find him staring at her with a strange, almost haunted look in his eyes. Even as she watched, he blinked, and the look was gone.

Or had she only imagined it?

"I'll leave you to your rest, Briana O'Neil." He

turned away abruptly and picked up the empty tumbler.

She watched as he set the tumbler on the tray. Then, knowing the blush was still on her cheeks, she rolled to her side, wishing she could pull the covers over her head and hide.

What had just happened between them? She wasn't quite certain. Perhaps he had merely reacted to her work-worn hands. Or perhaps he was simply trying to soothe her, or honor her. Whatever his reason, he'd had no way of knowing how deeply she would be affected by that simple gesture.

Oh, how she wished she knew how to deal with these strange feelings that had her so agitated. But the isolation of the convent had magnified everything in her mind. All she knew was that the simple press of Keane O'Mara's lips against her palm had started a fire in the pit of her stomach that was burning still.

She squeezed her eyes tightly shut, wishing she could shut out her feelings as easily. But they were there, fluttering like butterfly wings against her throat, her temple, her chest. She prayed the potion would soon have the desired effect. She wanted desperately to escape into blissful sleep.

In time her wish was granted.

There was no such escape for Keane. Throughout the long night he was forced to keep his vigil. He sat by the bedside and watched the steady rise and fall of the thin chest beneath the blankets as Briana slept, and wondered why a woman from the noble house of Ballinarin would give up a life of luxury to live like a peasant.

Whenever his gaze was drawn to those small callused hands, he would find himself pacing to the window, to stare moodily into the darkness. It was the only way to keep his gaze from being drawn to her mouth.

The strange desire to taste her lips, just once, had him muttering every hot, fierce oath he knew.

Chapter Four

"Good day, my lady." Cora swept open the draperies, then paused beside the bed. "You have a bit of color in your cheeks. A good sign. Do you feel strong enough to leave your bed?"

"I'm not certain." Briana touched her tongue to her dry lips. The days and nights had passed in a blur. But thanks to the opiates, and the prolonged rest, the deep, searing pain had eased. "I'm willing to try." She sat up and waited until the dizziness left, then swung her feet to the floor. "How long have I been at Carrick House?"

"A fortnight, my lady."

Could it really be two weeks? "How could I have slept so long?"

"Mistress Malloy said it is the opiates. And the fact that your poor body craved rest in order to heal."

"Whatever the reason, I feel almost alive again."

"The lord left orders that, as soon as you were able, we must prepare a bath. Do you think you're strong enough for that?"

Briana's smile bloomed. "For the offer of a bath, I'll muster all the strength I have."

Cora plumped pillows around her, then flew to the door. "I'll just summon Mistress Malloy and some servants, and I'll be right back."

Briana barely had time to close her eyes and steady herself before Cora had returned, trailed by the house-keeper and a string of servants.

"Well now." Mistress Malloy had plump apple cheeks and twinkling blue eyes. Her white hair was pulled back in a tight, neat bun at her nape. She stood with hands on her ample hips, studying the young woman who had occupied so much of the lord's time and energy. "Cora says you're feeling strong enough for a bath."

"I think I can manage."

"Good." Mistress Malloy took charge, seeing that another log was added to the fire while the tub was filled with warm water, and soft linens were laid out on a chair.

"You're not to attempt to stand alone, miss." With the housekeeper on one side of her and Cora on the other, they supported Briana from her bed to the tub. With the servant's help, Briana removed her nightshift and stepped into the water.

While Cora scrubbed her hair, Briana closed her eyes and sighed with pleasure. "Oh, it has been years since I've felt so pampered."

"You do not bathe in the convent?" one of the servants asked.

Briana laughed. "We wash in a basin of cold wa-ter." She shivered just remembering.

"Could you not heat the water over the fire?"

"There was no time. We had only minutes to wash before we had to hurry to chapel for morning prayers."

"Did you cry when your hair was cut off?" Cora asked.

"Aye. I wept buckets of tears. But later, when I was doing penance for my display of false vanity, Mother Superior reminded me that it's not what is outside a person that counts. It is what's in one's heart."

"Well said." Mistress Malloy nodded in agreement. She liked this lass. A refreshing change from most of the highborn women who thought themselves above the rest of the world. Of course, such humility was to be expected of a woman who'd promised her life in service to the Church.

"But your hair, my lady." Cora poured warm scented water to rinse away the soap. Then she held up one short gleaming strand, while the others gathered around to study it. "It is the color of fire. It must have been lovely before it was shorn."

"I always thought so. But it no longer matters." Briana snuggled deeper into the warm water, loving the feeling of freedom. "I have not seen my reflection, nor cared to, in three years now."

The servants exchanged looks before one of them said, "But my lady, you are truly beautiful. Even with your hair shorn."

"Beautiful? Now I know you jest. For Cora told me that even the old man who found me thought I was a lad."

"Because you were covered with mud and blood, my lady. Now that we can see you, you truly are pleasing to the eye."

Briana waved a hand in dismissal. "It matters not. What matters is that I am alive. And so enjoying all your tender ministrations." She found herself laughing, and loving the sound. "It has been so long now since I've felt this joyful. But it is the knowledge that I am free. Truly free.''

''Free? What do you mean, my lady?'' Cora asked.

''I am free of the confining rules and restrictions of the convent.''

''You are not going back?''

''Nay. I was heading home when we were attacked. And now, for the first time, I realize just how much I have survived, thanks to Lord Alcott. Not only the attack by the English soldiers, but the last threat to my freedom. You see, as soon as I am strong enough, I will be returning home, to my beloved Ballinarin.''

''You're certain she said she is not a nun?'' Vinson stood in the shadows of the hallway, his voice low.

''That is what she just told us.'' The housekeeper's eyes were shining. ''You saw how obsessed he was with her. She could be the answer to our prayers.''

The old man shrugged. ''Maybe. But you say she is eager to return to her home.''

''Aye. But she is far too weak to attempt the journey yet. It could be weeks, months even, before she could endure it.'' Mistress Malloy lowered her voice. ''She seems a lovely, simple lass. I see no harm in throwing them together and seeing what transpires.''

''This is a dangerous game we play with other people's lives.''

''Aye. But there's so little time. You said yourself he plans to leave. And he is our last, our only hope.''

Vinson stared off into space, mulling it over. Then he nodded. ''Leave it to me. I'll think of a way.''

''My lord.''

Keane looked up from the ledgers and was surprised

to see the evening shadows outside the window. Where had the day gone?

"Aye, Vinson."

"The lass felt strong enough to bathe."

Keane nodded. "A good sign."

"Aye, my lord. Very soon now, she will be well enough to leave."

"So it would seem." He had won the battle. The patient was not only alive, but growing stronger with each day. He took a certain amount of pleasure in the knowledge that he had played a small part in her survival. There'd been so little in his life to be proud of.

Vinson cleared his throat.

Keane tensed, waiting for the old man to say what was on his mind. He was eager to return his attention to the ledgers.

"I thought, since the lass is strong enough to bathe, you might wish to invite her to sup with you."

Keane frowned. "I'm certain she'd prefer to eat in her chambers."

"She has not left her room in a fortnight, my lord. The change might do her good."

Keane pushed away from the desk and strode to the window. His voice lowered. "I think the lass dislikes being in my company."

"Why do you think that, my lord?"

"Whenever I am near her, she watches me the way prey might watch a hunter."

"You can hardly blame her. She was, after all, nearly killed here on your land."

Keane's eyes narrowed. "I'm not her enemy. If she doesn't know that now, after all I've done to save her, she never will."

"It could be because of the horror of what she suffered, my lord."

Keane nodded. "There is that, of course."

"Or she could be shy, my lord. She is, after all, a lass educated in the convent."

"Aye."

The old servant decided to poke and prod a bit more. "You might find it pleasant to have someone with whom you could talk about the books you've read, the places you've been. She might prove to be an interesting companion, something in short supply here in Carrick."

Keane stared out the window, seeing nothing. Neither the green rolling hills, nor the flocks undulating across the valley, nor the way the sunset turned the cross atop the chapel to blood. All he saw was the emptiness, stretching out before him. Endless emptiness.

"She has nothing to wear. I doubt she would sup with me wearing a borrowed nightshift."

Vinson smiled. He'd anticipated the problem. "There are your mother's trunks. Mistress Malloy could no doubt find something that would fit the lass."

Keane turned and met the old man's look. "You've put a good deal of thought into this, haven't you, Vinson?"

"Aye, my lord." The old man remained ramrod straight. Not a hint of a smile touched his lips. "The lass needs a chance to properly thank her benefactor."

Keane gave the slightest nod of his head. "All right. Invite her to sup with me. And tell Mistress Malloy to rifle through the trunks for something appropriate." As the old man turned away he added, "Suggest that she find something modest. We wouldn't want to scandalize such an innocent.''

"Aye, my lord.''

When the door closed behind the servant, Keane glanced at the portrait of his father staring down from the mantel, and beneath it, a set of crossed ancestral swords. The two symbols he most detested. Bloodline and misuse of power. Life and death.

He could still hear his father's harsh tone, lecturing him on his weaknesses. "The man who puts the love of God, country or woman ahead of gold is a fool. For, in the end, gold is all that matters.''

He'd rebelled, determined to prove his father wrong. He'd have the rest of his life to regret it.

To occupy his mind, he returned to his ledgers. But as he bent over the page, he found himself thinking about the lass's strange voice. And the way her lips looked whenever she smiled. Odd. He hadn't felt this quickening of his heartbeat for a very long time. But it wasn't the lass that caused it. It was merely loneliness. He'd kept himself locked away with his ledgers too long now. But they were all he had now, since he'd become a stranger in the land of his birth.

"This will do nicely, Cora.'' The housekeeper held up a gown of pale lemon, which she had retrieved from the trunk in the tower room. Though it appeared to be far too big, it was the only one she'd found with a modest neckline. "Can you make it fit the lass?''

"I'll do my best, Mistress Malloy.'' Cora signalled for Briana to stand. Then she slid the gown over her head and began plying needle and thread, nipping and tucking, until the fabric began to mold to the shape of the slender body.

"Oh, my lady, this is lovely on you." Cora tied the waist with a lace sash, then, because there were no boots to fit, added satin bed slippers.

"Now, if you'll sit, I'll do what I can with your hair."

Briana did as she was told, closing her eyes as the little servant dressed her hair.

"Are you feeling weak, my lady?"

"Nay." Briana gave a dreamy smile. "It's just that these past hours have been so luxurious, I'm beginning to feel whole again."

Cora stood back, admiring her handiwork. "Now if you'll just step over here, my lady, you can see what I'm seeing."

Leaning on Cora's arm, Briana walked to the tall looking glass and stared in amazement.

"Oh, my." She lifted a hand to her mouth. Words failed her.

Seeing her reaction, Cora smiled. "Then you are not unhappy with what you see?"

"I'm…speechless."

Gone was the girl she had once been. In her place was a woman. A stranger.

It was the gown, she told herself. A pale lemon confection with a high, tight circlet of lace at the throat and wrists, and a full skirt, gathered here and there with lace inserts. With a critical eye she studied the slender body revealed in the gown. She hoped she wouldn't appear frail. In her whole life she had never thought of herself as anything but robust.

And then there was the hair. Or rather, the lack of it. The last time she had looked at her reflection in a looking glass, she'd had thick, fiery tresses that fell to below her waist. Now it was no more than a few inches long, a tumble of curls framing a face bronzed by the sun.

Oh, what had happened to her fair skin? It was not only tawny, it was freckled. Dozens of them. Hundreds, perhaps, parading across her nose, down her arms. And to think she had once protected her fair skin beneath bonnets and parasols.

"Come, miss." The housekeeper's voice broke the silence. "Vinson is here to escort you to sup."

She turned and saw the old man's look of approval before he lowered his gaze. When she accepted his arm, she was grateful that he matched his steps to her halting ones.

"I see Mistress Malloy found a gown that suits you, miss."

"Do you think it does, Vinson?"

"Aye, miss. And Cora worked her magic to make it fit."

"I've…" She swallowed. "…lost a bit of weight."

He patted her hand and slowed his steps.

As they made their way along the hall, she stared at the ancient tapestries that depicted the history of the O'Mara lineage.

"I see from the number of swords and battles that Lord Alcott comes from a family of warriors."

"Aye, miss. Do you disapprove?"

She shook her head. "My family can trace its roots to King Brian, whose sons were baptized by St. Patrick himself. And we are, proudly, warriors all."

She missed the old man's smile of approval as he whispered, "I must share a secret, lass. Lord Alcott disdains his title. He prefers to be known as merely Keane O'Mara."

"Thank you, Vinson. I'll keep that in mind."

The old man paused, knocked, then drew open the doors to the library.

"My lord. The lass is here."

"Thank you, Vinson." Keane set aside his ledgers and shoved back his chair. He'd been trying, without success, to keep his mind on the figures in neat columns. But it had been an impossible task.

Briana, leaning on Vinson's arm, walked slowly into the room.

Keane knew he was staring, but he couldn't help himself. He hoped his jaw hadn't dropped. Quickly composing himself, he called to Vinson, "Draw that chaise close to the fire for the lass."

"Aye, my lord."

The old man hurried forward to do his master's bidding, while Keane led Briana across the room. The minute he touched her he felt the heat and blamed it on the blaze on the hearth. He shouldn't have had the servants add another log. It was uncomfortably warm in here.

When she was settled, he asked, "Would you have some wine?"

It was on the tip of her tongue to refuse, feeling that such a luxury should be saved for important guests. Then, recalling the festive meals at Ballinarin, she relaxed. Before the convent, it had been an accepted custom. It was time she adapted to life outside the convent walls. "Aye. I will."

Keane turned to his butler. "We'll both have wine, Vinson."

"Very good, my lord."

Minutes later the old man offered a tray with two goblets. That done, he discreetly took his leave.

"Well." Keane lifted his goblet. "I need to know what to call you."

"I thought I'd told you. My name is Briana."

"Aye. You did. But I thought…" He sipped. Swallowed. "I thought perhaps you would want me to call you sister."

"Sister?"

"You said you spent the last three years in the Abbey of St. Claire."

"I did." She swallowed back her surprise. Was that why he had kissed her hand? Out of respect? "But only as a student. I took no vows."

"I see." He took another sip of wine and thought it tasted somehow sweeter. "So, you're not a nun."

"Nay." Was that disappointment that deepened his voice? She couldn't tell.

Keane relaxed. Not that it mattered to him whether or not the lass was a nun. All he wanted was a pleasant evening of conversation with a reasonably intelligent human being.

"Tell me a little about your family."

"With pleasure. But only if you agree to tell me about yours, as well."

"Aye." He forced himself not to frown as he glanced at the portrait above the mantel. That was his usual reaction whenever he thought about his family. He shook off his dark thoughts and concentrated on the lass.

"My father is Gavin O'Neil, lord of Ballinarin."

"Aye." His frown was back. "I know of him. All of Ireland knows of him. And your mother?"

"My mother, Moira, is a great beauty."

"I see where you inherited your looks."

She blushed, feeling suddenly self-conscious. She

had no way of knowing if he was merely making polite conversation, or if he meant to pay her a compliment.

Needing to fill the silence, she said, "I also have two brothers, Rory and Conor. And their wives, AnnaClaire and Emma. And Innis, who is like a brother to me, though he was orphaned when his entire family was killed at the hands of the English. He lives now with Rory and AnnaClaire." Her eyes lit with pleasure at the thought of those beloved faces. "And there is Friar Malone, who has lived at Ballinarin since before I was born, and who is like an uncle to me."

She took a deep breath. It was the most she had said in years.

Suddenly, spreading her arms wide she gave a husky laugh. "Oh, it feels so strange and so good to be able to talk without asking permission."

The sound of her laughter skimmed over him, causing the strangest sensation. "It would be a pity to stifle a voice as unique as yours, Briana O'Neil."

"Unique?"

"Aye." Instead of explaining, he said simply, "I like listening to you. Tell me more about your family and your home."

"Ballinarin is wild. And so beautiful. In all of Ireland, there is nothing to compare with it. We live always in the shadow of towering Croagh Patrick, with its wonderful waterfall that cascades to the lake below. There are fields of green as far as the eye can see. And rolling meadows, where I used to ride, wild and free with my brothers."

Keane refilled her goblet, then his own, before settling himself on the chaise beside her. Their knees brushed, and Briana's voice faltered for a moment. "It was...the loveliest life a girl could ever have."

"Why did you choose a convent so far away?" He found himself studying the way the soft fabric revealed the outline of her thighs, her hips, her breasts.

"I didn't choose. It was chosen for me."

He heard the change in her tone and realized he'd struck a nerve. "And you have not seen your home in more than three years?"

"Aye. There were times when I thought I'd die from the loneliness." She looked over at him. "I suppose that sounds silly."

"Not at all." He stared down into the amber liquid in his glass. "I know the feeling well."

"Have you ever been forced to leave Carrick House?"

He nodded. "For most of my life I've been away."

"By choice? Or were you forced by circumstances?"

She saw a look come into his eyes. "Like you, my education abroad was chosen for me."

"And then you returned?"

"Not immediately."

She smiled. "But you're home now."

"Aye." He didn't return the smile. He had gone somewhere in his mind. A place, Briana realized, that wasn't pleasing to him.

They both seemed relieved when Vinson knocked, then entered to announce, "My lord, dinner is ready. Mistress Malloy wishes to know if you will take your meal in the great hall or here in the library."

He had intended a simple meal here in the library, so that the lass wouldn't be drained by a longer walk. But now, glancing at the portrait over the mantel, he realized he wanted a change of scenery. He wanted, needed, to put some distance between himself and his past.

"Tell Mistress Malloy we'll sup in the great hall."

"Aye, my lord."

The old man took his leave, and Keane stood and offered his arm. "Come, my lady. It's time you saw more of Carrick House."

It was, he realized, his first opportunity to show off his home to a guest.

Chapter Five

"You'll let me know when you grow weary, Briana." Keane deliberately kept his strides easy, the pace slow so as not to tire her.

"I will, aye." She was grateful for the strong arm to lean on. "This weakness is most distressing."

"It will soon pass, and you'll be as you were before."

She looked up at him with an impish smile. "Do I have your word on that?"

His own features remained impassive. "You do." He thought about touching that cap of curls and resisted the impulse. "Now tell me how you were before."

"Before the attack? Or before the convent?"

"Why don't we begin with your life before the attack."

"Before the attack I had learned, at great cost, how to keep my head bowed in chapel, how to keep my thoughts to myself, and how to bear the unbearable."

Though she kept her tone light, he could detect the underlying sadness. "What was this great cost?"

"Penance. It seemed I was always on my knees. If

not in chapel, then scrubbing the cold stone floors of the refectory. And when I was allowed to stand, it was to harvest a crop or to fork dung from the barns and stables.''

He couldn't hide his surprise. ''You did all that?''

''Aye. But only after my classes and chores were completed to the liking of Mother Superior.''

''I'd say you were far from weak, if you did all that and survived.''

''I survived all that, and more.''

He knew, by the finality of her tone, that she had no intention of listing all that she'd been through. His admiration for her was growing by the minute.

''Now I would like to hear about your life before the convent.''

She smiled. ''That would take hours.''

He paused at the threshold to the great hall. ''We have all evening.''

As he led her to the table, the butler, the housekeeper and their army of servants stood to one side, awaiting his command.

Keane helped Briana to her chair, then took his place at the head of the table.

Briana surveyed the table, with its gleaming silver and crystal and the masses of candles that flickered and glowed. ''Oh, Mistress Malloy, this is indeed lovely.''

The housekeeper nearly burst with pride. ''Thank you, miss. We do our best to please.''

''I haven't seen anything this grand in years.'' Briana turned to Keane. ''Isn't it wonderful knowing this awaits you each night?''

He glanced around. ''I never think of it. I suppose I've begun to take such things as my due.'' He signalled to his housekeeper. "You may begin serving now, Mistress Malloy."

"Aye, my lord." At a word from her, the servants moved to the table bearing platters of fresh mussels and salmon, tender slices of beef and biscuits still warm from the oven, while Vinson filled their goblets with wine.

When Keane noted the small portions on Briana's plate he lifted a brow.

Seeing it she avoided his eyes. "It's my training at the hands of the good sisters, I suppose. I can't bear to waste."

"But you've taken so little, it wouldn't keep a bird alive."

"I'm afraid my appetite is slow to return." She took a bite of salmon and almost sighed with pleasure. "But if this is any indication of your cook's talent, it won't be any time at all before I'm eating like Sister Ascension." Seeing his questioning look she added, "Our sister cook at the convent. She was wider than she was tall. We used to whisper that she tasted everything before she served it. And sometimes, we thought, she surely must have tasted many times over."

Keane found himself smiling as he dug into his meal.

Briana broke open a steaming biscuit. At once a servant approached with honey.

Drizzling it over her biscuit, Briana tasted, closed her eyes and sighed. "Surely I've died and gone to heaven."

Keane arched a brow. "If you can fall into ecstasy over Cook's biscuits, I worry what will happen when you taste her brandied currant cake." He looked up.

"Mistress Malloy, will you see that Cook bakes one for our guest?"

The housekeeper couldn't hide her surprise. In all the time Lord Alcott had been back in Carrick House, this was the first time he had ever mentioned a favorite food, or requested anything in particular. Cook had long puzzled over what to fix for him, since he ate, without comment, whatever was placed in front of him.

"Aye, my lord." She couldn't wait to tell Cook the news. "I'll see that she bakes one on the morrow."

"And salmon," he added. "Our guest seems to have a fondness for it." At the housekeeper's steady look he felt compelled to add, "We have a duty to see that Miss O'Neil's strength returns."

"I'll see to it myself." Pleased, Mistress Malloy nudged a servant with another tray.

"Now." Keane returned his attention to the lass beside him. "You promised to tell me about your life before the convent."

He saw her smile bloom. This, then, was something she enjoyed talking about.

"It was a grand life. Such freedom, which I took completely for granted. I roamed the hills with my brothers and Innis. I learned to hunt with them, to fish with them, even to handle weapons with them."

"Weapons?"

"Aye. The knife and sword. The crossbow, as well as bow and arrow. Each day was a grand adventure."

She saw the way he was staring at her and added, "On market day I sampled the wares from the booths, or bought lace or frills with my mother."

"Tell me about her."

She could see her mother in her mind. It was an

image that never faded or wavered. "She's tall and slender and beautiful. And very kind. Though she married into wealth, she never forgets that she came to the marriage with no dowry. This then is her payment. She looks after the women and children in the villages around Ballinarin. If they are ill or in need, they know Moira O'Neil will come calling with whatever they need, be it a packet of herbs, or a brace of pheasants, or a warm cloak to ward off winter's chill. She loves the people of Ballinarin as though they were her children. And in a way, they are. She's fond of saying we're all of the same family."

He loved the way her eyes looked as she spoke of her mother. All soft and warm and loving. "She sounds like a saint."

"Aye. She is that. She would have to be to remain wed to my father."

"Tell me about him."

He saw a wariness come into her eyes before she looked down at her plate. "Gavin O'Neil is lord of Ballinarin. His word is law. His temper is fierce. But all who know him will tell you he's a fair man."

"Was it your father who sent you to the convent?"

She nodded. "But as I've learned these last years, under the tutelage of Mother Superior, what he did, he did out of love. Because it was necessary for my growth and education. I was willful. And far too proud and unyielding."

He would know a little about such things. And how such decisions, no matter how noble the intentions, hurt. Without thinking he closed his hand over hers.

Her head jerked up. Her eyes went wide before she managed to compose herself.

For Keane, it was equally shocking. He hadn't

meant to touch her. He had merely reacted reflexively, hoping to offer her a measure of comfort.

Knowing the servants were watching, he removed his hand and, needing to do something, lifted the goblet to his lips.

At once Vinson was beside him, refilling it.

Keane glanced at Briana. "You haven't touched your wine."

"It's been so long, I'm afraid to drink more than a few sips, for fear it'll go straight to my head. And then I'd have to be carried to my chambers."

For some strange reason, the very thought had his blood running hot. He kept his tone deliberately bland. "That would not be a hardship, my lady."

At the deep timbre of his voice, Briana felt a little thrill. But a quick glance assured her he was merely being polite. He had already returned his attention to his meal.

"You've told me nothing of yourself, except that you were educated abroad." She lifted her goblet. "Where did you study?"

"A few years in Paris. A few more in Spain."

"How wonderful. My brother, Conor, studied there, as well as in Rome."

"Did he like it?"

She shook her head. "I think he had some marvelous adventures. But he said he was often lonesome for the sights and sounds of Ballinarin. Was it the same for you?"

He nodded. "One doesn't have to be in a convent or a prison to feel confinement."

She thought about it a moment, then said softly, "Mother Superior once said we all carry a prison inside our hearts. But we also carry freedom. It's up to us to choose which door we open, and which one we close.''

When he remained silent, she knew which door he had chosen to open.

''What did you study, while in France and Spain?''

He shrugged. ''Much as you at the convent, I suppose. History, literature, mathematics. My father wanted me to be prepared to take over the family estates.''

''And what did you want?''

He turned to her and saw the understanding in her eyes. ''I didn't know what I wanted. I only knew I didn't want what my father wanted for me. When he told me to go left, I went right. When he told me to sleep, I defied him by staying awake all night.'' His voice lowered. ''And when he ordered me to join him in England, I went. But I did everything I could that was harmful and hurtful.''

''Perhaps your father should have sent you to a monastery.''

Despite his dark mood, he had to smile. ''Hearing your tales of the convent, I wonder if I would have survived. In my earlier, arrogant days, I would have been horrified if I'd been forced to shovel dung in a stable.''

''Oh, you'd have survived. And you would have returned, like me, humbled and work-worn.''

''Is that how you see yourself?''

She nodded. ''Or perhaps I should have said chaste and chastened.''

Chaste. His laughter died. If only he could make such a claim. He would have been spared untold misery.

Seeing his sudden grim mood, Briana took a sip of

wine before setting down her goblet. Though the meal had been excellent, she could feel her strength beginning to ebb.

The housekeeper approached. "Will there be anything else, my lord?"

He glanced at Briana, who shook her head.

"Nothing more, Mistress Malloy." Then, for no reason he could fathom, he felt compelled to add, "Everything was perfect. You'll give my compliments to Cook."

"Aye, my lord." Bursting with pride, the housekeeper motioned for the servants to leave, then followed them out the door.

Lost in thought, Keane sipped his wine and stared at the closed door.

Across the room, Vinson cleared his throat.

Keane looked up with a frown, wondering what he had forgotten to do or say.

The butler glanced toward Briana, then at Keane. "Perhaps the lass is growing weary, my lord."

Keane turned to her. Seeing her pallor, he shoved back his chair and got to his feet. "Forgive me, my lady."

"There is nothing to forgive." She accepted his hand and stood beside him. "I only wish I were stronger. But for now, I must go to my chambers and rest."

He offered his arm, and she leaned on him as they crossed the room and bade good-night to Vinson. The old man held the door and watched as they moved slowly down the hall.

"I detest this weakness." When the words slipped from her mouth, she gave a sigh of annoyance. She had thought, after the years of coaching by the good sisters, that she could keep such thoughts to herself. It would seem that within mere days of freedom, her old nature was returning. Or perhaps, it had always been with her, awaiting the chance to show itself.

"I know you are impatient for your strength to return." His voice was so close beside her ear she had to struggle not to shiver. "But you have been through so much, Miss O'Neil. Be patient just a bit longer."

"Is patience one of your virtues, my lord?"

"If only it were."

By the light of candles burning in sconces along the walls, she turned to study his profile. It showed a proud, haughty man. She had a feeling there was much more to Keane O'Mara than mere pride and arrogance. She sensed an underlying sadness in him, as well. A deep and abiding wound that had never healed.

At the door to her chambers they paused.

She turned to him, her face tilted. "I never properly thanked you for saving my life. Cora told me how you fought for me when she and the others had thought me beyond saving."

"You were the one who fought your way back to life, Briana O'Neil." It occurred to him that hers was the loveliest name he'd ever spoken aloud. "I knew, the moment I saw you fighting to hang on to the smallest thread of life, that you had the heart of a warrior. But I'm glad I was here to help."

Her voice lowered to a whisper. "I can never repay you."

"You already have." He took her hands in his. "Your presence tonight was more than enough payment. You shared your past with me. For a little while, you made me forget about my own. I don't remember when I've had a more pleasant evening."

He lifted her hands to his lips and kissed one, then the other. It was the merest brush of his lips to her flesh, but he felt the sizzle of excitement and found that he couldn't release her just yet.

Turning her hands over, he pressed kisses to each of her palms. He heard her little intake of breath and knew that she had been unprepared for this. As had he, if truth be told. But there was a demon inside him that had suddenly taken over his control. Without giving a thought to what he was doing, he released her hands and lifted his to frame her face.

"Have I shocked you, my lady?"

"Aye." She started to draw away and found herself backed against the door.

"Forgive me. But I've never before seen a woman with amber eyes. They fascinate me." He drew her closer. "You fascinate me, Briana O'Neil."

And then, before he could reconsider, he lowered his head and covered her lips with his.

Briana stood absolutely still. Though her heart was racing like a runaway carriage, and her blood was pumping furiously, she didn't move. Couldn't.

The hands framing her face were the gentlest of prisons. But they held her all the same. As did the kiss.

And oh, what a kiss. His mouth moved over hers with such sure, practiced ease. This was a man who'd had a great deal of experience, if his lips were any indication. They nuzzled and coaxed and tasted until, on a sigh, she returned the kiss. And became lost in it.

He tasted of wine and tobacco and some other, darker taste that was distinctly male. And purely intoxicating.

Years before, she'd been kissed. By village boys, eager to impress the daughter of the O'Neil. By friends of her brothers, who'd taken care not to anger the powerful O'Neil men. But none of those chaste kisses had caused this strange ripple of feeling that had her feeling as if her entire world had suddenly tipped upside down.

She reached out to steady herself, and her hands made contact with his waist. As soon as she touched him, she heard his little moan. Whether of pleasure or impatience, she knew not. She responded with a sigh of her own.

Keane could have told himself that this was unplanned, but it would have been a lie. He had thought of nothing but this all evening. From the first moment she'd walked into the library, he'd wanted to kiss her. To feel the heat. The fire. To feel her heart pounding in rhythm to his.

He knew he'd shocked her by his boldness. It couldn't be helped. Just being around her made him want things he had no right to. And her sweetness, her innocence, only made him want them more.

On a moan he took the kiss deeper. His fingers tangled through her hair, drawing her head back. He heard her little sigh as she brought her hands to his chest. But instead of pushing him away, her hands clutched at the front of his tunic.

Dear heaven, he was starved for the touch, the taste, of one as sweet as this. He hadn't known his heart could respond like this. He'd buried his feelings deep, consigned to the grave forever. But now, with the simplest touch of her, the merest taste, he could feel his heart beginning to beat again.

He knew he had to end this, but not just yet. He wanted, needed one more moment, one more taste.

Her sweetness, her innocence, aroused him as nothing ever had. Dangerous, he knew. For he was far from innocent. And the thoughts he was entertaining at this moment would shock and scandalize this unspoiled, untouched lass.

Finally, detesting this weakness in himself, he lifted his head and took a step back, breaking contact.

When she put a hand to the door, he covered it with both of his, to still her movements. Inside, he knew, Cora would be awaiting her mistress. What he wanted to say was for Briana's ears alone.

"I'm sorry if I've shocked you. But I can't say I'm sorry for the kiss. Given the chance, I'd no doubt do it again. So beware, Briana O'Neil. For, as I'm certain the servants will tell you, you're in the home of a man with no conscience."

She looked up and met his gaze. For the past three years, the virtue of honesty had been preached on a daily basis. She wasn't certain if this was the time or place for it, or just how other women would deal with this situation. But she wasn't other women. And so she said the only thing she could.

"I can't say I'm sorry either." Her lips curved in a most beguiling smile. "And if that be a sin, it was a most enjoyable one, Keane O'Mara. One I'd gladly commit again."

She shoved open the door and walked inside without a backward glance.

As the door closed behind her, Keane stood perfectly still. Then, as he began to walk along the hall, he threw back his head and roared with laughter. Briana O'Neil was the most unexpected surprise. An absolute delight.

He was still laughing when he reached his own chambers.

It was a sound the servants at Carrick House hadn't heard since his return from England.

Chapter Six

"Good morrow, my lord." Vinson entered Keane's chambers and found him standing on the balcony, naked to the waist, wearing only his breeches and boots.

The look on his face was dark and bleak as he turned to his butler. "I learned something last night."

"Aye, my lord? And what might that be?"

"Briana O'Neil is not a nun. She took no vows. She was merely a student at the convent."

"Is that so, my lord?"

"Aye." His scowl deepened as the elderly servant helped him into his tunic and removed a waistcoat from the wardrobe.

After a sleepless night, he'd come to several decisions. As pleasant as he found the lass's company, he needed to avoid any further contact with her. He had no right to lead the lass on. She was completely open and guileless. And he…

If she were to learn the truth about him, she would run, weeping and praying, back to the safety of the convent.

He'd best walk a very wide circle around Briana O'Neil. And see that he returned her to her family as he'd found her. Untouched. Unspoiled. With her trust—and her heart—intact.

"Though the village elders have been requesting a meeting, I've been putting them off, Vinson. Perhaps it's time I saw to it."

"Aye, my lord. If you'd like, I'll send a messenger. When would you like to meet with them?"

"Today. This morrow." He needed to get away. To put some distance between himself and Briana O'Neil. He may have been undecided before, but last night had convinced him. If he didn't take drastic steps to avoid the lass, he might end up doing something they'd both regret. He had no desire to hurt her. Or to complicate his already complicated life. "You'll see to it, Vinson?"

Instead of a reply, the old man cleared his throat.

Keane braced himself.

"Mistress Malloy and I have been discussing the lass."

"Aye." Keane waited, tapping his foot.

"We think she needs a bit of prodding."

"Prodding?"

"Aye. A push or two in the right direction."

Keane crossed his arms over his chest. "And which direction might that be, Vinson?"

"She eats almost nothing from the trays sent to her chambers. But last night she ate quite a bit of meat and biscuits."

"Her appetite will improve as her strength grows."

"But how can her strength grow if she doesn't eat? Mistress Malloy and I were thinking that if you were to take your meals with the lass, you might be able to persuade her, in a nice way of course, to take more nourishment."

There was no way he could possibly explain to this old man that the very thing he was suggesting was the thing Keane most needed to avoid. The more time he spent in Briana's company, the more complicated all this would become.

"Isn't it enough that her life was spared?"

"What good will it do if the lass never recovers her strength, my lord?"

"It will come back. Slowly. But I don't believe that taking my meals with Miss O'Neil will do anything to improve her appetite. In fact, it might have quite the opposite effect."

"If I may say so, my lord, the lass was in high spirits last night. And I do believe it was due in some small measure to the fact that she was in the company of a kindred spirit."

Aye. Just what he'd feared. A kindred spirit. With kissing on both their minds. And he knew what kissing led to, even if she didn't. Complications.

His tone hardened. "There's the matter of my meeting with the village elders."

"Aye, my lord. If you'd like, I'll arrange a meeting for midmorning. After you've had a chance to sup with the lass."

Keane expelled an impatient breath. Stubborn. The old man had been this way with him since he'd been a lad. And, if anything, Vinson seemed to be growing more stubborn with every year. It was the problem with elderly retainers. They felt as if they ruled the manor. And this one, who had been more a father to him than his own flesh and blood, was becoming especially vexing.

Still, what was the harm? Didn't he owe it to the lass to help her recover completely?

He gave a reluctant nod of his head. "All right, Vinson. I'll break my fast with her this morrow." He waved a hand. "Tell Mistress Malloy to prepare her morning repast. Then I'll be on my way."

"Very good, my lord." The old man took his leave. Then, smiling broadly, he hurried off to tell the housekeeper that everything was going along as planned.

"Good morrow, my lady."

Briana squinted against the bright sunlight as Cora threw open the heavy draperies and began to move efficiently about the room. She'd been having the loveliest dream. A dark angel had lifted her onto his steed and carried her home to Ballinarin. But when it was time to bid her goodbye, he had gathered her into his arms and proclaimed his undying love, kissing her until she was breathless.

In fact, she was still breathless. And her heartbeat most unsteady. If only she could have finished the dream. Would he have stayed with her?

She roused herself enough to return the servant's greeting. "Good morrow, Cora. How I wish I had just a little of your energy."

"You shall, my lady. You'll see. But you must be patient a while longer."

Briana sighed. All her young life she had heard that admonition. Patience. The lack of it was her downfall. Mother Superior had called it her cross in life. But there was nothing to be done for it except hope that one day she would acquire a least a small measure of patience.

Cora held up a simple morning gown of pale pink. "Mistress Malloy chose this for today. Does it meet with your approval?"

"Oh, Cora. It's lovely. I do thank you for all the work you're forced to do on my behalf. But please explain to the housekeeper that it matters not to me what I wear. For so long now I've worn nothing but the coarse robes of the convent. I've no need of such finery."

"I don't mind the extra work, my lady. You make it a joy to serve you." The servant drew back the covers and offered her arm, leading Briana across the room to a basin of rose-scented water.

While Briana washed, Cora laid out a petticoat and chemise, as well as dainty kid boots.

"We found these in a trunk and thought they might suit you better than those slippers, my lady."

Briana nodded in appreciation. "They're lovely, Cora. Thank you. But why all this fuss?"

"Lord Alcott sent word that you were to join him this morrow to break your fast."

"He did?" Briana felt a rush of pleasure. Though she knew little about her host, she had enjoyed his company. Not to mention his kiss. Her cheeks felt warm at the very thought of it.

"Keane was most reluctant to speak of himself or his family last night, though I know not why. Perhaps he will speak of them this morrow."

The little servant's voice lowered. "It is rumored that he has known much sorrow in his lifetime, my lady. He has only recently returned from England to claim his inheritance."

"He spoke of England. And France and Spain, as well. But after traveling afar, I should think he would be delighted to finally return to his childhood home."

Cora turned. "There is much speculation among the servants."

"Such as?" Briana looked up.

"Whether he will remain in Ireland, or become an absent owner as his father was. No one knows whether or not he will, of course." Cora kept her voice just above a whisper. "For Lord Alcott has not chosen to confide his plans to anyone. But there are those who wager he'll soon tire of the life of a landowner in this poor country."

"Oh." Briana covered her mouth with her hand. "It would be a sin to turn his back on a place as lovely as this."

"Aye, my lady. But it's done all the time by titled gentlemen." The little servant held up a comb, trying to decide if it could be secured in such short hair, then seemed to change her mind, placing it back atop a dressing table. Seeing that Briana had finished washing, Cora approached and began to help her into the gown. "That's why the household staff has made wagers that the master is merely biding his time until he leaves here to make his home in some exotic land." Her voice lowered. "Where he will never again be reminded of his troubled past."

"His past?"

"Aye. There are stories. Rumors. That he chose a life of debauchery." She led Briana to a chair and began dressing her hair. As she worked she added, "Of course, our lord is merely doing what was done to him."

"And what is that?" Briana studied the servant's reflection in the mirror.

"After his mother died, and shortly thereafter his grandfather, I'm told his father had hardly a minute for the young lord. He was sent off to boarding schools so that his father could entertain with lavish masques and dinner parties here at Carrick House, until he took himself off to England, where he lived out his days in the company of the titled noblemen and their ladies. I suppose it was natural that the present Lord Alcott would feel like an outsider when he finally returned to his home.''

''But after so many years of wandering, I should think Carrick House would bring him such joy.''

The serving wench shrugged. ''Mistress Malloy says there are some people in this world who simply cannot find happiness anywhere. Perhaps Lord Alcott is one of them.'' Cora stood back to admire her handiwork. Satisfied, she said, ''Now, my lady, I'll summon Vinson to escort you to the great hall.''

''Thank you, Cora.''

When she was alone, Briana turned to stare out the window at the green, rolling hills of Carrick. The scene was not as wild and primitive as Ballinarin. But it was obvious that Keane O'Mara had inherited something of great value here. How truly sad it would be if he should turn his back on his birthright.

Her own problems faded into insignificance. If the last three years away from Ballinarin had seemed interminable to her, what must it have felt like for a young, lonely lad? The loss of a mother and grandfather would have left him adrift. But to lose the love of his father, and to be turned out of the comfort of his home, would have left him devastated.

Still, the servant had suggested that much of this was Keane's own choice. If it be true, he had no one to blame but himself. Still, for now, she would not forget that this man was the one who had saved her life. For that, she owed him an enormous debt.

* * *

"You did what?" The housekeeper looked aghast as Cora repeated what she'd told Briana. "You discussed Lord Alcott with the lass?" With her hands on her hips, the older woman turned to the butler. "Now what're we to do?"

Vinson sighed. "There's nothing to be done about it now. Besides, it may not cause any real damage. The lass isn't like most females. She doesn't strike me as someone who'd be put off by the lord's past. In fact, Cora, you might have done more good than you know. After all, if she's as tenderhearted as I suspect, it may be just the thing the lass needed to hear."

The servant gave a sigh of relief. "I truly didn't mean any harm. It's just that it's so easy to talk to the lass. There's a real goodness in her heart and soul. I can see it in her eyes."

Vinson nodded, then motioned for her to leave. When they were alone he turned to the housekeeper. "There's nothing to do now but go on as planned."

"Aye." Mistress Malloy nodded. "And hope that scatterbrain Cora keeps at least a few of the family secrets to herself."

"My lord, the lass is here." At the sound of Vinson's voice, Keane took a deep breath and turned to face her.

She was leaning slightly on the old man's arm. Keane's frown deepened. Why did she have to look so young and fresh and lovely?

All night he'd seen her in his dreams. Smiling up at him with such trust. He could have sworn he'd even tasted her. As sweet as spring rain. With just a hint of roses.

When Vinson stepped away, Keane had no choice

but to cross the room and offer his arm. The mere touch of her made him bristle. Dear heaven, how was he going to get through an entire meal?

He forced himself to make pleasant, innocuous conversation. ''How are you feeling this morrow, my lady?''

''A little better,'' she said as she laid her hand on his sleeve.

He absorbed the touch of her and felt his blood begin to stir. ''Are you still in need of opiates for the pain?''

''At times. But each day the need seems to lessen.''

''That pleases me.'' He led her to the table and settled her in a chair, then took his place.

Another mistake. His knee brushed hers, and he felt a rush of heat that had him clenching his hand into a fist.

Mistress Malloy motioned for the servants, who approached the table with platters of roasted quail, thin slices of beef swimming in gravy, and a basket of steaming bread. Another servant held a bowl of fruit conserve, while another offered tea and mead.

Vinson cleared his throat. Keane turned his way. Seeing the old man's arched brow, Keane was reminded of the reason for this meal. He served Briana's plate first, making certain that it was heaped with food. Then he served his own plate.

The old man nodded his approval.

Briana's eyes widened. ''I couldn't possibly eat all this, Keane.''

His tone was rougher than he'd intended. ''You need to eat if you're to regain your strength. After all, it's the only way you'll endure the journey to Ballinarin.''

At the mention of her home, she felt the momentary thrill of pleasure. "It sounds as though you're eager to see me gone, my lord."

He frowned at the very thought. "I should think you'd be eager to be on your way."

"I am. Aye."

"Then I shall be happy to oblige, my lady."

Neither of them smiled as they fell silent.

The housekeeper used that moment to step forward. "Have you tried the fruit conserve, my lady?"

"Nay. But I will, Mistress Malloy. Thank you." Briana spooned some onto her plate, then spread a bit on her bread.

Her smile was back. "Oh, that's the finest conserve I've ever tasted." She turned to Keane. "You must try some."

She spread a little on a piece of bread and held it to his lips. He opened his mouth and accepted the offering, keeping his gaze fixed on her. As her fingers brushed his lips, she saw his eyes narrow slightly. Then, as he tasted, a slow smile spread across his lips.

"You're right, my lady." He addressed his words to the housekeeper. "You'll tell Cook that she has made another conquest."

Mistress Malloy was grinning from ear to ear. "I will, my lord."

He turned to Briana. "Now, I believe you were going to tell me about Innis, the lad you call almost a brother."

He could see the joy that came into her eyes. "Aye. Innis. His entire clan was slaughtered by English soldiers. From that day on he made his home with us at Ballinarin, until my brother Rory wed AnnaClaire Thompson. Innis adores them, and they feel the same about him. So, by happy circumstances, I acquired another brother.''

''Is he older or younger?''

''Just four years younger, at ten and four.''

He blinked. ''You're ten and eight, my lady?''

Out of the corner of his eye he could see Vinson and Mistress Malloy exchange a quick look. They appeared to be as surprised as he.

''I thought you much younger, Miss O'Neil.''

''Perhaps it is the simplicity of life in the convent,'' she mused as she spooned fruit conserve on another piece of warm bread.

But Keane knew it was not the simplicity of the convent, but the simplicity of the woman beside him. She was absolutely without pretense. But a woman, nonetheless. A beautiful, simple, and most desirable woman.

He fell silent, lost in thought. Seeing it, the housekeeper turned to the butler with a knowing look. Perhaps they had all made a dangerous miscalculation. A woman as old as this, who was still a maiden, would be thinking of marriage and permanence and ties that would bind for a lifetime. Not things Lord Alcott would ever consider.

''Oh, that was heavenly.'' Briana sat back with a sigh. ''But I simply can't eat another bite.''

''Nor I.'' Keane set aside his napkin. ''Do you feel strong enough for a walk in the garden?''

She nodded. ''I'd like that.''

She leaned on his arm as he helped her from the table. He felt the quick rush of heat and struggled to dismiss it. But as they walked slowly from the room he became aware of the scent of roses that lingered on her skin, in her hair.

"You must see the rose garden. They're just beginning to bloom."

"I do love roses." She breathed in the fresh air as they stepped outside. "Oh, Keane, this is lovely."

He nodded, seeing it through her eyes. It was, in fact, the first time he'd bothered to walk in the garden since his return to Ireland. He realized now that it had become neglected.

He remembered as a lad playing here while his mother and grandfather looked on. The jolt was swift and painful.

"Here we are." He led her along a stone-paved path. "We can sit over here and admire the roses."

He settled her on a garden bench, then took a seat beside her. It was a lovely, peaceful setting, with rows of hedges between beds of roses. If the hedges were in need of trim, and the roses in need of pruning, they detracted little from the view.

In the center of the garden, a fountain spilled into a circular basin. The sound, the scents, were a soothing balm.

Briana watched the antics of a bird, splashing in the waters of the fountain, before turning to Keane.

"My mother has a lovely garden at Ballinarin. She's especially proud of her roses. They're considered some of the finest in all of Ireland. Villagers come from all around to admire them. And though she has several gardeners, she prefers to tend the roses herself."

She suddenly laughed, remembering an incident from her childhood. "Once, when I was a wee lass, I snipped off all the blooms from my mother's roses, then proudly raced inside and presented her with my lovely gift.''

Keane chuckled. ''If I had committed such an offense as a lad, I would have tasted the rod. What was the reaction of your parents?''

She smiled. ''As you can imagine, my father was horrified. He pounded his fist on the table, and I fully expected that I'd be avoiding anything that required sitting down for many days to come. But before he could exact punishment for my crime, my mother clapped her hands and laughed and said it was the nicest present she'd ever been given. And she gathered all the blooms into her apron and carried them outside to the fountain, scattering them into the waters of the pool.''

''For what purpose?''

Briana shook her head. ''At the time, I hadn't the vaguest idea. I just thought all those pretty blossoms looked so perfect, floating in the water.'' She smiled, remembering. ''That night, when I was supposed to be asleep, I heard laughter from outside. I crept to my balcony, where I saw my father and mother seated in the pool, sipping from goblets and whispering words that were unintelligible from such a distance. But I fell asleep with the sound of their laughter still ringing in my ears.''

The image her story had painted in his mind had him looking at her with a bemused expression. ''What an amazing family yours must be. It sounds as though your parents actually enjoy one another.''

''Of course they do. Why are you surprised by that?''

He shrugged. ''I suppose because I have observed

so few husbands and wives who are truly happy with their state in life.''

"Theirs is a great love, despite their differences in personality and temperament.'' Briana's voice softened. "All who see Gavin and Moira O'Neil marvel at the love for one another which shines in their eyes.''

Without thinking he linked his fingers with hers and studied her small hand. "Did you ever pick your mother's roses again?''

She laughed, to cover the little tremor that raced along her spine at the touch of his hand on hers. "Nay. But there were so many other offenses committed, I often couldn't sit down for days at a time.''

"You, lass?''

She grinned. "From the day I was born, I have been the bane of my father's existence. He wanted me to emulate my mother. To be sweet and silent, and...'' She wrinkled her nose. "...subservient. And all I wanted was the freedom my brothers take for granted.''

"Such as?''

"The freedom to ride a horse bareback, without thought to modestly covering my legs. The freedom to wield a weapon. The freedom to swim in the river with my brothers and Innis.''

He glanced down at their linked fingers. "Perhaps what you see as freedom, they see as duty.''

"Then why must men's duties be so enjoyable, while women's duties are so confining?'' She turned to him with a frown. "While my brothers were tumbling about in a meadow, I was expected to sit at my mother's knee and learn needlework. While they were swimming on a summer's day, I was assisting my mother in birthing a villager's babe. And while they were hunting, I was kneeling in prayer at chapel with my mother and Friar Malone.''

He felt a grin tugging at the corner of his lips, but he managed to keep his tone even. ''It does sound as though your brothers were having a great deal more fun at their chores than you, lass.''

''Aye. It's why I constantly ran away and joined them. For which I always paid. And paid dearly.''

''And did you never learn the virtue of obedience?''

''Not according to my father. He called me his foolish, headstrong female. But, as comfort, my mother used to say it is up to the young to make foolish mistakes, so that their elders can cluck their tongues and feel superior.''

Keane's voice lowered. ''If it is any consolation, Briana, I've also made my elders feel very superior indeed.''

He seemed about to say more when he caught sight of Vinson hurrying along the garden path. Briana swallowed back her disappointment. She'd felt certain that he'd been about to discuss his own childhood.

''My lord.'' The old man came to a halt when he drew near. ''Have you forgotten your meeting with the village elders?''

Keane looked thunderstruck. His time spent with his lovely companion had wiped every other thought from his mind.

''Your horse is saddled, my lord. Your valise is packed.''

''Thank you, Vinson. You'll see the lass back to the house?''

''Aye, my lord.''

Keane turned to Briana and lifted her hand to his

lips. "Forgive me, my lady. In your pleasant company, I'd forgotten the time."

As he brushed his lips over her knuckles, he felt the jolt to his heart.

"I must be gone for several days, to oversee my estate. If you need anything at all, you need only ask Vinson and he will see to it."

"You are most kind."

He continued to hold her hand between both of his. Then, seeing Vinson watching, he lowered her hand and turned away.

Chapter Seven

Keane wiped a sleeve across his forehead and urged his mount up a wooded hill. As he started down the other side, he could see below him the village of Carrick. It spread out, the valley green and lush, the huts and farmhouses clean, if less than prosperous. As he passed through the fields he noted the flocks and herds, wishing they looked a bit more healthy. The village cemetery caught his eye, and he noted the fresh graves. So many. Too many.

An occasional villager would look up as he rode past. And though the men doffed their hats out of respect and the women nodded, there was no real display of affection. As he had noted everywhere he rode, his reputation had preceded him. Not that he minded. He'd learned to deal with it as he'd dealt with everything unpleasant in his life. He put it aside and moved on. And if, in some small part of his mind, he felt a twinge of pain, it mattered not. Pain, he'd learned, was to be endured. As life was to be endured.

The long, winding path to Carrick House snaked through a delightful stretch of woods that was cool and green, with moss-covered timbers and shrubs tak-

ing root in every available space. When horse and
rider emerged from the woods, Keane caught his first
glimpse of the silver-gray facade of Carrick House.
For a moment his heart stirred in his chest. Odd. He
hadn't felt that way in such a long time. In fact, he'd
been a young lad the last time he'd felt anything at all
for his boyhood home. It was just as well. He wanted,
needed, no attachments. It would make it all the less
difficult to leave, when his business here was con-
cluded.

His horse splashed gratefully through an age-old lily
pond, pausing a moment to drink. Then, sensing an
end to the journey, exited on the far shore and started
across the meadow that led to the stables.

Keane was as eager as his stallion to be home. The
journey around his property had stretched into more
than a week. A week of crude taverns and inns, where
the food and ale had been barely tolerable, and the
people only slightly more so.

He handed his horse over to the stable lad, and
made his way to the house.

"Welcome home, my lord." Vinson accepted
Keane's cloak and hung it on a hook before trailing
him upstairs to Keane's room. "Gone a bit longer than
you'd planned, my lord."

"Aye." Keane waited while his butler poured him
a glass of ale to wash away the dust of the road. "Most
of the meetings with the village elders didn't last very
long after they learned that I had no intention of
throwing good money after bad."

"They want money, my lord?" Vinson handed him
the goblet, then took a poker to the smoldering log on
the fire.

"To buy arms to be used against the English. I told

them there isn't enough money in all of Ireland to
defeat the English.''

"You said that, my lord?''

Keane nodded. ''But the meetings the last day or
so went much better. Probably because I remembered
to compliment the village elders on the fine job
they've done with the fields in my absence.''

Vinson turned. ''You did that, my lord?''

"Aye.'' Keane smiled at the look of pride on the
old man's face. Vinson had been his first tutor. And,
at times, throughout his lonely childhood, his only
friend. ''I might not have thought of it earlier. But
since the arrival of Briana O'Neil, I've been reminded
how fortunate I am to have all this. I find her humble
gratitude refreshing. Don't you, Vinson?''

"Oh, aye, my lord. Most refreshing.''

"What has she done in my absence?''

"You'll be pleased to know that she grows stronger
with each day. She can take the stairs without help.
Fairly flies along the halls. Has been known to race
from room to room searching for Cora or one of the
other servants. And her appetite seems to be improving. In fact, she has begun taking her midday meal in
the kitchens, with the staff.''

Keane's hand paused in midair. ''In the kitchens?
Why?''

"I don't know, my lord. She asked Cora where she
ate, then offered to join her. I think she just likes to
be around people.''

Keane sipped, thought. ''Was the household staff
put off by her presence?''

"Put off, my lord?'' Vinson shook his head. ''Not
at all. Everyone enjoys the lass's company. She's quite
delightful.''

Delightful. The perfect description of Briana O'Neil. "Do you join them as well, Vinson?"

"Aye, my lord. The first day, I was passing through and heard the laughter and decided to join the others. After that, it became a bit more routine."

"I see." Keane stared at the amber liquid in his glass. "What else has she done in my absence?"

"Chatted up Fleming, the gardener, a good bit, my lord. Puttered with the roses, with his help, of course. She walked to the stables and asked to ride, but Monroe, the stable master refused until he first learned how you feel about it."

"Do you think she's strong enough, Vinson?"

The old man shrugged. "It's hard to say, my lord. She seems filled with energy. Still, Mistress Malloy has insisted that the lass rest every afternoon. We thought it best to wait until you return, and you can decide what's best for our lass."

Keane noted the use of the term *our lass*. When had Briana O'Neil ceased being a guest, and become an accepted part of the household?

"Where is she now?"

"The last I saw her, she was going up the stairs. Probably to bathe. She's put in quite a day. Perhaps a bit taxing for one still recovering from such serious wounds. But the lass has spirit. It's her saving grace." He moved to the wardrobe and began laying out fresh clothes. "Will I tell Mistress Malloy to prepare a late supper?"

"Aye. And you might ask if Miss O'Neil would care to join me." Keane was already setting aside his glass as he strolled toward the basin of water. Not that he was eager to see her. But it was nice knowing he had someone to talk to after his long absence. "Tell her I'll be in the library."

As the old man turned away Keane called, "And Vinson."

"Aye, my lord?"

"There's a cask of wine from our French vineyards in the cellar. Have one of the servants open it for you."

"I thought you'd told me you were saving that for a special occasion."

"I was." His smile was quick. And dangerous. "I've just decided to make tonight special."

"French wine." Mistress Malloy sniffed and darted a look at Vinson while the cask was being tapped. "Our lass isn't much for drinking."

"A bit of wine won't hurt." Vinson filled a crystal decanter, then corked the cask.

"How can you be certain?"

He added two sparkling crystal goblets, then lifted the silver tray and headed for the door. "Because I'll drop by the library often enough to keep an eye on things."

When he walked away, the housekeeper returned to her duties. She'd been able to let down her guard with her lord away all week. Now she'd have to get back to the tiresome task of trying to keep one step ahead of him. A man with a reputation like Lord Alcott's required considerable watching around an innocent like the lass. She shivered just thinking about all the scandals. Drink and women and cards and all manner of unmentionable behavior. There probably wasn't much Keane O'Mara had missed in his youth. But now that she and the others had tossed their young lass into the lion's den, they had a duty to see that she wasn't devoured before she had a chance to tame him.

"Oh, Cora." Briana stood on a little stool in the middle of the room, while the servant finished turning up the hem of her latest gown. This one was the color of heather, with a softly rounded neckline edged in lace. Catching sight of her reflection in the looking glass, her voice was tinged with awe. "This gown is…"

"…much too big." Mistress Malloy paused in the doorway, with an armload of fresh linen. She felt a little twist of fear. The lass looked far too fetching. What man could resist such a vision?

"Too big?" Cora stopped her work and got to her feet.

"Aye. Look here." The housekeeper crossed the room and deposited the linens on the bed before turning to Briana. "This neckline is too low. Why, I can see…too much of the lass's flesh. And this fabric is much too soft. Look how it clings to her body."

Cora considered. "It's too late to change it now. I could add a shawl."

"Aye." Mistress Malloy nodded vigorously. "A shawl would help." But she knew it was pointless. Nothing short of a nun's habit would hide the lass's beauty. Not that they wanted to hide her. But they did have an obligation to keep her virtue intact. Given Lord Alcott's appetite, they were playing a dangerous game. And with an innocent who had not a clue.

"Is this better?" Cora picked up a soft white shawl that might have been spun from angel hair, and draped it over Briana's shoulders.

"Aye. Some." The housekeeper studied her with a

critical eye. Even with the hair cut shockingly short, Briana O'Neil was a striking lass. A man would have to be blind not to notice her beauty. And Lord Alcott was far from blind where pretty women were concerned.

They looked up at a knock on the door. When Mistress Malloy opened it, Vinson was waiting.

"I've come to fetch the lass. Is she ready?"

"Aye." The housekeeper turned. "Come, lass. The lord is waiting."

As Briana crossed the room, the butler and housekeeper exchanged a look.

The old man cleared his throat. "You look...splendid, lass."

"Thank you, Vinson."

As they started along the hall he noted that she was no longer leaning on his arm. He thought wistfully, for just a moment or two, how much he missed it.

"How is Keane? Did he talk to you about his journey? Was he glad to be home?"

"Aye, to everything." So many questions. It was quite plain that she could barely contain her excitement. "The lord is fine, lass. He said little about his journey, though I'm sure he'll have more to say when the two of you are together. And he seemed most happy to be home."

She danced along beside him, smiling broadly. "Did you tell him that I'm feeling much stronger?"

"Aye, lass. I told him."

"What did he say?"

"He said he'd see for himself soon enough."

"Do you think he'll allow me to ride?"

"I don't see why not. But you must be patient, lass."

"Patient." She gave a little hiss as they reached the door to the library.

Vinson knocked, opened the door, and called, "My lord, Miss O'Neil is here."

Keane stepped away from his desk and watched as she stepped into the room, looking like a vision with her cap of red curls dancing around cheeks that were bright with color. He'd been actually pacing the room in anticipation.

"Welcome home, Keane." With no trace of her earlier weakness, she hurried forward, her hands outstretched.

"Thank you." He took her hands in his, and was caught off guard by the jolt. After his little absence, he'd forgotten her effect on him. It was as potent as a tumbler of fine aged whiskey. And just as intoxicating.

Rather than release her, he continued to hold her hands as he spread them apart and stared at the vision before him. "Look at you, Briana O'Neil. You look..." Like an angel, he thought. An angel caught in a whirlwind. "...like you're healing nicely."

"Oh, I am." She squeezed his fingers and gave him a radiant smile. "I'm feeling ever so much stronger."

"I'm pleased to hear it."

"Your wine, my lord." Vinson stepped between them, offering two tumblers on a silver tray.

"Thank you, Vinson." Keane was forced to release his hold on her as he accepted the two glasses, handing one to Briana, keeping the other for himself.

Vinson returned the tray to a nearby table, then busied himself at the windows, drawing the draperies against the night.

"Let's sit here by the fire." Keane motioned toward a chaise positioned in front of the fireplace.

Like his butler, he noted that she no longer needed his aid in walking. And though he knew he ought to be cheered by her returning strength, he found himself missing her dependence on him.

Briana sat, sipping her wine. "Tell me about your time away. How far did you journey?"

"I tried to visit every town and village that make up the estate, though I fear I may have missed a few. The weather grew quite stormy in the north, and I found myself yearning for the comfort of my own bed."

"Is your estate that vast, then, that you couldn't see it all in a week?" She was thinking about Ballinarin. Her father was considered one of the wealthiest landowners in Ireland. But he rarely journeyed more than a few days at a time to explore the estate.

"Aye. It's vast," he said almost wearily.

"Where did you sleep?"

"In taverns and inns. Sometimes I had to ride until well past dark to find one that was habitable."

"Couldn't you have stayed with your overseers?"

He seemed surprised by the question. "Why do you ask?"

She shrugged. "It's where my father always stays when he travels across his estates. He knows all his overseers by name. And every addition to their families as well."

Keane took a moment to sip his wine before replying. "I suppose I could have invited myself. But I'm new to them and unknown, except for my name. Many of the overseers are the sons of men my father once knew. I found them to be stiff and uncomfortable with me." He didn't add that many of the villagers had been openly hostile, as well.

"Perhaps what you mistake for stiff and uncomfortable is really shy and reserved."

He glanced at her over the rim of his glass. "I think I would know the difference."

"Aye. One would think so." She dismissed the hint of impatience in his tone as mere weariness. "Are you pleased with the crops?"

He nodded. "I'm told the yield would have been twice that of last year. But the English soldiers' attacks have left many of the farmers afraid to even venture from their homes into the fields. The soldiers have been stealing from the flocks and herds as well, leaving the farmers without profits." He crossed to the table and returned with the decanter, topping off her glass and his own. "What do you think of the wine?"

"It's excellent."

"I'm glad you approve. It's very special to me. It's from my French vineyards."

"You own property in France?"

"Aye. As well as Spain and Italy."

Briana thought about what Cora had told her. No wonder the servants expected him to leave this poor land and make his home in some exotic location. He could afford to live anywhere in the world.

"Is that why you seem unconcerned about the damage to the crops and herds?"

"I'm not unconcerned. Merely at a loss as to what to do about it."

"What to do? Why, you fight the English soldiers, of course."

Before Keane could frame a reply, Vinson stepped between them once more. "Excuse me, my lord." With a little frown, the butler took note of the half-empty decanter. He'd have to pay more attention to such details. He couldn't permit the lass to drink too much. "Do you wish to sup in here or in the great hall?"

"I think we'll take our meal in here tonight, Vinson. It's smaller. More...intimate."

Vinson nearly groaned. "Very good, my lord. I'll tell Mistress Malloy."

The old man hurried away to give the housekeeper her instructions.

There would be no early bed for him or for the housekeeper. Both he and Mistress Malloy would have to stay alert this night. For there was a look in their lord's eyes that Vinson had seen before. It was a look he always dreaded. It meant Keane O'Mara was feeling especially...frisky.

Chapter Eight

"Here we are, my lord." Mistress Malloy entered the library, trailed by half a dozen servants, who proceeded to set a table with fine linen and crystal and silver.

More servants entered carrying steaming trays and platters, which were set on a side table, until it groaned under the weight of so much food.

"Are you certain that's all for us?" Briana couldn't help laughing. "It looks as though you've cooked enough to feed an army."

"Aye. Cook was worried. What with the master away so long, she thought he'd be wanting a few of his favorites." The housekeeper lifted a lid, sniffed. "There's beef and mutton. And salmon as the lord requested for you, lass. Biscuits and some fresh spring vegetables. And Cook baked one of her brandied currant cakes as you'd asked, my lord."

When the servants were finished with their tasks, they stood to one side, waiting to serve the lord and his guest.

Keane glanced over from his position by the fireplace. "Thank you, Mistress Malloy. You and the servants may leave now."

"But, my lord, you'll be wanting our help."

"Nay, Mistress Malone. Miss O'Neil and I will be fine." Keane topped off Briana's glass, then his own, before turning and handing the empty decanter to his butler.

The housekeeper shot a withering look at Vinson as she and the servants took their leave. A moment later, when Vinson walked from the library carrying the silver tray, she was waiting for him in the hallway.

"You said a little wine wouldn't hurt. But they've already emptied an entire decanter."

"Aye," he said, tight-lipped. "I can see that."

"Well? Now what are we supposed to do?" Her voice was an angry whisper.

"I suppose there's nothing to do but hover outside the door and listen."

"Hover and listen? What good's that going to do?"

"Whenever things get too quiet inside, we'll have to invent a reason to intrude."

"Oh. I knew it. I knew this was going to get out of hand." She stomped away, wiping her sweating palms on her apron.

Vinson followed a bit more slowly, wondering how many excuses he could come up with for interrupting Lord Alcott from whatever it was he was planning for his evening's entertainment.

"Ah, this feels good, doesn't it?" Keane took the seat beside Briana on the chaise and stretched out his long legs toward the fire.

"Aye. It's a lovely surprise. I'd expected to take a quiet meal in my room and be abed early."

"Vinson tells me you've been spending time at midday with the servants in the kitchens."

She nodded. "You have a wonderful staff. I had no idea that Cora was a great-niece of Mistress Malloy."

Keane nodded. "Nor did I. Though I'm not surprised. Most of the staff at Carrick House is related through blood or marriage. They've been serving the O'Mara family for generations."

"Cook told me she has a sister who lives in a village just east of Ballinarin. She's knitting a blanket for her sister's baby, expected at the end of summer. I promised her that when I return home I'll drop by for a quick visit, to drop off the blanket and send her love."

"You'd do that for my cook?"

"Aye. Of course. Why wouldn't I?"

He studied her in the glow of firelight. "You're a most unusual woman, Briana O'Neil."

"Am I now? And why do you think that?"

"I've never known a highborn woman who mingled with the servants."

"Highborn." She gave a snort of derision.

"You have to admit that the O'Neil family is far from poor."

"Aye. But it's none of my doing. Mother Superior said we're all accidents of birth. We have no say over where we'll be born or how we'll be taught. What we can choose is how we'll live our lives once the decisions are in our own hands."

"And so you choose to live without boundaries."

She thought about it a moment. "If you mean without boundaries of wealth or poverty, aye. It isn't the coin in a man's pocket that makes him hero or knave. It's what's in his heart. His soul."

"And which do you suppose I am? Hero or knave?"

"That isn't for me to judge. You know what's in your own heart. But I'm thinking that you are a harsh judge of yourself, Keane O'Mara."

He sipped his wine a moment, gathering his thoughts. She was more than just unusual. She had an amazing capacity for insight that startled him.

"If you were to ride over your newly acquired estates for the first time, Briana, what would you do?"

She found the question odd, but after a moment said, "I'd chat with everyone I could. I'd ask them how to improve their herds or flocks, or how to enrich the soil. I'd ask the mothers what their children most need, and ask the village elders how to improve the lot of their citizens."

"And when would you tell them what you wanted them to do?"

She smiled. "I wouldn't."

He blinked. "Not ever?"

"Nay." She shook her head. "Instead, I'd let them know that, as lord of the manor, I wanted what was best for them."

"Why?"

"Because anything that improves their lives, improves mine as well. After all, doesn't the lord of the manor live by the sweat of his people?"

For the space of a moment or two Keane seemed thunderstruck. He went very still. Then he got to his feet and began to pace. That's what he'd done wrong. He'd behaved, from the beginning of his journey to end, like lord of the manor. Instead of asking, he'd given orders. Instead of listening, he'd given his opinion. Instead of learning from those who knew the soil and the herds, he'd lectured. No wonder they'd resented him. It wasn't just his reputation which had buried him. It was his attitude.

When had he found any cooperation among them? When he'd complimented the village elders on the condition of their fields. He'd tossed them a single crumb of kindness, and they'd returned it tenfold.

As he mulled all this over, he began to smile. Aye. The lass was right, of course. And he'd been right about her. She had an amazing insight.

All the while that he paced, lost in thought, Briana said not a word, allowing him time to work out in his mind whatever it was that troubled him.

A sudden loud knock broke the prolonged silence. The door was thrown open and Vinson charged into the room, carrying a full decanter on a silver tray. He glanced around, then seemed relieved to see his lord some distance from the lass.

"Your wine, my lord."

"Thank you, Vinson." Distracted, Keane motioned toward the table. "You may fill our goblets." He turned to Briana. "I'd forgotten all about our meal. Come, we'd best eat before our food grows cold."

He caught her hand and led her toward the table, then held her chair as she took her seat.

"Perhaps I should stay and serve," Vinson suggested.

Keane slanted him a look. "Aye. A fine idea."

He settled himself at the table and lifted his glass. "I believe a toast is in order."

Briana picked up her glass. "What are we drinking to?"

"To pearls of wisdom, my lady."

"I don't understand."

"Ah, but you do. You, Briana O'Neil, seem to understand things better than anyone I've ever met. And when you explain your thoughts, they make more sense to me than all the lessons I was forced to learn as a lad in those hated boarding schools."

"Then I'm pleased to know I make you so happy, my lord."

He touched his glass to hers. "Oh, you do, Briana. You make me very happy." He turned to Vinson. "You may serve now."

Puzzled, the old man did as he was told. But when, minutes later, Keane sent him on his way with a wave of his hand, he wondered just what had transpired to erase his lord's usually dour expression. The reason that came to mind left him more concerned than ever.

"You didn't really invite a sword fight with English soldiers."

Keane and Briana were once again seated comfortably in front of the fire. Dinner had been relaxed and slow and easy. They had polished off beef and mutton and salmon. Had finished six biscuits between them and even managed to share a piece of Cook's special cake. But neither of them could recall a single thing they'd eaten.

He couldn't remember ever talking this much. Or listening with such intensity. Or laughing so often and so easily.

Briana had regaled him with stories of her youth, of growing up in the shadow of two strong, warrior brothers.

"I did. Aye. All my life I've had to live with the cruelty of those soldiers. I've watched as villagers were helpless against their swords. I've seen my father and brothers fight back against them. And I've heard my family rage endlessly at the table, or after dinner around the fire, about the injustice of such a presence in our land.''

"But watching and listening aren't the same as leaping into battle with the enemy.''

She nodded. "I know that. But that day, I just seemed to cross over a line. I saw the soldiers going into the village tavern. I heard their coarse words and laughter as a lass walked by. Saw the tears in the eyes of that helpless lass who had been so humiliated by what they'd said to her. And something seemed to take hold of me. I rode home to Ballinarin and took down my grandfather's sword, then rode back to the village and stood waiting for them to emerge from the tavern.''

"God in heaven, Briana.'' His hand tightened on the stem of the goblet. "Couldn't anyone in the village stop you?'' Restless, he got to his feet and walked to the fireplace, where he rested his hand along the mantel while he watched her.

"Nay. I was Briana O'Neil, daughter of the lord of Ballinarin. They wouldn't have dared to stop me.'' She frowned, remembering. "And when the soldiers emerged, amid drunken laughter and good-natured bantering, I challenged them to fight. After their shock at such a bold, foolish prank as they called it, their leader knocked me from my horse and ordered his men to leave. I was so angry, I fought back, and he was forced to wound me, just to keep me from killing him.''

She winced, thinking back to that terrible, fateful day. "By the time the village lads carried me home, all bloody and dirty, my father was half-mad with worry.''

''He had every right to be.''

Her voice lowered. ''All of Ireland knows that Gavin O'Neil has a fierce temper. I knew, the minute I saw his face, that I'd gone too far. With half the village watching and listening, he ordered me off to a cloister.''

He saw the pain that clouded her eyes. ''What else could he do, lass, if he loved you?''

''I don't know.'' She stood and began to pace. ''Over time...'' She stopped to glance at him. ''...and there was plenty of that in the long, sleepless nights I passed those first few weeks in the convent...I realized that I'd forced my father's hand.'' She resumed her pacing. ''But I had this wonderful hope that sustained me. The hope that he'd send for me. And when he didn't, and the weeks stretched into months, and the months into years, I began to despair of ever seeing my home again.''

''And now, very soon, you shall.''

''Aye.'' She stopped her pacing. Her eyes were troubled. ''But it wasn't my father who sent for me.''

''It wasn't?''

''Nay.'' She shook her head. ''Mother Superior told me it was my mother who'd sent for me, after my father sustained a minor wound and became difficult to care for.''

''I see.'' He could see so much more. Though she was eager to return to her home, she was fearful of the sort of greeting she would receive from the man who had banished her.

Keane would know about such things. He placed a

hand on her sleeve. "Don't you think he's missed you every bit as much as you've missed him?"

"I hope so. I want to believe he has."

"Then trust that his love for you is as great as your love for him. And that he will rejoice when he hears that you are safe and will soon be returned to his care."

She looked up into his eyes. "How is it that you understand how troubling this is to me?"

His tone hardened. "Whatever I've learned about familial love, it wasn't taught to me in this house."

Briana thought about what Cora had revealed. "Was there no one here at Carrick House who loved you, Keane?"

"Aye. My mother and grandfather, I suppose. But they died when I was young. I was devastated, for then I was left with my father, who felt he was burdened with one small boy who was more bother than he was worth."

"You can't be certain of that."

He nodded. "Oh, but I am. My father saw me merely as an heir. Someone to carry on the name. But, until I was old enough to be of some use to him, he wanted me out of the way. And so I was sent abroad. And left there, with Vinson as my only connection with the past, until I was summoned home to carry on the family tradition."

"At least your father summoned you home."

"Aye. But not here, to Carrick, but rather to his new home in England. I was so filled with hatred and bitterness at the loss of all I'd held dear, I decided to exact revenge. I wanted to punish my father the way he had punished me all those years. I drank too much and spent money like a drunken sailor, and..." He paused, thought better about what he'd been about to say, and amended, "...and did a number of things I'd like to forget. And in so doing, I nearly destroyed myself just to spite my harsh, unyielding father."

Briana shook her head, trying to deny what she'd heard. It was her turn to offer comfort. She placed a hand on his. "We all make mistakes, Keane."

"Ah, but not all of them on such a grand scale as mine. I managed, in a single season, to destroy everything my ancestors held dear. Our name. Our reputation. Our bloodline." He turned away, staring into the flames of the fire. "I had no pride left. Not a shred. My behavior was despicable. What I did was unforgivable."

"Don't say that." Without thinking, Briana caught his arm, turning him to face her. "There is nothing we can ever do that is beyond forgiveness."

"Oh, lass." His eyes mirrored his torment. "If only I had your faith. And your sweet innocence."

"Believe me, Keane." Her voice lowered with feeling. "I know it to be true. But first, you must forgive yourself."

He touched a hand to her cheek. "If only I could."

There was such pain in his eyes. She couldn't bear to see him suffering so. Without thinking she pressed her lips to his. It was the sweetest of gestures. Meant to soothe. To heal. But the moment their lips met, everything changed.

He seemed to shudder. And then a spark passed between them. A spark that leapt into flame.

His mouth took hers with a fierceness that spoke of hunger, of pain. The hands at her shoulders were rough with impatience. He dragged her close, then closer still as his lips moved over hers, taking, demanding.

Her wispy shawl drifted to the floor and lay, discarded at their feet.

She could taste the need. Desperate. Deep. Endless. And she had an equally desperate need to satisfy it. She poured herself into the kiss, opening her heart, her soul.

He lifted his head for a moment, staring down into her eyes. "Ah, Briana. You're so sweet. So good for me."

And then his mouth was everywhere. Across her face, as he whispered unintelligible words. Down her throat, until she arched her neck and sighed with pure pleasure.

His mouth came back to find hers, drawing out the sweet, innocent taste that was hers alone. She tasted of French wine and spring roses. Like the clear, pure water of a Derry stream.

He was desperate to taste her. All of her. And yet he lingered over her lips while his hands began a lazy exploration of her back. He could feel her soft sigh of pleasure as his hands pressed, massaged, aroused. He moved his hands along her sides, until his thumbs encountered the swell of her breasts.

She gasped in shock as her body reacted to his touch. She felt her nipples harden, her blood heat, as a pulse began throbbing deep inside. But before she could push away, he took the kiss deeper, swallowing her protest. And then she was lost in a rush of sensations that robbed her of all thought.

In some small corner of his mind, Keane knew that he had crossed a line. This innocent in his arms deserved better, for she had no defenses. But he needed desperately to cling to her, to take what she so generously offered. He filled himself with her goodness, her sweetness. And as he did, he took them both higher, until they were battered by need.

He felt as if he were standing on the brink of a high, steep precipice. One misstep, and they would both fall. The decision was his. The power to save her, or to take her crashing down with him lay in his strength of will.

For a moment longer he lingered, tempting himself.

At last he lifted his head and held her a little away.

"Briana. God in heaven, lass, I need a moment." With his hands at her shoulders he pressed his forehead to hers, taking in deep draughts of air to clear his head.

He could feel her doing the same.

"My lord." The door was thrown open, and Vinson stopped short in the doorway.

Two heads came up sharply. Keane and Briana stepped apart.

"What is it?" Keane's tone was sharp with impatience as he bent and retrieved her fallen shawl.

"I have a lad here with fresh wood for the fire." Vinson stepped aside to indicate a burly servant struggling under the weight of a log.

"We've no need for a fire." In fact, Keane realized, he was damp with sweat.

"Then I'll have him take it up to the lass's chambers." Vinson paused a moment, aware of what he'd interrupted, and determined to see that it went no further. "Perhaps you could accompany the lass upstairs now."

"Aye." Keane took a deep breath, avoiding Briana's eyes. "I think that would be wise."

Still trembling with need they made their way from the room and climbed the stairs as if in a trance. When they reached Briana's chambers, they paused, aware of Vinson and the servant standing silently behind them.

"Good night, Briana." Keane lifted her hand to his lips, then took a step back, breaking contact.

"Good night, Keane." She glanced at his face, but could read nothing in his eyes. They were, like the man, once again cool, composed, devoid of all emotion.

She followed the servant inside her chambers. And stood, on legs that threatened to fail her, until his chore was complete. When she was alone, she sank down on the edge of the bed, praying the trembling would soon pass.

Chapter Nine

Keane stood on the balcony, watching the first faint light of dawn begin to slide over the horizon. He'd been too restless to sleep. He knew the cause.

Briana O'Neil.

He'd never expected to feel this way again in his lifetime. Was it because this lass was so sweet, so innocent that she made him feel that way, too? He'd felt a kind of cleansing as he'd kissed her, held her. As though her goodness was enough for both of them. In fact, he was almost beginning to think he could begin anew. That somehow, despite all that had gone before, he could overcome his past and start over.

Oh, not that he'd been fooled into believing he could ever be innocent again. There'd been a demon inside him that made him want, more than anything in the world, to seduce her. To take her there in the library, with the fire playing over her face, and the taste of wine on her lips.

It would have been so easy. She was such a willing participant. Her kisses, though chaste, were generous. There was so much passion simmering inside of her.

Passion and fierce, all-consuming energy. It was intoxicating. It was exciting. It was far too tempting.

He found himself wondering what would have happened if Vinson hadn't interrupted them.

Looking back on the evening, he realized there'd been several such interruptions. Could it be that the servants didn't trust him and were looking out for "their lass"? Perhaps they saw it as their obligation to keep the innocent from being led astray by the jaded lord of the manor.

The very thought had him chuckling. Perhaps he was the one who needed protection. The lass, by her very sweetness, was far too irresistible. And her mind was as fascinating as her body.

He began to pace as he thought about all he and Briana had talked about. There were so many things playing through his mind. Ideas, thoughts, all of them planted by their conversation last night.

He had thought he would have to go far away to put his ideas into practice. Ideas about crop rotation and importing stock from other countries for breeding. Ideas about improving the lives of those who lived on the land by becoming self-sufficient, and perhaps even trading with those from other lands.

But if he could learn to put aside his tarnished reputation and express his true interest in the people and land here at Carrick, they just might open up to him. And perhaps, in time, this place could even feel like home again.

A knock on the door interrupted his musings.

"Come," he called with annoyance.

"Forgive me, my lord." Vinson stood on the threshold, holding a candle aloft. "I saw the light and thought you might have need of me."

"Nay. Go back to bed, old man."

"Aye, my lord."

As he backed away Keane changed his mind. His harsh tone softened. "Wait. As long as you're up, Vinson, come inside and close the door."

The elderly servant did as he was told, bracing himself for the expected reprimand for the number of times he'd interrupted his lord and the young lady the previous evening.

"Tell me, Vinson. Do you think a soul blackened by sin can ever be wiped clean again?"

The old man blinked. This was the last thing he'd ever have expected to be asked. "We are taught so by our church, my lord."

Keane waved a hand. "I'm not interested in what the good friars preach. You know I turned my back on my faith long ago. I want to know if you believe it to be so."

Vinson cleared his throat. "I believe that a man will be judged by the deeds of his entire lifetime, not just the deeds or...misdeeds of his youth. If a man should find one noble purpose to pursue for purely unselfish reasons, it could wipe away a multitude of sins."

"A multitude of sins." Keane turned away to stare at the pale golden light beginning to creep over the horizon. "But sometimes even the most noble purpose pursued for the most unselfish of reasons, can cause pain to innocents."

"That may be true, my lord. But that cannot stop the good man from trying. He will still know in his heart that his motives were pure."

"Aye. Purity." He made a sound that might have been a grunt or a chuckle. "A word I'd not believed in, until recently."

A moment later he heard the door close as the old man returned to his bed. Then he was alone again. Still unable to sleep as he pondered. And brooded. And paced.

"Good morrow, my lady." Cora drew open the draperies, allowing morning sunlight to spill into the room.

"Good morrow, Cora." Briana yawned, stretched, then lifted her arms high. "Oh, isn't it a glorious day?"

"Aye, my lady." Cora filled a basin with warm, rose-scented water and laid out an assortment of linens and soaps. "Lord Alcott sent word that he must ride to the village this morrow. But he hopes you will join him for a midday meal in the garden."

"He's riding to the village?" Briana flew to the balcony, and could see a horse, saddled and ready, in the courtyard below. "Oh, Cora. I must hurry and dress. For I wish to ride with him."

"It's much too soon for you to attempt to ride, my lady. And there's no way you can be ready to leave in time to accompany Lord Alcott. Why, you haven't even broken your fast yet."

But Briana was already stripping off her nightshift. A few swipes with a soapy cloth, a few rinses, and she was struggling into her chemise and petticoats.

"My lady, I have nothing in your meager wardrobe appropriate for riding. I had planned that you would wear this lovely white gown of lawn for your lunch in the garden."

"It'll be fine, Cora. Help me into it." Briana was already slipping it over her head.

With fumbling fingers the little servant fastened the

row of buttons, and had barely run a brush through Briana's curls before the lass was hurrying down the stairs and out the door.

The courtyard was empty.

Despite her haste, she had missed Keane's departure.

Lifting her skirts, she flew across the courtyard and ran to the stables.

When she found a lad mucking stalls she called breathlessly, "I desire a horse, saddled and ready as quickly as possible."

"Aye, my lady. I'll fetch the stable master."

"Nay. The stable master will never..." Briana stopped. The lad had already ambled away.

She spied a horse already saddled, standing quietly in one of the stalls. Without waiting for permission, she opened the stall and led the horse outside. Using an overturned bucket as a stool, she managed to pull herself into the saddle, though it meant hiking her skirts to her knees.

Out of the corner of her eye she could see old Monroe, the stable master, coming at a run. Anticipating an argument, one she would surely lose, she urged the horse into a gallop.

Minutes later, ignoring the shouts coming from the vicinity of the stable, she leaned low over the horse's head and urged him even faster.

She knew it was just a matter of time before the stern old stable master would have another horse saddled. She was fairly certain he wouldn't give up until he caught her. Unless, of course, she caught up with Keane first. She would use all her powers of persuasion to convince him that she was completely mended and more than capable of riding to the village and back, despite the decidedly unladylike posture.

Up ahead, across a field dotted with ancient standing stones, she could see a horse and rider trotting smartly.

A laugh of delight escaped her lips.

"Keane." She shouted his name. Once. Twice. "Keane." She cupped her hands together and shouted with all her might.

When at last he heard her and turned in the saddle, she waved a hand. "Wait for me. I'm coming with you."

She was surprised by his reaction. She'd expected him to be pleased. But after his initial surprise, he appeared to be signalling her to halt.

Ridiculous. Why would she stop now? She hadn't gone to all this trouble, only to miss this opportunity to ride with him.

She gave her horse its head. It raced, full gallop, across the field. When they approached the piles of stones, Briana tugged on the reins, intending to make a wide circle around them. The horse, ignoring her signal, headed straight for them. In a flash, Briana realized her mistake. This horse was a jumper. He'd been bred for that solitary purpose. And now, acting on instinct, he was determined to clear the hurdle.

It was too late to stop the inevitable. She gathered herself for what was coming.

All her life she had been a highly skilled, fearless equestrienne. But as the horse headed toward the hurdle, she saw out of the corner of her eye, a contingent of horsemen on the far side of the field.

Soldiers. English soldiers. For the space of a moment her heart seemed to stop.

As the horse leapt, the distraction caused Briana to lean just a fraction too far forward as she attempted to shout a warning. Her body arched, snapped. She felt herself flying through the air, then tumbling, before crashing to the stones below.

As if from a great distance she could hear Keane's voice, shouting, swearing fiercely. And then rough hands closed around her, lifting her, holding her.

Just before she slipped into unconsciousness, the hands gentled. She was being cradled against her father's chest. He was rocking her, and weeping, and murmuring words that were oddly soothing. But the voice didn't belong to her father. It was another's voice. Low. Deep. Tortured.

His name, his face, were lost somewhere in the blackness that had stolen everything from her mind. Everything but the pain.

"How is she, Mistress Malloy?"

Keane was beside himself. The sight of Briana, so still, so quiet in the bed, was almost worse than the bloody, broken figure he'd carried home.

His clothes still bore the stains of her blood. He'd refused to change. Had refused to even leave her side since he'd stumbled, dazed and trembling, into Carrick House. He'd carried her up the stairs, while the housekeeper shouted orders to the servants to fetch water, towels, opiates and ointments.

They'd had to work around him, since he had insisted upon remaining by the bedside, his hand constantly stroking her brow whenever she moaned, or squeezing her hand when she slipped back into unconsciousness.

"She has sustained several deep cuts and her poor

body is badly bruised. But none of those things is too serious, my lord. Still, I can't revive her. It appears she's hit her head, as well. There's quite a big lump there. It could be nothing or it could be…'' She saw the hot, fierce look that came into his eyes and let the words trail off.

She glanced helplessly at Vinson, who stood to one side, watching in silence.

The old man approached and said softly, ''You can do nothing for the lass, my lord. Perhaps you should see to yourself now. You might want to take the time to wash away that blood and change into a clean tunic.''

Keane ignored him and knelt on the floor beside the bed. Keeping one hand holding tightly to Briana's, he lifted his other hand to smooth the hair from her forehead.

The housekeeper and butler exchanged silent looks. Then, signalling for the servants to leave, they set about stoking a fire in the lass's chambers, and seeing that all her bloody clothes were removed from the lord's sight.

When they exited the room, Keane was still kneeling beside the bed, murmuring words to the woman who lay ominously silent and unmoving.

''My lord.'' Vinson entered Briana's chambers, bearing a tray on which rested a decanter and goblet. ''Since you've taken no sustenance, I thought a bit of ale might revive you.''

''Thank you, Vinson.'' Keane never took his eyes off Briana as the old man poured, then pressed a goblet into his hand.

''Has she moved, my lord?''

"Nay." There was a world of pain in that single word. "Neither moved, nor sighed, nor given any sign that she even knows I am here. This is all my fault, Vinson."

"Now why do you say that, my lord?" The old man set the tray on a table and came to stand beside the bed. "The lass ignored the stable master's warning, and took off at a reckless pace. We've all known, since she first began to mend, that our lass is more than a bit headstrong. In the past few days she's been tearing around the castle like a little whirlwind."

"Aye. That's just it. We've all seen that she was mending nicely. I knew it. But I made no move to send her home to Ballinarin. I selfishly wanted to keep her here with me a while longer." Forever, if truth be told.

"But you couldn't have known the lass would do something like this. There was no way to prevent this accident."

"Nay." He shook his head. "But I'd rather die than see her harmed." Keane's eyes were so bleak, they tore at the old man's heart. "Oh, Vinson, I feel so helpless. What can I do?"

"When all else fails, my lord, one can sometimes find solace in prayer."

"Of all people, I have no right to petition heaven. Not after what I've done in my life."

The old man cleared his throat. "If you don't mind my saying, my lord, the prayers might be even more acceptable, coming from you. It's said that heaven looks most kindly on a reformed sinner."

When the door closed behind him, Keane sank to his knees beside the bed, his lips moving in silent prayer.

Chapter Ten

Briana was crawling through a long, dark tunnel. With each forward movement, there was tremendous pain. Whenever she slipped back into the darkness, the pain would ease. But, though it seemed easier to surrender to the darkness and forego the pain, she sensed that she needed to keep crawling toward the light. She was exhausted, but knew she couldn't stop. There was something, or someone, waiting just beyond. Someone worth whatever pain it would take.

Aye. Someone. She couldn't recall his name. But she could see his face. A darkly handsome man. Her angel.

After one last tremendous effort, she surfaced, and lay, breathing heavily, bathed in sweat.

She felt something soft against her hand. When she could focus, she saw that he was here with her, kneeling beside the bed, his head bowed as if in prayer. A single candle burned on the night table, casting his face in light and shadow. Her dark angel. Handsome. Mysterious.

She brushed a hand over his hair, as if to soothe.

At once he lifted his head and stared at her.

When he managed to find his voice he whispered, "Briana. Oh, lass. You've come back to me."

"I feared I'd dreamed you. But I didn't, did I? You're real. And here with me." She touched a hand to the growth of hair that covered his cheeks and chin. His eyes, she noted, were red-rimmed and bloodshot. "I thought I heard you calling me."

"I was. Summoning you from that netherworld that held you in its grip."

"How long have I been there?"

"Two days and nights. I'd feared you would never return."

She struggled to sort through the bits and pieces of memory. "I took a horse. I wanted to ride with you. Oh." She clapped a hand to her mouth, seeing in her mind the pile of stones, the horse leaping, and then feeling herself falling. "There was something I needed to tell you. Something…" She struggled to hold on to the thought, but it drifted just out of her grasp, like a wisp of fog.

She sighed. "Father always said I was too reckless."

"It doesn't matter now, lass. Nothing matters now that you're back with me."

"Aye. But from the looks of you, I've put you through a terrible time."

"I'd go through hell and back for you, Briana O'Neil." And had. Though she'd never know it. He'd bargained with heaven, promising his fortune, his health, his very life, in exchange for hers. He would have bargained his soul, as well, except that he'd already sold it to the devil years before. "Do you need anything for pain?"

She nodded, and felt her head swim at that small movement. "I'll take all you have."

He jumped up and returned moments later to hold a glass to her lips. She sipped, moaned at the pain it caused, then emptied the glass.

"Will you sleep now, lass?"

"Aye. And from the looks of you, you'd better do the same."

Instead of leaving, he crawled in beside her and wrapped his arms around her, cradling her to his chest. And was asleep instantly.

"It is a miracle."

Mistress Malloy was holding forth in the kitchens. All the servants had gathered around to hear the tale again.

"Two days and two nights without a movement. But Lord Alcott wouldn't give up, even when the rest of us had. He'd even resorted to prayer, according to Cora, who saw him more than once on his knees. It was Vinson who found him, curled up beside her. The two of them sleeping as soundly as babes, they were. Lord Alcott hasn't stopped smiling since. I tell you, he's a changed man."

The others were nodding in agreement.

One of the servants bobbed her head. "He sent me to the village to invite Friar Murphy to make use of the chapel here on the grounds of the keep." She laughed. "It was the first time I've ever seen the old priest struck speechless. But he seemed pleased with the invitation and said he would agree to meet with Lord Alcott."

Fleming, the gardener, chimed in. "I saw Lord Alcott cutting roses in the garden. I offered to help him, but he merely asked which ones were the lass's favorites, then cut them himself. He said he wanted to brighten her chambers.''

''That's nothing,'' Cora added. ''He won't let me do a thing for our lass. He insists on feeding her himself, cutting her meat, lifting a spoonful of broth to her lips. He helps her to sit up, to lie down. If it were left up to Lord Alcott, our lass would never again lift a hand for herself.''

''All right now.'' Vinson, overhearing their remarks, strode into their midst. ''Is no one seeing to the chores around here anymore?''

The crowd of servants scattered.

When they were alone, Mistress Malloy dusted an imaginary spot with the hem of her apron. ''What do you make of it, Vinson?''

He shrugged. ''I think we have what we wished for. Now we'd better hope it's good. For us and, more importantly, for the lass. For it's surely done a world of good for Lord Alcott.''

''What are you doing?'' Briana's lids fluttered, and she saw someone at the window, drawing the draperies against the afternoon sunlight.

Keane turned. ''I didn't want anything to disturb your sleep.''

''Oh. Nay. Open them wide. I want to see the sunshine.''

He started toward her. ''But you should be sleeping.''

''If you had your way, I'd sleep away my life.''

He sat on the edge of her bed, studying her carefully. ''Mistress Malloy says sleep is healing.''

''Then we'll send Mistress Malloy off to her bed.

But I want to see the sun, Keane. And I want to leave this bed.''

He caught her hands in his, lifting each of them to his lips. ''Then you shall have your wish.''

She felt dizzy with heat at the touch of his lips. And knew, from the way his eyes narrowed, that he felt it as well. But just when she thought he might draw her into his arms and kiss her lips, he suddenly pushed himself away from her.

He crossed the room and tore open the draperies, allowing sunshine to spill into the room. Then he returned to her side and said, ''Shall I carry you to the window?''

''Can't I walk?''

''Not yet. But I'll carry you if you wish.''

''Oh, yes. Please.'' She was hungry for the touch of him.

She tossed aside the bed linens, and he lifted her in his arms, cradling her against his chest. It was the most natural thing in the world to wrap her arms around his neck as he carried her to the window.

''You still weigh little more than a bird. I worry that you're so thin.''

''Stop worrying.'' She traced a fingertip over the little furrow between his brows. ''You worry far too much about me. Besides, if Mistress Malloy has her way, I'll soon be as round as an old sow.''

''I'd not worry about that,'' he muttered, and turned away to avoid her touch. For there was a fire building inside him. A fire he was determined to put out before it could flame any higher.

He had, after all, bargained with heaven. And he'd been granted his miracle. Now it was up to him to keep his part of it.

They stared down at the rolling green hills and colorful valleys of Carrick.

"You've such a lovely home, Keane."

He turned his head so that their lips were almost brushing. "I've just begun to appreciate it, thanks to you."

She saw his gaze drop to her mouth and felt a thrill of anticipation. Her arms tightened around his neck, and her eyes closed as she waited for his kiss.

Keane tore his gaze from her and looked toward the window, willing himself to be strong enough to resist what she seemed so eager to give.

"My lord." Cora skidded to a halt in the doorway.

Briana's eyes snapped open. She nearly groaned in frustration.

"What is it?" Keane turned slightly.

"Mistress Malloy wants to know if our lass will be taking her meal below stairs with you."

"Certainly not."

"Oh, please, Keane," Briana whispered. "I do so want to leave this room."

"I'll not have you risking your health."

"How can it hurt?"

"You could take a chill. Or tax your strength."

"I won't, Keane. I promise I'll tell you the moment I'm feeling chilled or weary."

He knew it was impossible to deny her. Still, he tried to consider every argument for keeping her here to himself. Safe. All he wanted, all he cared about now, was that she be kept safe. Still, how could he dismiss the pleading in her eyes?

At length he turned to the servant. "Aye, Cora. Tell Mistress Malloy that the lass will join me for a midday meal in the library. And after you've told her, find a suitable robe so your mistress doesn't catch a chill.''

"Aye, my lord." With a delighted laugh, the servant raced off to inform the housekeeper. It was good news indeed. For it meant that Briana O'Neil had taken another step back from that dark place they had all feared.

"A little more broth, lass?"

Briana shook her head. "It was most tasty, Mistress Malloy. But I couldn't manage another sip."

"Perhaps a sip of wine then? It's said to stimulate the appetite."

"I couldn't. But thank you."

"Tea, my lady?" a servant asked.

"Nay, thank you. No more." Briana glanced around the table. Besides Keane, who sat beside her, there were half a dozen servants hovering, eager to do her bidding. And Vinson, positioned by the door, looked as though he'd turn somersaults in the air if she but asked.

"You must all stop this at once."

She could almost hear the astonished gasp from the assembled.

"Whatever do you mean, lass?" Keane placed a hand over hers.

"This…treating me like some helpless infant. I'm not ill. Or frail. I'm just a little weak from my fall."

"Of course you're weak." Keane patted her hand. "You were at death's door, Briana. You frightened us half to death."

"That's just it. Now, you're doing the same to me. Frightening me with all this attention. I need…to be treated as I was before."

Keane motioned to the servants, and they took two steps away from the table. "All right, my lady. But you must promise me that you will ask for help when you feel weak."

She gave him a bright smile. "Agreed." As she got to her feet, she felt her head swim. She quickly gripped the edge of the table to keep from falling.

At once the servants surged forward.

Keane scooped her into his arms, a frown darkening his brow. "Cora, prepare the lass's bed."

As he strode from the room he muttered, "Now we'll do things my way. And you'll not leave your bed again until I say you will."

"Please, Keane. You can't keep me confined to my room." Briana sat in her bed, surrounded by plump pillows.

As he had every morning for a week, Keane himself carried in her tray and proceeded to sprinkle sugar and cinnamon and sweet thickened cream over a bowl of porridge. "Try this," he murmured in his most persuasive tone. "I've embellished Mistress Malloy's recipe."

He dipped the spoon into the confection, and lifted it to her mouth.

She tasted, swallowed, nodded her approval. "It's very good, Keane. But porridge isn't enough. Even your excellent recipe. What I need is fresh air. And sunshine. Please."

"One more bite, lass. And then I'll consider your request."

With a sigh she obliged him, taking a spoonful of porridge and swallowing it down.

"Well?" She drew the single word out like a plea.

He couldn't hold back his smile any longer. "All right. I'll indulge your request for sunshine and fresh air. Would you like to walk in the garden?"

"You'll let me walk?" She was already tossing aside the bed linens and swinging her legs to the floor when he caught her hand in his, stilling her motions.

"A figure of speech. I'll do the walking. You'll be enjoying the sunshine and fresh air in my arms. And then, if the air isn't too chilly, on a bench."

"Keane." She nearly stomped her foot in frustration. "I'm not a child."

His eyes were warm with admiration as he looked her up and down. "On that point we quite agree."

He loved the flush that touched her cheeks and the impish grin that sprang to her lips. Oh, she was a saucy lass. How he would love to tempt himself with but a single kiss. But he would do well to remember his bargain. A bargain that would surely test his strength of will to the limit.

"Just remember that you were dealt a very serious blow to the head. I've seen seasoned warriors in the field of battle who didn't survive such a blow."

"And where would you have seen such a thing?"

It was his turn to look just a little flustered as he sprang to his feet and handed her the bowl. "Finish your porridge, while I go in search of Cora to fetch you a warm wrap."

When he exited the room she thought about setting the bowl aside. But then she remembered the weakness that still plagued her, and decided she would do whatever it took to regain her strength. Even if it meant eating an entire bowl of hated porridge.

While she ate, she thought again about what he'd said. Now where would Keane O'Mara have seen warriors on the field of battle? Hadn't he claimed he'd led a life of privilege and decadence?

Perhaps he had merely used such a colorful phrase to validate his silly rules. No matter. She had more pressing things to occupy her mind. Such as how to convince Keane that this enforced idleness was nearly as difficult to bear as the confining rules of the convent had been.

"Here we are, my lady."

Keane stepped into the garden, cradling Briana against his chest.

"Oh, Keane." Like a flower, she lifted her face to the sun.

He stood a moment, allowing her to bask in the warmth of the summer day. Then he carried her along the path until he came to a stone bench that had been warmed by the sun's rays.

As soon as he had settled her, the gardener looked up from his chores, then got to his feet, dusting his hands on his breeches, and hurried forward.

"Ah, 'tis good to see you looking so well, lass." In his hand was a single deep red rose, which he offered her in a courtly gesture.

"Thank you, Fleming." She buried her face in the bloom, inhaling deeply. "My mother used to say that heaven can be found in a single rose."

"Aye, lass." The old man's ruddy cheeks seemed infused with even more color as he added softly, "Or in the smile of a beautiful woman."

Keane watched this exchange in amazement. In his lifetime he'd never known the elderly gardener to speak more than half a dozen words. In fact, in his youth, Keane had thought him to be mute. It was known by all in the O'Mara household that Fleming much preferred the company of his plants to that of people.

As if by some sort of prearranged signal, servants began drifting out to the gardens on one pretense or another. Scullery maids, baskets on their arms, slipped out to the gardens to pick herbs. They smiled and bowed as they stopped to ask Briana how she was faring.

"I'm fine now. In no time I'll be as I was," she called.

They waved and laughed as they moved on.

More servants stopped to chat as they went about their chores. Keane was surprised to note that Briana knew them by name and had a kind word for each of them.

Monroe, the stable master, hearing that the lass was finally out of her chambers, came timidly across the garden with a look so grave, so contrite, he might have been preparing his own eulogy.

"Oh, lass." The old man dropped to his knees before Briana and bowed his head. "I hope you can find it in your heart to forgive me."

"Forgive you, Monroe?" She appeared stunned. "Whatever for?"

"For leaving such a dangerous animal as Peregrine unattended."

"Peregrine? That is the name of the jumper?"

"Aye, lass. So named because he can fly."

"He can, indeed. He's a most magnificent animal."

The old man's head came up. On his face was a look of astonishment.

"But the fault is not yours, Monroe. It is mine. I made a hasty and very foolish decision. Though I can't, for the life of me, recall why I took such a fall. It's never happened to me before. I must have been weaker than I'd thought.'' The lack of memory over that incident still worried her more than she let on.

She laid a hand on the stable master's shoulder. ''I give you my word, Monroe. I'll not ride again unless I first ask your permission.''

The old man blushed clear to his toes.

Shortly after that exchange, Mistress Malloy managed to find a reason to be needed in the garden. She claimed to have come in search of the scullery maids, but when told where they were, she remained to chat with Briana.

''How well you're looking, miss.'' The plump old woman paused beside the stone bench. ''I've always thought that sunshine is healing. Don't you agree?''

''Aye. My mother claims she found not only solace in her gardens, but health in both body and mind.''

''A wise woman, your mother.'' Mistress Malloy looked up at Keane, who hovered beside his patient like a mother hen. ''Perhaps you and our lass would like to take tea here, my lord?''

''Nay, Mistress Malloy. A few more minutes out of doors will be sufficient. Then I'll be returning Briana to her chambers.''

''Oh, Keane.'' Briana's smile faltered. ''Why must I leave so soon?''

''Lord Alcott is right, miss. You wouldn't wish to overtax yourself.'' The housekeeper squeezed Briana's hand before hurrying off along a stone path.

Minutes later Vinson moved toward them, his hands behind his back. His face creased into a smile when he caught sight of Briana.

''Ah, lass, it's good to see you out of doors.''

"Thank you, Vinson."

"The sunshine is putting color back in your cheeks, I believe." He glanced at Keane. "See how even the flowers cannot compete with our lass."

Keane arched a brow. Coming from this reserved old man, it was the highest of compliments.

When, minutes later, Vinson walked away, Keane lifted Briana in his arms. As he carried her back to the house, he thought about the extraordinary effect this woman had on every member of Carrick House. He'd never met anyone quite like her.

She wrapped her arms around his neck, and whispered in his ear. "Where are you, Keane? Where have you gone?"

He felt the jolt, as shocking as any lightning strike, and steeled himself against it.

Turning his face, his lips brushed hers. All the blood seemed to drain from his head.

He jolted back. "I'm here. With you, Briana."

"Aye. But your mind has gone somewhere else. What were you thinking?"

That he wanted her. Desperately. That being this close to her, and not permitting himself to taste her lips, was pure torture. And that he would soon go mad with the need for her.

But all he said was, "Tomorrow, if you're strong enough, I may let you ride in the carriage."

Chapter Eleven

"Well, lass, what do you think?"

Keane pointed to the carriage standing in the court-yard below.

Briana leaned on his arm, permitted, for the first time since her recovery, to actually walk. "Oh, Keane. Are you really taking me for a ride?"

"I promised, didn't I?" He turned to her, loving the excitement in her glowing eyes. "Now you must make me a promise, as well."

"Aye. Anything."

"Promise that you will tell me when you're weary."

She nodded. "I promise."

"Then Cora will help you make ready for our little adventure."

He waited while the servant helped her into an er-mine-lined hooded traveling cloak of dark green vel-vet. Then, moving at the pace of a snail, he escorted her down the stairs and through the wide front foyer, where Vinson stood, watching with a nod of approval.

Once in the courtyard, Keane settled her into the

carriage, then took the seat beside her. With a flick of the reins, the horses trotted smartly.

As they rolled along the curving ribbon of road leading away from Carrick House, Briana gave a delighted laugh. "Who would have ever believed I could get this excited about a simple carriage ride? But oh, Keane, how happy I am."

"Has it been that terrible, being confined to my home?"

"Nay." She touched a hand to his arm. "Never think that. I love your home. And I'm most grateful for your many kindnesses to me. But I was beginning to believe I would never again be able to know the freedom I once took for granted."

He closed a hand over hers. "Just be patient with me, Briana. I was so afraid of losing you. And now that I have you back, I realize I can't afford to be careless. One misstep and you could be snatched away again."

"Now you're beginning to sound like my father."

"Am I?" He shot her a dangerous smile. "Believe me, my lady, my feelings for you are not those of a father."

Her heart did a little flip. Coming from Keane O'Mara, that was quite an admission. Especially since her accident. She had become worried about him. Worried about the fact that, though he hovered and fretted over her, he seemed to have erected a wall between them. A wall that kept him from feeling any emotion other than fear for her safety.

She snuggled closer, feeling a sudden rush of joy. She breathed in the familiar fragrances of newly turned earth and the perfume of rhododendrons and azaleas, that bloomed in profusion on the hillsides.

Was her freedom sweeter because it had been lost to her for so long? She knew not. But she found herself revelling in it.

"Oh, look, Keane." She pointed to a family up ahead. A father, mother and half a dozen sons and daughters were walking along a dirt path, with an assortment of dogs chasing after sticks the children were tossing.

"Could we please stop?"

"But why, lass? They're strangers to us."

"During my years at the convent, such scenes made me yearn for family. But, because of our rule of silence, I was never allowed to speak to the strangers who passed by. And now, I am free of such rules. Oh Keane, please stop."

How could he deny her? He tugged on the reins, bringing the carriage to a dust-churning halt.

"Good morrow," she called, waving and smiling.

"Good morrow, my lady." It was the children who responded first, gathering around the carriage and staring wide-eyed at the beautiful couple inside.

Their parents, recognizing the lord of the manor, held back.

Briana stepped from the carriage and bent down to scratch the ears of one of the hounds. She was rewarded by long, loving licks of its tongue and a body that wriggled in delight.

"Where are you headed on this fine day?"

"To market," said a bold little boy of about six. His brothers and sisters, noting the lady's fine cloak, had all been struck speechless.

"And where is the market?"

An older lad, not to be outdone by his little brother, pointed. "In the village of Carrick."

Briana shielded the sun from her eyes and peered in the distance. "I always loved market day. Tell me. Are there booths where one might buy pastries?"

A little girl overcame her shyness to nod. "They're my favorites, my lady."

"They were always mine, as well." Briana turned to the parents. "You've a lovely big family."

Though he didn't smile, the father stood a little taller. "Thank you, my lady."

"We were just headed to Carrick." Briana's smile encompassed the entire family. "Why don't you ride with us?"

The children were overjoyed at the chance to ride in an elegant carriage. But as they started to scramble forward, their father said, "You couldn't possibly have room for so many."

Briana glanced at Keane. Though her spontaneous gesture had caught him by surprise, he managed to nod his head. "We'll make room. Climb aboard."

Briana moved close to Keane, so the parents could squeeze in beside her. The children scrambled over them to crowd into the back . The dogs circled the carriage, barking their excitement at the horses.

Spying the blanket-clad bundle in the mother's arms Briana gave a little cry. "Oh, a wee one. Is it a lad or a lass?"

"A lad, my lady." The mother was so shy, she could barely speak above a whisper.

"A lad. What's his name?"

"Daniel, my lady."

"Daniel. What a fine name. May I hold him?"

The parents exchanged glances before the mother handed her baby over to Briana. With the children peering over her shoulder and the parents looking on with a mixture of awe and unease, she uncovered the tiny bundle.

"Oh. Oh, aren't you just beautiful." She watched with delight as the infant grabbed hold of her fingers. She turned to Keane. "Oh, look at him, Keane. Isn't he perfect?"

All Keane could do was nod. The discomfort at having strangers suddenly thrust upon him was forgotten. As was the noise of the barking dogs. The reins lay unused in his hand. He seemed mesmerized by the sight of Briana balancing the cooing baby on her lap.

She gathered the tiny bundle against her chest and pressed her lips to his temple. "Oh, Daniel, you smell so good."

In reply, the baby closed a chubby fist in her hair and tried to eat it. She gave a delighted laugh and hugged him fiercely.

Finally, when Keane was able to compose himself, he flicked the reins and the carriage rolled forward.

The entire family seemed enchanted by the sight of the grand lady cuddling baby Daniel.

"Do you work for Lord Alcott?" Briana asked.

The father nodded. "I farm the north field. As my father did before me."

"The north field?" Keane searched his memory. "Was your father Colin McCann?"

"Aye, my lord. I am Hugh McCann."

"Your father was once kind to me, Hugh. I was no more than six when my horse stumbled and I was thrown. As I recall, your father took me home and your mother fed me broth until a carriage was sent for me. I remember your family with much fondness."

Briana watched as Hugh McCann shot a sideways

glance at his wife, who proudly linked her fingers with his.

When they reached the village green, Keane brought the carriage to a halt. The parents climbed down and the mother reached up for her infant. While Briana returned him to his mother's arms, the father doffed his hat to Keane.

"I thank you, my lord, for this kindness. It will not be forgotten."

"You're welcome, Hugh."

As the dogs circled the children who had climbed out of the back, Briana leaned close to whisper a request to Keane. At once he reached into his pocket.

"Lord Alcott has something for each of you," she said.

The children gathered around, and he pressed a coin into each of their hands.

"For the pastry booth," Briana said with a smile. "Because that was always my favorite."

The children let out little squeals of excitement, until, at a dark look from their father, they remembered their manners.

"Thank you, my lord. Thank you, my lady," they called as they bowed and curtsied, as though in the company of royalty.

Then they raced away in a daze of pleasure. For the first time in their lives, they could buy anything their hearts desired.

When the McCann family was swallowed up in the crowd, Keane turned to Briana. "Would you like to join them at market?"

"Oh, Keane. Could we?"

"Aye. But only until you begin to feel weary."

He climbed down and tied the reins, then helped her

to the ground. As they strolled among the colorful
stalls boasting everything from fancy lace to pigs' en-
trails, Briana's weakness seemed to vanish. Here,
among people like those she had known at Ballinarin,
she was completely at ease.

"Oh, look, Keane." She paused at a booth where a
weary-looking woman stood beside a boy of perhaps
ten or twelve, seated on a straight-backed wooden
chair. From a tray on his lap, he was fashioning an
assortment of buttons. There were some carved out of
wood, others made of colorful stones, and some from
bits of hide.

Briana held up a button made of mother-of-pearl.
"Oh, how pretty. See how the sunlight brings out all
the colors of the rainbow, Keane."

"Aye." But it was her eyes he was looking at. It
gave him such joy to see them sparkling with newly
restored health and vitality.

She turned to the lad. "You do beautiful work."

His smile was quick and bright. "I thank you, my
lady."

"Did you make all of these?"

"Aye."

"It fills his hours," the woman added. "Since my
Paddy can't run and play with the other children."

"And why can't you?" Briana asked the boy.

"I cannot walk, my lady."

It was then that she noticed, beneath the tray, the
withered legs barely covered by shabby breeches.

She touched a hand to his. "Perhaps you can't walk,
but you have a rare talent, Paddy."

The boy's smile was radiant.

Keane took the button from Briana's hand and examined it carefully, then turned to the lad. "How many of these do you have?"

Paddy opened a soft pouch and counted them out. "Ten, my lord. Would you like to buy one for the lady?"

"I'll take the lot of them." Keane reached into his pocket and counted out a handful of coins.

From the look on the lad's face, he'd never before seen so much money.

"My lord, that's far more than they're worth."

"Not when they make the lady so happy."

The lad returned the buttons to the pouch, and handed it to Briana.

As they turned away, Keane caught sight of the woman placing a hand on her son's shoulder, a single tear coursing down her cheek.

"Pastries." Briana stopped, studying the assortment of treats with a sigh. "Ah, this is what I'd been searching for."

"You mean this is why we visited every stall?" Despite Keane's mutterings, he was smiling broadly. "Had you but told me, I could have saved us both a great deal of walking. Not to mention the gold I've spent."

"But think of how many people you've met, my lord."

"Aye, there is that." He'd met half the village, thanks to this amazing lass. She had the most charming way of drawing people out of themselves. She was truly interested in them, and they, in turn, found themselves opening to her as they would a friend. In no time they had lost their shyness with her. And that had led them to accept the man who accompanied her, despite their initial mistrust.

She looped her arm through his as she made her choice. "That one, I think. And one of those." She turned. "What about you, Keane? Which pastry appeals to you?"

He leaned close, so that the old woman tending the booth wouldn't overhear. "The hunger I feel will not be satisfied with mere pastries."

His words, murmured against her temple, caused such a rush of heat she had to take a step back. Keeping her tone light she said, "A pity. I have it on good authority that these pastries are the best in all of Carrick."

The old woman handed her the pastries with a warm smile. "Thank you, my lady. And who would have told you that?"

"Your daughter, I believe. The pretty dark-haired lass who was selling eggs." Briana bit into one and sighed as she rolled her eyes. "I see I was not misled. It is I who thank you, mistress."

When Keane had finished paying, Briana lifted the pastry to his mouth. "You must taste this."

He took her offering, warmed by the brush of her fingers against his lips. He swallowed, then nodded. "Excellent."

The old woman was still beaming when they walked away. And, like everyone else in the village of Carrick, she would have something fascinating to tell her family this night as they sat around the table. For she had not only seen the mysterious new lord of the manor, but the pretty stranger who seemed to have captured Lord Alcott's heart, as well. And both had complimented her on her fine pastries.

* * *

"Tired?" Keane held the team to a slow, easy trot as they headed toward home.

"Aye. A little. But it's a satisfying fatigue." She turned to him. "Thank you for this day, Keane. I so enjoyed myself."

"As did I, my lady."

"Truly?"

She tilted her face and he found himself dazzled by her smile. "Truly. I met more people today than I met in an entire week of riding across my estate. And all because of you." He laid his hand over hers. "You have a most extraordinary gift, Briana O'Neil. A gift that attracts people to you. You are a rare treasure."

Briana laughed. "If I am a treasure, it is a well-kept secret. Mother Superior called me her cross in this life. She said that if she should ever succeed in teaching me silence, she would have earned her reward in heaven."

"What that good nun didn't understand is that some things were not meant to be silent."

"If you would say such a thing to Reverend Mother, she would accuse you of heresy."

"Then how can she explain the song of a bird? Or the laughter of children?"

Briana glanced at him in surprise. She had never expected Keane O'Mara to give voice to such lofty thoughts. She fell uncharacteristically silent, mulling these strange, new feelings that bloomed inside her. Feelings that had her at the same time joyous and uneasy.

"Ah. Here we are." The carriage entered the courtyard with a clatter, and the stable master hurried over to take the reins as soon as the team came to a halt.

"Welcome home, my lord. My lady."

"Thank you, Monroe." Keane stepped down, then reached up and helped Briana. But instead of setting her on her feet, he scooped her into his arms and carried her through the open doorway.

"Keane, I'm not too tired to walk."

"I know." He nodded a greeting at Vinson, who held the door, and then at Mistress Malloy, who was standing to one side, smiling and wiping her hands on her apron. As he started up the stairs he pressed his lips to Briana's temple and whispered, "But it was the only excuse I could think of to get you into my arms."

She wrapped her arms around his neck and smiled. "All you had to do was ask."

He carried her to her room and was disappointed to see Cora inside, awaiting her mistress. As soon as the door was opened, the little maid leapt up from the chaise where she'd been sewing a gown.

"My lord, my lady, welcome back. I have a new gown ready for your approval, should you care to wear it to sup tonight, my lady."

Keane banked his feelings. "The lady will be taking her evening meal in bed, Cora. The only thing she'll need will be a nightshift."

He stood a moment longer, holding Briana in his arms as easily as if she weighed nothing at all.

Her lips formed a pretty pout. "I'm not that tired, Keane."

"You put on a brave face, lass. But I know the day has been long for you. Especially since you're so recently recovered from your wounds."

He set her gently upon the bed, then stepped back as Cora crossed the room to assist her.

As he made his way to his own chambers he found himself smiling. This had been an extraordinary day.

One he would not soon forget. And the fact that Cora had been in Briana's chambers was a good omen. He'd been feeling entirely too weak-willed at that precise moment. He would certainly have given in to the desire to kiss those tempting lips. And that could have led to all sorts of other...desires.

No need to throw himself into temptation's way. After all, he was still a novice at this heroic nobility. One slip, and he could drag them both into the abyss.

He decided quickly. He would dine alone. And get back to his ledgers. And if necessary, go for a long midnight ride until he was ready to face his bed. Alone.

Chapter Twelve

"Excuse me, my lord." Vinson stepped into the library, pausing just inside the door.

"Aye, Vinson." Keane tore his gaze from the columns of figures he'd been studying for the past hour. "What is it?"

"Hugh McCann has asked to speak with you. He is one of your tenant farmers."

"Aye, I know of him. Send him in."

Minutes later the two men were shaking hands.

Keane indicated a chair by the fire. "Will you have tea, Hugh? Or a glass of ale?"

"Nothing, my lord."

Ignoring his refusal, Keane turned to his butler. "Fetch two ales, Vinson."

The old man did as he was told, then took up his position by the door while the two men lifted their glasses and drank.

Keane settled himself in the chair beside Hugh's. "What brings you to Carrick House?"

"I had no wish to disturb you, my lord. But my wife and children can't stop talking about the kindness of you and your lady. And my wife thought…that is, we both thought, you and the lady might join us for a meal this evening.''

''A meal.''

''It won't be anything fancy. But we would like to repay you in some small way.''

Keane could barely hide his surprise at this unexpected gesture. ''I would be honored to sup with you and your family, Hugh. And I'm sure the lady Briana will be pleased at your invitation.''

''Then we'll expect you this evening, my lord.'' Hugh set his empty glass aside and got to his feet. ''The children will be so delighted. They've talked of nothing but the lovely lady since market day. Oh.'' He seemed to catch himself. ''And you, of course. You were most kind to them, my lord.''

Vinson escorted the visitor to the front door, then returned to the library. Keane was standing at the window, hands behind his back, staring at the rolling hills beyond. Hearing the footsteps he turned.

''Tell Mistress Malloy that Miss O'Neil and I will not be taking our evening meal here at Carrick House.''

''Aye, my lord.''

As he went in search of the housekeeper, Vinson wondered if the tenant farmer had any idea of the importance of his visit. Hugh McCann was the first to set foot in Carrick House since Keane O'Mara had become lord of the manor. And the first to extend the hand of friendship.

It could mean nothing more than a simple meal. Or it could prove to be something quite momentous.

''What is all this?'' Keane looked up as Briana, wearing a simple woolen gown of palest pink and a matching shawl, descended the stairs, trailed by Cora and Mistress Malloy, whose arms were laden with packages.

"Gifts for the McCann family." Briana paused at the foot of the stairs. "I hope you don't mind, Keane. I asked Fleming to cut some roses for Hugh's wife."

He nodded. "A thoughtful gesture. But what are all these others?"

"I asked Cook to bake something special for the children. And she seemed to get a bit carried away. And then I wanted a gift for baby Daniel, and Cora sewed him a lovely soft coat to ward off the evening chill. And I made him a silly play toy. And..." She paused a moment to catch her breath.

He seized the moment to mutter, "You'd think it was a holiday instead of a simple meal." He took her arm and called to the others, "Stow those things in the back of the carriage."

"Aye, my lord." The housekeeper and servant followed him outside, where Monroe stood holding the reins of the team.

"Shall I drive you, my lord?" the old man asked.

"Nay, Monroe. I need no driver." Keane helped Briana into the carriage, then climbed up and took the reins.

The team trotted smartly as the carriage rolled along the curving ribbon of drive, then turned off to head across a flat green meadow.

Briana lifted her face to the late afternoon sunshine. "Oh, Keane. Look around you. What do you see?"

His tone was deliberately unemotional. After a day spent poring over ledgers, he knew exactly what there was here in Carrick. "I see barren, rocky soil that challenges the farmer every day of his existence. I see poor, tired people in a poor, sad little country.''

"If that's all you see, I pity you." She turned her head to watch as a flock of sheep moved slowly across a distant hill. "In all your travels, did you ever see a lovelier scene than this?"

"Aye. It is lovely," he admitted grudgingly. "I'd forgotten just how lovely until I came back home. But that doesn't change my mind about it."

"Your servants are making wagers among themselves on how soon you'll take leave of your home."

He pressed his lips together. In truth, were it not for the woman beside him, he'd have probably been gone by now.

They rolled along a narrow lane edged with a tangle of wildflowers growing in such profusion, they formed a wall of color and sweet perfume that filled the air. They came to a stop in front of a thatched-roof cottage. The door opened, and the children came tumbling out, eager to greet their company. Behind them stood Hugh McCann and his wife, holding the infant.

"Welcome, my lord."

"Welcome, my lady."

The children's voices were high-pitched in excitement as they shouted their greetings.

Keane helped Briana from the carriage, and the two of them greeted their host and hostess, then learned the names of Hugh McCann's wife, Bridget, and each of their children.

"We thought you might like some roses from the gardens at Carrick House." Briana handed them to her hostess.

Bridget blushed with pride as she accepted her gift.

"Who are those for?" A little girl pointed to the packages in the back of the carriage.

Her father quickly reprimanded her for her boldness.

Briana merely smiled. "I'm glad you reminded me, Keely. These are for all of you. A gift from Lord Alcott's cook. I do hope," she added as she passed one to each of the children, "that you'll wait until after your meal to sample them."

As the children unwrapped the parcels, they squealed with delight.

"Look, da. Look, ma. They're little cakes, made in the shape of animals."

Everyone gathered around to examine the clever pastries, cut in the shape of dogs and cats and horses, with bits of frosting outlining eyes and ears.

Foregoing formality, Keane knelt down and lifted one for closer inspection. "Well, I'll be... I'd forgotten all about these." He looked up. "Cook used to make these same little cakes for me when I was just a lad."

"She did?" Little Keely smiled, showing a missing tooth. "Was she your cook when you were as little as baby Daniel?"

Before he could answer one of the other children piped up, "Don't be foolish, Keely. Lord Alcott was never a baby. Da said fancy lords and ladies aren't like other people."

"They aren't?" Keane turned to the lad.

"Nay, sir. Da said they don't work the fields or tend the flocks. They just 'herit all the gold in the world, then grow fat and lazy off the sweat of other men."

While their host turned several shades of red, Keane surprised him by throwing back his head and laughing.

"Your father's right, lad. We do inherit wealth. And we also inherit enormous debts, if our fathers and grandfathers weren't good managers of their estates."

"What did you 'herit, sir. Wealth? Or debt?"

Keane winked. "A good bit of both. But most of what I have today, I earned." He turned to his host and hostess. "I believe we brought gifts for your baby, as well."

The young parents seemed relieved to change the subject. Leading the way inside their cottage, they set the baby down on the floor, while Briana and the children gathered around to open the last of the gifts.

"This is from Cora, one of the servants at Carrick House," Briana said as she unwrapped a lovely little coat of softest wool.

"Oh, my lady." Bridget McCann held it up, her eyes shining with excitement. "Never have I seen anything so fine."

"I'll tell Cora you approved. She's a fine seamstress, as well as a lovely young woman." Briana unwrapped a small square. "And this is something I made to amuse baby Daniel."

It was a softy, spongy ball, stuffed with fabric and tightly sewn with hide. As soon as she handed it to the infant, he clutched it to his mouth and began to chew.

"I believe he likes it, my lady."

His antics brought a smile to Briana's lips. "I recall that my mother often made such toys for the children of our village."

Hugh led Keane to a chaise pulled in front of a cozy fire, where two glasses of ale were already poured and waiting on a side table.

"Come, my lord. We'll have a drop before we sup."

"Aye, Hugh. Thank you." Keane stretched out his legs and sipped his drink, while Briana and the children knelt in a circle around baby Daniel, tossing him the ball, and watching as he scooped it up to his mouth, drooling and grinning with delight.

From the kitchen came the most enticing aroma of beef roasting over a fire, and biscuits browning on a warming shelf.

While the men talked of land and crops and weather, and the children continued to entertain the baby, Briana walked to the kitchen and offered her help.

"Oh nay, my lady. You'll soil your lovely gown."

"You're not to worry about my gown. Here." Briana reached out and took a heavy platter from Bridget's hands. "Where would you like this?"

"In the center of the table, if you please."

The two women worked in companionable silence, enjoying the rumble of masculine voices and the laughter of the children. Soon the dinner was ready, and the others were called to the table.

As they sat, the family reached out to link hands, while Hugh led them in prayer. Briana and Keane followed suit.

"We ask a blessing upon this food, this fine land, and most especially on our guests, who honor us with their presence."

With her head bowed Briana glanced at Keane. But his face showed no expression as he listened to the words.

Then they began passing platters. It was simple fare. Beef. Potatoes. Biscuits. But the meat had been cooked until it fell off the bone. The potatoes were swimming in rich dark gravy. And the biscuits, spread with freshly churned butter, melted in the mouth.

Keane accepted a second helping, and a third, and even Briana was surprised by her appetite, eating more than she could ever remember.

When Bridget brought tea to the table, the children began to fidget, in anticipation of the special dessert awaiting them.

Their father glanced around the table, then said with a smile, "I think it's time you enjoyed those fancy cakes Miss O'Neil brought you."

With sighs of delight they began to eat until there wasn't a crumb left.

"Those were the bestest I've ever tasted," little Keely said solemnly as she licked her fingers.

"I'm glad to hear that, Keely." Briana laughed. "Shall I tell Cook that you approve of her surprise?"

The children nodded as they drained their glasses of tea laced with milk.

"If you've had enough to eat," Hugh said, "we can take our ale outside, where we can sit and watch the sunset."

"What about the dishes?" Briana asked.

Bridget scooped up the baby, who was still seated on the floor, playing with the new ball. "The older ones will see to them. Come, my lady. The air is pleasant tonight."

They wandered outside and sat on wooden benches positioned beneath the branches of a gnarled old tree. Already the sun had dipped below the horizon, leaving a sky streaked with gold and rose. Night shadows were gathering close.

Bridget opened her dress and held the babe to her

breast. Seeing mother and child, Briana felt a sudden tightness in her throat. By now, all of her young friends in Ballinarin would be wed with children of their own. Her brothers, too, had taken wives, and would no doubt soon have families. And all the while, she had been suspended in time and place, unable to go forward with her life. In these past three years, the world had moved on, leaving her behind.

Keane sipped his ale and looked off across the meadow, watching the flight of a hawk. "You're a lucky man, Hugh. A lovely wife, a fine family."

"Aye, my lord. A lucky man, indeed. And I'd like to keep them all here, safe around me." He turned to Keane, daring to look him in the eye. "But I wonder how much longer I can do that, with the English soldiers roaming the land, seeking new victims daily for their bloodletting."

When Keane said nothing he asked, "You've seen what these madmen do to our women and children?"

"Aye. I've seen, Hugh."

"We've no weapons with which to defend ourselves, my lord."

Keane sipped, nodded.

Hugh's voice lowered. "The men of Carrick wish to band together and form a militia, my lord. We want your permission to forge some of our farming implements into weapons. And we would ask you to teach us how to wield them."

"You want me to teach you how to handle a sword?"

"Aye, my lord. And a longbow and knife."

When Keane held his silence, Hugh stood and faced him. "There was a time, when your grandfather was alive, that the people of Carrick knew such things. We were proud of our warlike abilities. But during the time of your father, such things were lost to us. He…'' It was obvious that Hugh was struggling to choose his words carefully, not wishing to offend the new lord. But the words needed to be said. They burst forth from between clenched teeth. ''He cared more for grand balls and fine dinners than he did about the people whose work made those things possible. There's even talk that he deliberately relieved us of our weapons, because he'd gone over to the English.'' He glanced toward his wife, then lowered his voice. ''Forgive me, my lord. But after our chance meeting, I'd begun to think, that is, I'd hoped, that you might prove to be more like your grandfather.''

''I see.'' Keane stared down into his glass.

Perplexed, Hugh McCann did the same, avoiding his guest's eyes.

After a prolonged silence, Keane drained his glass and got to his feet. ''I thank you for the lovely meal, Bridget.''

The young woman fastened her gown and lifted the infant to her shoulder. ''You're welcome, my lord. I hope you'll come again.''

''And I hope one day you will accept the hospitality of Carrick House.'' He took Briana's hand and helped her to her feet.

When he turned, Hugh said, ''You'll think on what I've said, my lord?''

''Aye, Hugh. I will.''

The children gathered around the doorway, calling their good-nights. Little Keely ran up to hug Briana, who, in turn, lifted her in her arms and kissed her soundly before setting her down.

Keane helped Briana into the carriage. With a wave of their hands, they took their leave.

Briana waited until they were some distance from the cottage before turning to Keane. "Tell me the truth. Do you love this land?"

His voice, so close beside her in the darkness, vibrated with feeling. "You know I do. But soon enough it will be bathed in the blood of its people. How lovely will it seem then, I wonder."

Her voice trembled with anger. "Do you hear yourself? Do you know what you're saying?"

"Aye." He nodded. "Would you have me lie to myself?"

"I would have you care enough about your land to do something about it. Hugh McCann made a simple request. Arms for his people, and someone to teach them how to use them."

"What would you have me do, Briana? Should I encourage all of Carrick to die for their country? Would I then prove to you how much I love Ireland?"

Her voice lowered with conviction. "I would rather die for my country than turn my back on its troubles."

"Is that what you think I'm doing?"

"Isn't it?"

He didn't answer. Couldn't. For in truth, he was no longer certain just what he was doing.

He had returned to Ireland simply to put his affairs in order. And then he had fully intended to leave this unhappy land with its unhappy memories, and never look back. Now he found himself tempted to do what he'd sworn never to do again.

And all because of this fiery little woman who had fought her way back from the dead. And would no doubt fight until the day she breathed her last.

Dear heaven, he was sick of the fighting. He cursed the day he'd ever stumbled across Briana O'Neil. Were it not for her, he would already be on his way to Spain or France. To safety. Not to a life of inherited titles and lands and debts, but wealth he'd earned with his own two hands and clever mind. To a life of untold wealth and ease. With no demanding little female like a millstone around his neck. A female who made him think too much. And want too much. And ache for things he could never have. Like respect and respectability. And love, such as he'd seen between Hugh McCann and his Bridget.

Aye, love. It was the one thing he'd always wanted in his life. And had despaired of ever finding.

Chapter Thirteen

Keane leaned a hip against the balcony, watching the sunrise. He'd slept badly. All because of a certain female, who was taking up entirely too much of his time lately.

He ought to be grateful for their harsh words of the night before. At least he hadn't been tempted to ravish her. It was probably the first night since she'd been under his roof that he could make such a statement.

He was still angry with her. She had him tied up in knots. She'd questioned his loyalty. His integrity. His courage.

What's worse, he was now questioning them himself.

What right did she have to plant such seeds in his mind? Hadn't he suffered enough? Paid a high enough price? And all because of some misguided sense of duty to the land of his grandfather. To atone for the sins of his father.

No, by God. He slammed an open palm against the balcony. He'd paid his dues. He'd be damned if anyone would question such things again. He was done with all that. He had no intention of paying a further price for his father's weakness.

He watched a horse and rider top a ridge in the distance. Sunlight glistened on a cap of dancing curls. If he didn't know better, he would think it was Briana. But that couldn't be. She wouldn't attempt to ride again after the horrible fall she'd taken on Peregrine. Would she?

He turned away and slipped into a tunic, then pulled on his boots. That done, he strode down the hall toward her chambers.

The door to her sitting room was standing open. Inside, Cora was tidying the room.

She looked up as he entered.

"Where is Miss O'Neil?"

"I know not, my lord. She left here not long ago, dressed for riding. I assumed that she was joining you."

His eyes narrowed as a sudden thought intruded. He swung away and stalked toward the library. Inside he stared at the mantel where his ancestral swords usually hung. The space was empty.

With a muttered oath he stormed out the door and headed toward the stables. Minutes later the stable master confirmed that the lass had indeed gone riding, "with the lord's permission." With a look of fury Keane took off on his own mount, following the direction Briana had taken.

It didn't take him long to figure out where she was headed. The McCann cottage.

Tigers, it would seem, never changed their stripes. And his resident tiger, Briana O'Neil, had decided to take matters into her own hands once again, and fight the English in the only way she knew—by leaping into battle without a thought to the consequences.

When he got his hands on her this time, he'd throttle her within an inch of her miserable little life.

"Nay, Hugh." Briana, standing atop a hillock in a neatly plowed field, held aloft her weapon and shouted commands at the man who was attempting to disarm her with his upraised sword.

Standing around in a semicircle was a cluster of more than a dozen farmers and their sons, watching and listening intently.

"If you charge directly toward me, I'll be able to run you through with my blade. Don't you see? You must twist, turn, dodge. Whatever it takes to avoid injury."

"Unless you'd like to die a bloody, and very painful death," came a familiar deep voice from behind.

Briana whirled. And found Keane advancing toward her, with a look of fury smoldering in his eyes.

"My lord." Hugh McCann stepped forward, holding out his sword. "It was kind of you to permit us the use of your ancestral weapons. At first we thought Miss O'Neil was jesting when she said you'd sent her to teach us to fight. But now that we've seen and heard her, we are most grateful. The lady has real skill with a sword."

"Aye. She does, doesn't she?" Keane accepted the sword, testing the weight of it in his palm for several moments before turning to Briana. The murderous look in his eyes had her backing up as he said softly, "Let's give them a demonstration of your skill, Miss O'Neil."

She was aware of the temper that flared in his eyes.

Was aware, too, of the deadly softness that masked a blazing fury.

She would show him that she didn't fear him or his temper. She lifted her chin a fraction. "Aye, my lord. As you wish."

She raised her sword and waited. Keane did the same, his gaze never leaving hers. When she advanced, he moved to one side and easily deflected her thrust. But she surprised him by turning on the balls of her feet, and striking out quickly, catching his arm with the point of her sword.

The stab wasn't enough to draw blood. It merely sliced a long tear in his sleeve. But it was enough to make the crowd gasp. For they realized that these two had no intention of holding back. If it was, indeed, a mere demonstration of skill, it very nearly resembled a true battle.

"You're quick, my lady."

"Thank you." She smiled as she backed away from his thrust.

It was true. What she lacked in strength, she more than made up for with speed and grace. She was, he realized as he backed her across the hillock, a worthy opponent.

As the fight took them across toward a stand of trees, the crowd of farmers moved with them, watching each thrust, each parry with avid fascination.

"But what will you do when I pin you?" Keane brought his sword up, catching hers in midstrike. Metal clanged against metal, and Keane could see, by the look on Briana's face, that she had felt the blow clear to the tips of her fingers. She'd had to, since his own were still vibrating from the force of it.

Still, to her credit, she didn't drop her sword and

break into tears as he had half expected. That would be the way of most females. But this one was like no other.

"I was taught to never surrender." Her breath was coming hard and fast now as she danced, spun, avoided and, whenever possible, charged . "And never retreat."

He deflected another thrust and tempered his blow with the flat of his blade, knowing that if he were to use all his strength, he'd send her facedown in the dirt. He didn't want to humiliate her, after all. He merely wanted to test her skill. Though the thought of inflicting just a little pain and a little embarrassment, was tempting.

"Most unwise, Miss O'Neil," he said between clenched teeth. "For sometimes retreat is necessary, in order to live to fight another day."

She felt the rough bark of a tree against her back and knew she'd gone as far as she could. No more evasive tactics. Now she would have to stand and fight.

"A true son of Ireland would rather die than retreat from the sword of an Englishman, my lord."

His smile was dark and dangerous. "Tell that to the sons of Ireland who lie buried beside the chapel. And tell it to their widows, and their children, who now have no one left to provide for them or defend them."

"They have me." She lifted her sword, prepared to make one last valiant effort in her own defense. "And soon they'll have these brave men, who have come here to learn how to defend, not only their own loved ones, but all of Ireland as well."

"Then I suggest they watch closely." Keane easily

brought the point of his sword to her hand, and in one deft movement disarmed her.

Her mouth dropped open in stunned surprise as her weapon fell to the earth at her feet. Before she could bend to retrieve it, Keane caught her roughly by the shoulder and dragged her in front of him, holding the sharp blade of his sword against her throat.

"And that is how you disarm your opponent and render him helpless." He gave a sardonic grin to the circle of men. "Or in this case, render *her* helpless."

The men roared with laughter, before doffing their hats to congratulate Lord Alcott on his superior skill.

Keane released her and picked up her fallen sword, jamming both weapons into the earth at his feet in a symbol of victory.

As she stepped back, heat stained Briana's cheeks. Even her brothers, Rory and Conor, who were perhaps the most skilled swordsmen in all of Ireland, had never managed to disarm her without so much as a drop of blood being shed. To fight and win without inflicting serious wounds demonstrated a superior skill such as she had never before encountered.

Her eyes narrowed. Just who was Keane O'Mara? And where had he learned to fight like this?

More importantly, why was such a man reluctant to take up his sword against his enemy?

"Are you ever going to speak to me?" Briana held her horse to an easy trot beside Keane's mount. "Or are you still smarting because I took your ancestral swords without permission?"

He turned to study her, and she nearly flinched at the hard, cold look in those smoky eyes. "That is but a small part of my anger."

"Someone had to come to the aid of these people. It is cruel and inhuman to leave them defenseless against the English."

He snagged her reins, drawing their horses close. "You speak to me of cruelty? Inhumanity? Woman, you have no idea about either."

"And you do?"

"I've had a taste of it. Enough that I want no more." He shot her a fierce look. "Do you have any idea what you're doing to these people?"

"I'm offering them hope."

"Hope." He spat the word. "What you're offering them is a lie. A cruel lie that will come back to haunt you."

"If that is true, why did you agree to come back tomorrow and help them hone their skill with a sword?"

"Because." He released her reins and nudged his horse into a run. "Now that they're determined to forge weapons of death, I have a responsibility to see that they have at least a fighting chance when they take them up and use them."

She had to urge her horse faster, to keep up. "Will you let me help?" she shouted.

He pretended not to hear. There were too many emotions still churning inside him. He had a feeling that his life had somehow slipped from his cool, careful control. In the blink of an eye, he found himself heading in a direction he'd sworn never to go again.

Because of Briana O'Neil. The most pigheaded, obstinate, frustrating lass he'd ever known.

He rode ahead, leaving her in his dust. But even that gave him no satisfaction.

* * *

"My lord." Vinson stood waiting at the door as Keane and Briana stepped inside.

"Something is wrong, old man."

"Aye, my lord." Vinson glanced toward Briana, then away. "The messenger you sent to the lass's family…met with English swords."

"Is he…?"

"Aye, my lord. His body was just returned by some lads from a nearby village."

"No." Brianna's cry was torn from her lips.

Keane's face was devoid of emotion as he turned away. "I'll go to his family at once."

Briana touched a hand to his. "I must go with you."

He understood. The lad's death was a burden they would both have to bear.

The sky was still dark when Keane made his way to the stable. He was pleased to see his horse saddled and ready in the courtyard, as he'd requested. Also waiting was a horse and wagon. In the back of the wagon were more than two dozen weapons he'd located throughout Carrick House. Swords, longbows, knives, many of them rusted and forgotten, gathering dust in unused storerooms. After a night of work by more than a dozen servants, the blades had been honed to a razor edge. The hilts, highly polished, caught and reflected the wink of starlight.

It was a start. Not nearly enough to arm a militia, of course. But the men had been told to scour their own homes and fields for whatever weapons they could find. The local smiths would fashion even more weapons from farm implements.

As Keane was about to pull himself into the saddle,

he saw one of the stable lads approaching.

"Good, lad. You're up. I was afraid I'd have to wake you. Let's be on our way."

The lad pulled himself to the seat of the wagon and took up the reins. As they started off along the curved drive, Keane rode ahead, lost in thought. Scant weeks ago, if anyone had told him that he would be agreeable to training the men of Carrick to fight the English, he'd have scoffed. Yet here he was, up before dawn, ready to do just that.

How had he become so entangled in this web again? Hadn't he come here with but one thought in mind? To settle his father's debts and make a new life for himself. Somewhere far from anyone who had ever heard of his damnable title and his disgusting past. And now, look at him. About to jump in again. And all because of a female. Would he never learn?

Briana O'Neil. He'd half expected to find her in the stable this morrow, begging to be allowed to ride to the McCann cottage with him.

He slowed his mount. In fact, he'd been sure of it. So sure, he'd already planned his arguments.

This was completely uncharacteristic of the lass. Nothing could hold back that little firestorm when she made up her mind about something.

He reined in his horse and looked back at the horse and wagon, plodding slowly up the hill. The driver was hunched over, as though more asleep than awake. A wide hat completely covered the hair and hid the face from view.

Keane felt a tingling at the back of his neck. Through the years he'd learned to trust his instincts. And at this moment, his instincts were shouting a warning.

He suddenly wheeled his mount and headed toward

the wagon. As he approached, the driver glanced up, then ducked his head.

"Just as I thought." Keane pulled up alongside and reached over, yanking the hat from the driver's head, revealing a tumble of red curls. While Briana shrank back, Keane let loose with every rich, ripe curse he'd ever known.

"Just how did you think to keep your identity secret once the sun came up?"

"I figured by then it would be too late to send me back."

"You did, did you?" He looked her up and down, noting the men's breeches and tunic, the mud-spattered boots. He bit back the smile that threatened. "And where did you find such lovely clothes?"

"Cora borrowed them from one of the stable lads."

"Cora." His eyes narrowed. "Now you've even dragged the servants into this."

"They were already in it. Don't you see, Keane? Everyone in Ireland is in this. There isn't a family left that hasn't felt the pain of an English sword. Cora, Vinson, Mistress Malloy. It is their brothers and sons and fathers who are buried beside the chapel. And all are cheered by the fact that you've agreed to train the villagers in the use of weapons."

When he didn't respond, she glanced up at him. He wasn't looking at her. He was staring off across the green hills, glistening with dew in the first rays of the morning sun.

She felt a glimmer of hope. "You aren't going to send me back, are you?"

He turned to meet her eyes. And though his look was still stern, his tone was brisk and businesslike. "We'll divide the group into two and begin with the basics. The advantage of the longbow for distance. How to wield a sword when fighting three or more. The need for a concealed knife, when all else fails.''

She knew her jaw had dropped. For the space of a moment, all she could do was stare. Then, when he wheeled his mount and raced ahead, her heart bloomed with relief and joy.

She flicked the reins, and the horse and wagon rumbled across the meadow toward the McCann cottage, where more than three score men and boys stood waiting in the dawn light.

Chapter Fourteen

"Watch it, lad." As late afternoon shadows gathered, Keane stood on the sidelines, shouting instructions as two burly farm boys came together in a clash of ringing swords.

The taller of the two was swinging his blade wildly, clearly caught up in the excitement of the moment.

"If you don't slow down, you're apt to separate your best friend's head from his shoulders. Is that what you want, lad?"

"Nay, sir. But you told me to defend myself."

"Aye. But save the blood and pain for the English."

"Speaking of which." Hugh McCann leaned close. "I've heard that a band of soldiers attacked a field near Derry and left an entire village in shock. More than half their men and boys were cut down as they were reaping their crops."

Keane made a quick calculation. "From Carrick to Blaire, and now to Derry. It sounds as though they're circling back."

"Aye. My thoughts exactly."

"Is it the same band that struck our villages before?"

Hugh shrugged. "We can't be certain. They never leave any survivors who can identify them."

Keane glanced toward Briana, who stood nearby, coaching a group in the art of defense using a knife at close range.

In the past few weeks she had become a familiar figure, garbed in breeches and tunic and work-worn boots. At first the men had treated her with great care, fearing they might do harm to the slender lass. But they soon learned to overlook the fact that she was a female, as she leapt into the thick of every skirmish with sword flashing. She was absolutely fearless. A fact that caused many of the men to work even harder than ever, in the hope of becoming her equal.

Through her usual diligence and determination, Briana had become an accepted member of their militia. As had the lord of Carrick House, who had once been considered their enemy.

Keane's voice lowered to a whisper. "Briana can identify the English. It is how I met the lass. She survived the attack that bloodied the fields of Carrick."

Hugh McCann looked aghast. "Has she spoken of it? Has she described any of the English dogs?"

Keane shook his head. "Not a word." A fact that puzzled him. She'd made no secret of her hatred of the English. Yet she'd never spoken about that day, or about the men who had taken her to the brink of death.

He shrugged. She was as entitled to her private demons as he was to his. He wouldn't poke or prod her memory. Perhaps it was simply too painful to bring out into the light. Something he understood all too well.

"Come lads," one of the farmers called as he carefully laid aside his weapon. "We've been up since dawn, working the fields, then honing our skills with weapons of war. 'Tis time to wash away the day with an ale or two at the tavern.''

The others nodded, and, one by one, began to fall into line marching toward the village.

When Keane and Briana made ready to leave, Hugh shook his head. ''Nay, my lord. You and the lass must join us. The men have been talking among themselves. They wish to thank you for all you've done for us.''

Keane glanced at Briana and wondered if she was thinking about the fine meal awaiting them at Carrick House, and the long, soaking bath Cora would surely have ready. But what Hugh was offering was far more than a drink with the men. It was an acknowledgment that they had been accepted by the villagers as one of their own. It was a rare honor.

He nodded. ''Aye, Hugh. The lass and I would be grateful for a sip.''

They walked to the village, leading their horses, and stood around the warm fire while the tavern owner and his wife filled their tankards.

''To Lord Alcott,'' one of the men shouted, as they raised their glasses.

''And to Briana O'Neil.''

They drank, wiped their mouths, and smiled as the tankards were filled a second time.

''To Ireland,'' called a small, wiry man with skin the texture of aged leather, and a thatch of white hair.

''To freedom,'' shouted another.

''And to all of us, who will give our last drop of blood to keep it free.''

They drank more slowly, allowing the ale to snake through their veins and warm their blood.

Hugh ordered another round for the men, then set

his tankard on the mantel and turned to Briana. "I'm told you survived an English attack in our village, my lady."

"Aye." She sipped her ale, feeling warm and content among these good people.

"Could you identify the soldiers?"

She noticed that the others had gone very still, watching her. She swallowed the ale, feeling it burn a path of fire down her throat.

Her fingers tightened on the handle of the tankard, and she had to force herself to relax her grasp. "I suppose I could." Her voice lowered. "At least their leader."

"Is there something about him? Something that sets him apart from the others?"

She could see Keane watching her. After all her self-righteous lectures to him about courage, she was about to reveal her own cowardice. "I...see him sometimes, in the night. It is a vision that leaves me filled with terror and revulsion. But when I awake, afraid and trembling, the image is gone. And I am left with only the sound of his voice, damning all Irish to death." She shuddered. "And the sound of his mocking laughter. It torments me. And wakes me often from a sound sleep."

The men glanced around and nodded, and Hugh patted her arm much as her brothers might. "You've nothing to be ashamed of my lady. We understand what you're going through. It's a rather common reaction when a warrior faces his own death."

"Do you recall anything else?" one of the farmers asked gently. "The way this English soldier looked? His name, perhaps?"

She thought a moment, struggling to pull something, anything, out of her clouded memory. So many fragments. Bits and pieces that seemed to flash through her mind, then go blank. "Aye. His name." She thought long and hard, then nodded. "His men called him...Halsey."

Some of the men grew agitated, looking at each other for confirmation, for they'd heard the name before.

"Halsey enjoyed the killing." Briana closed her eyes a moment, then stared down into her ale. "He actually laughed as he sent my companions to their death. Lads who had done nothing more than try to defend me. Lads who'd had so little time to laugh, to love." She shivered. "To live."

"How did you survive when no others did, lass?" a farmer asked.

Her eyes hardened. "I know not. I was filled with a rage that seemed to take over me. I took up the sword Halsey had thrust through one of my defender's heart. And when that braggart feared I would best him with his own sword, he ordered his men to hold me."

There was a collective gasp from the men. Briana looked over and saw Keane's lips moving in a fierce oath. It was all coming back to her. So clear now. So vivid. So fearsome. "And as Halsey drove his sword through my chest, he told me that this land, and all who live in it, will answer to an English sword." For a moment her voice wavered, and Keane started toward her. But seeing it, she lifted a hand to hold him at bay and began to speak faster. It was important that she get everything out, for it had been festering in her soul all these long days and nights. "I remember his face now." She closed her eyes as a feeling of blackness came over her. With her eyes closed she saw his hated face come into focus. In a near whisper she described what she saw. "His face is scarred from many battles. His nose is flattened from having been broken. And only a puckered scar remains where his left ear should be." She opened her eyes. Her voice caught in her throat. "As I lay near death, I heard Halsey order his men to a tavern, where they could wash away the taste of…the filthy Irish."

Keane's fingers were grasping the tankard so tightly it shattered in his hand. A tavern wench hurried over to clean up the shards and to press a towel to his bloody hand. He flung it aside and made his way to Briana, while all around her the men muttered and swore.

"Come, lass." He caught her hand. "I know what this must have cost you. It's time we returned to Carrick House."

"Wait. There is one more thing. I saw him. Halsey." As the image rushed into her mind, she felt herself sway. "The day I was on Peregrine. I saw him leading a group of soldiers through a nearby wood."

"You only dreamed it, Briana. It was the fall."

"Perhaps. Aye. Nay." She stiffened, tried to push away. "I did not dream it. I saw him, Keane. I saw Halsey. That's why I fell. I remember it all now."

Her eyes were wide with shock.

As if in a daze she allowed herself to be led through the crowd of men. She was only dimly aware of them squeezing her shoulder, or calling out words of encouragement.

"You showed 'em, my lady."

"Next time, it'll be our turn, my lady."

"You're a hell of a scrapper, my lady."

"Death to the English."

"Aye." A great roar went up from the crowd. "Death to the English."

Outside, Keane lifted her tenderly into his arms and mounted his horse, then took up the reins of her horse, leading it behind.

As they rode through the village, the voices from the tavern faded.

Keane wrapped his arms firmly around her, drawing her against him. He could feel the shudders ripping through her slender body. Tremors of horror and revulsion that she no longer had the strength to fight.

"You're safe now, Briana."

She shook her head. "I'll never be safe. Not as long as Halsey lives. None of us will be."

Though Keane wanted to deny it, he couldn't. He'd known so many men like Halsey. Bullies who enjoyed the killing.

They crested a hill and began the descent toward Carrick House. All around them there was only the silence of the night.

And Keane's voice, low and fierce with passion. "Then we'll have to see that he lives no longer."

Keane's order to the servant was issued sternly. "You'll see that the lass has a warm bath, Cora. And then she's to go straight to bed."

"Aye, my lord." The servant studied Briana, who, beneath the tumbled hair and garb of a stable lad, looked pale and drawn. "Has our lass been wounded?"

"Aye. But it is a wound to her soul. She needs her rest. See to it."

"Aye, my lord." As soon as he'd stormed out of

the chambers, Cora helped Briana to bathe and dress for bed.

"What about food, my lady?"

Briana shook her head. "I couldn't. But thank you, Cora. You may go to your room. I'll sleep soon."

"Aye, my lady." Troubled by the look in her eyes, the servant blew out the candle and let herself out of the room.

Minutes later Keane stopped Cora in the hallway. "Is the lass asleep?"

"Nay, my lord. She seems agitated. But she asked me to leave her alone. Would you like me to go back and sit with her?"

He shook his head. "Go to bed, Cora. I'll see to her."

At Briana's door he knocked, then entered. The room was in darkness. But as his eyes adjusted, he could see, by the light of the fire, that Briana was standing by the window.

"You should be in bed, lass."

She turned. For the longest time she merely stared at him. Then, in a voice just above a whisper she asked, "Why do you call me lass?"

"It suits you."

"Nay. It suits you to call me that. It implies that I'm still just a wee lass, and not a woman, doesn't it?"

"Is that what you think?"

She nodded.

He stayed where he was, afraid to walk closer. "You're in a strange mood tonight."

"Aye." She hugged her arms about herself. "I suppose it was talking about the attack of the soldiers. And Halsey." She shivered. "And thinking again about those brave lads who'd been sent to accompany me home.''

"You said yourself they died bravely. Nobly.''

"Aye. But they're dead just the same. And I'm not.''

"Is that what's bothering you? That you lived?''

She shook her head. "You don't understand. They died without ever having a chance to live. And I lived, but for what? I'm no better off than they. What have I done with my life? I've no husband to look at me the way Hugh McCann looks at his Bridget. No babes, clinging to my skirts and smiling up at me with absolute trust.''

"You'll have all that.'' Even as he said it, the thought brought a knife to his heart. He didn't think he could bear to see another man look at her with love. Or to hear that she'd borne another man's children.

"How can you know what my future will hold?'' She took a step toward him and saw a wary look come into his eyes. "I could face Halsey's sword again tomorrow. And then, all my fine dreams would be gone forever.''

He reached out a hand and caught her more roughly than he'd intended. "Don't say such things, Briana.''

"And why not? Do you know, Keane, that I've never shared my dreams with anyone?''

He hadn't meant to touch her. But now that he had, he couldn't seem to let go. He drew her even closer, his hands moving across the tops of her shoulders, down her arms, trying vainly to dispel her chill and warm her with his touch. "You'll share them someday.'' His voice roughened. "With someone who deserves to share them with you.''

Her head came up. He could see her eyes warming, softening. "I want to share them with you, Keane."

He could feel the blood draining from his head. And rushing straight to his loins. "Be sensible, Briana. Any day now you'll be going home. I'm sure in Ballinarin there are any number of men eager to be a part of your dream."

"I don't want any number of men in Ballinarin." She stood as tall as she could and brushed her lips over his. "I want you, Keane."

It wasn't possible to resist those lips. Perhaps, if he had been a saint, he would have made a more valiant effort. But Keane did what any mere man would do, taking what she offered with a greedy hunger that rocked them both. His mouth closed over hers in a long, slow, deep kiss, pouring out all the passion, all the desire, all the loneliness in his heart.

She answered with equal passion and hunger.

His hands were greedy, touching, massaging, arousing. He pressed soft, moist kisses to her neck, her shoulder and the sensitive hollow of her throat.

With a sigh she arched her neck and clung to him, loving the feel of his lips on her flesh.

He continued kissing her while his hands began a lazy exploration of her back, her sides. His thumbs encountered her breasts, stroking until her nipples hardened.

He swallowed her gasp, taking the kiss deeper until they were both struggling for breath. And still he savaged her mouth, wanting more, needing more.

His words, spoken inside her mouth, were rough with urgency. "God in heaven, Briana, what am I to do with you?"

She wound her arms around his neck and sighed

with sheer pleasure. "You could try loving me, Keane."

He lifted his head and stared down at her. She was smiling in the most seductive way.

When had the lass learned to flirt? And why did she have to be so appealing as she tried to ply her newly discovered womanly charms?

He took a deep breath to steady the ripple of nerves that threatened to send him over the edge at any moment. "You don't know what you're saying."

"Aye. I do, Keane. I want you to lie with me. And love me."

"That isn't possible." He took a step back, needing desperately to break contact. When he was holding her, touching her, he couldn't think. And right now, he needed a clear head, so that he could do the right thing. The honorable thing. The only thing.

"I don't understand. I thought you..." She paused. Licked her lips, that had gone suddenly dry. "I thought we...cared about each other."

"I do care about you, Briana. That's why I'm leaving now. This minute. Before we both do something you'll later regret."

She felt tears dangerously close to the surface, and blinked furiously. "Is it me? Is there something about me that you don't like?"

Before he could answer, she shook her head. "Aye. Of course. It's as my father said. I don't know how to be a woman. I suppose that would put off most men. But I'd thought, somehow, that you were different from other men. That you would like me despite my...imperfections."

He caught her arm and dragged her roughly against him. His voice against her temple was a rasp of fury.

"Don't be a fool, Briana. You're more woman than any I've ever known. A man would have to be a fool not to want you. But this is about me. About what I am."

She pushed away. "And what are you, Keane? Some sort of monster?"

"Aye." His eyes were hard. As was his voice. "You've led a sheltered life, Briana. You have no idea about men like me. Believe me, you're better off without me in your life."

"Don't you think that should be my decision?"

"Nay." He hated the pain and confusion in her eyes. But there was no way he could explain. "The decision is mine. I made a vow to see you returned to your father as I'd found you, or die trying. And, by God, I intend to keep it."

"And my feelings don't matter?"

"Your feelings…" He lifted a hand, as though to touch her, then seemed to think better of it and closed his hand into a fist at his side. "Your feelings are bound to be confused, Briana. But one day you'll see things clearly, and you'll be grateful that you saved yourself for someone worthy of you. You're a very special woman, Briana O'Neil. The man who finally wins your heart will be the luckiest man in all of Ireland."

Because he could no longer bear to look at her, he turned away. "Now go to bed. And I'll do the same."

Briana stood perfectly still, watching as he let himself out of her room. In a state of shock she listened to the sound of his footsteps recede along the hall. And then, with her arms wrapped around herself to ward off the sudden chill, she listened to the silence of Carrick House as it closed around her.

Chapter Fifteen

Filled with self-loathing, Keane paced his room. His tunic lay in a heap beside the bed. It had given him little satisfaction to kick off his boots and watch them bounce, one after the other, against the wall. He had downed a tumbler of ale in one long swallow. But all it had done was leave a bitter taste in his mouth.

As had this whole horrible night.

He stormed to the balcony to stare into the blackness, but all he could see was Briana's eyes. The sweet lass was as transparent as glass. All her emotions were there for him to see. The self-doubt. The confusion. The pain of rejection.

That had been the worst. He'd hated hurting her like that. But it was the only way it could be done. It would have been so easy to take what she offered. In fact, it had taken all his willpower to refuse. But afterward she would have hated him. And would have always resented the fact that she had given herself to a man like him.

A man like him.

Aye, he thought, running his hand through his hair.

This was better. A quick, clean amputation. Like cutting off an arm to save a life.

Or cutting out a heart.

He caught the edge of the balcony at the sudden pain. He'd survived so much. He would survive this, as well. But the pain of this loss would linger for a lifetime.

He exhaled a long, slow breath, and allowed his shoulders to slump for just a moment. Then he straightened and made his way back to the bedside table, where he poured himself another glass of ale.

Briana sat shivering on her balcony, staring off into the distance. She had no idea how long she'd been sitting there, her chin resting on her arms atop the railing. It could have been hours or mere minutes. Time was a blur.

She hadn't cried. The pain was too deep for tears. She had thought her father's rejection the most crushing blow of her young life. But it had been nothing compared with this. The knowledge that she had offered herself to Keane, and that he had refused her, left her shattered.

She couldn't let him crush her spirit, she thought as she got to her feet and began to pace. She wouldn't permit it. Still, when she thought about how calmly, how coldly he had rejected her, she had to bite back a sob.

He'd called her feelings "confused." As though she were somehow a child who didn't know her own heart. She clenched her hands at her sides and stalked around the room, fueling her anger. It was so much better than self-pity. Anger was something she could deal with.

Confused, was she? She hadn't been confused about

the things she'd felt whenever he'd touched her, kissed her. And there was no confusion in her mind about his reaction to her either. Oh, there were times when he'd worked hard to bank his emotions. She'd been aware of that. But there were other times when he hadn't been able to hide his true feelings. When he'd crushed her in his arms and kissed her until they were both breathless. Like tonight, before he'd managed to compose himself.

She paused. Aye. Tonight, when he'd first come to her room, there had been real concern in his eyes. And tenderness in his voice. And a rough possession in his touch that left her no doubt of his intentions. But then it was as if he'd closed a door on his emotions. He'd called himself a monster. And hinted that she would have to live with regrets if they should give in to their passion.

What else had he said? She struggled to remember. At the time she'd been so stunned, she'd hardly paid any heed to the words. Now it was important to recall them clearly.

He'd spoken of a vow he'd made to return her to her father as he'd found her.

She clapped a hand to her mouth. Sweet heaven. Of course. It all made sense now. Ever since her fall from Peregrine, Keane O'Mara had been a changed man.

Cora had told her he'd never left her bedside until she regained consciousness. And from that moment on, he'd been so different, it had become a matter of great discussion among all the servants.

Since that time, whenever he was in her presence he'd been concerned, compassionate, almost brotherly. As though he'd shut down any other passions.

She stood in the middle of the room, giddy with

relief, as the truth dawned. Her heart swelled with such joy, she feared it would burst.

Keane loved her. Loved her so much, he'd bargained with heaven on her behalf. And now he felt honor-bound to protect her virtue, by whatever means possible.

Without taking time to think about what she was doing, she raced out of her chambers and down the hall.

Keane slouched in a chair in front of the fire. The room was dark except for the red glow of hot coals.

After the day he'd put in, he ought to be sleeping. But sleep, he knew, would be impossible this night. How could he rest knowing that all that he'd ever desired lay just a room away? And he, like some sort of noble hero, had just cast all his dreams aside. For what?

He wasn't feeling noble right now. All he felt was empty. And cold. So bone-jarring cold, he would probably never know warmth again.

He'd spent the past hour thinking of ways to spirit Briana away to his chateau in France or his villa in Spain, where her love would wash him clean, and he could put away his past forever. It was a foolish wish. For his past was real. And sordid. And nothing and no one, not even someone as innocent and good as Briana, could change it.

Briana. It was time he started thinking about her needs. She had a home to return to. A family she loved, who loved her. She hadn't seen Ballinarin in three years now. It was time he returned her to the one place she really belonged. A place where she would be safe. Especially from him.

He didn't even bother to look up when the door to his chambers was opened. He pressed an arm over his eyes as light from the hall sconces spilled into the room. "I don't wish to be disturbed, Vinson."

He heard the door close and expelled a tired breath. He leaned back, closing his eyes. If only he could close his mind as easily.

"Can't sleep, my lord?" The familiar voice was soft, breathless, as though she'd been running.

His eyes snapped open. He got to his feet, staring at her as if he couldn't quite believe his eyes. "What are you doing here?"

He was barefoot and naked to the waist. Something she hadn't counted on. It took her a moment to absorb the jolt to her already charged system. "You once said I live my life without boundaries."

"We were talking about class boundaries, if I recall."

"You were." She took a step closer and saw his eyes narrow. The fact that he was nervous only made her all the bolder. She laid a hand on his and he reacted as though he'd been burned, dropping his hand to his waist, where he clenched it into a fist. "I was talking about crossing all boundaries, Keane."

"This is one I wouldn't advise." Needing something to do, he walked to the fireplace and tossed a log on the fire.

She watched the way the muscles of his back and shoulders bunched and tightened with each movement. Her throat went dry, but when he stood, she forced herself to calmly walk to him, to boldly touch a hand to the naked flesh of his back.

It was only a touch, but it had him frozen to the spot.

Fighting for composure he kept his back to her. "The servants would have plenty to talk about if they were to find you in the lord's chambers, dressed in that nightshift."

"Is it the servants you're worried about, Keane?"

He pulled away from her and crossed to the night table. Earlier he'd tossed away his ale. Now he wanted, needed something to steady his nerves.

"Nay, lass. It's your fine, upstanding reputation I'd like to preserve. Believe me, you wouldn't like to have rumors about yourself and Keane O'Mara filtering back to your fine family at Ballinarin." He poured himself a tumbler of ale and lifted it to his lips.

But she stalked him, laying a hand on his chest, before looking up at him from beneath her lashes. The mere touch of his flesh burned her fingers like fire. "I thought we'd give them more than rumors to whisper about, Keane."

He felt as if he'd taken a blow from a broadsword. All the air seemed to leave his lungs.

"I've finally realized why you've been avoiding me." Her voice, low and sultry, seemed to cloud his mind. "You made some sort of vow, didn't you?"

He nodded, needing a moment to find his voice. To collect his thoughts.

"But it wasn't a formal vow, made in church, before witnesses, was it?"

He shook his head, struggling to clear his mind. He couldn't think when she was so close, touching him like this.

Her smile bloomed. "There. You see? But such vows are not binding."

"They aren't?"

"Nay. Mother Superior said most people make such

bargains with heaven, whenever they're feeling fearful. And afterward, they realize the foolishness of their impulsive behavior.''

"It wasn't foolish." His voice was stronger now. And tight with anger. "A vow is a vow. And I vowed to return you to your father as I'd found you."

"Aha. It's as I'd thought." She gave a low, throaty laugh. "And I vowed that this night I would lie with you and love you." She gave a meaningful pause before asking, with a knowing smile, "I wonder, Keane, which of our vows is the stronger?"

Her smile, her laughter only made him more determined. Though he was quickly losing his strength, he had to find a way to make her see the danger in this course of action. He would do and say whatever it took.

"I warned you before, lass." He kept his tone deliberately cutting. "But I see that you'll accept nothing more than cold, hard facts. And the fact is, I'm a man accustomed to much more worldly women. I have no intention of indulging you, simply so you can amuse my servants with something to whisper about."

He saw the hurt in her eyes as she took a step back. He cursed himself for his cruelty. But she'd given him no choice. Somebody had to save her.

"You'd best get back to your chambers before Cora finds you gone. She and the others will have a fine laugh over their sweet innocent lass pursuing the wicked lord of Carrick House." He lifted the glass to his lips and took a long drink.

Briana felt as if a knife had pierced her heart. Damn him. How could she have been foolish enough to open herself up to more humiliation? Her chin came up in that familiar way. And then she noticed something.

His hand was trembling. Some of the ale sloshed over the rim as he brought it to his mouth.

Seeing it gave her a strange rush of exhilaration. She'd been right about Keane. It was all an act. For her sake. Because he cared about her. Truly cared. And she wasn't leaving here until she proved it.

"Run along now, Briana." Keane's voice sounded hoarse in his own ears as he set the tumbler down on the night table and strode to the balcony.

When he heard a light footfall, he breathed a sigh of relief, until he realized she was heading toward him instead of toward the door.

He watched the way she moved, head high, hips undulating in the way of beautiful women from the beginning of time. On her lips was a mysterious, woman's smile.

He backed up all the way to the railing before he caught himself. "What are you doing?"

She opened the first button of her nightshift. "I'm about to tempt fate."

"Stop that." He caught her hand, then realized his mistake. Despite the cold night air, the touch of her had him burning for more.

"I didn't come to your chambers to stop, Keane." She reached a hand to his cheek.

Though he wanted to resist, he couldn't help moving his face against her hand as if starved for the touch of her.

"I came here to start something." Her words whispered over his senses and wrapped themselves around his heart.

He caught her by the shoulders to hold her a little away. Instead she boldly stood on tiptoe and brushed her lips over his. He felt all the breath leave his lungs.

There was no way he could deny her anything while she stood here, pressing that slender body to his, offering him everything he'd ever wanted in this world.

Though he knew it was futile, he gave her one last chance to consider what she was doing. "Once it's started, Briana, it's like being one of a vast sea of warriors swept along in a field of battle. A battle not of your choosing. But whether it's your war or someone else's, there's no stopping it. No going back." His eyes were hot and fierce as they stared into hers, trying vainly to hold her at bay. "Do you understand?"

In answer she wrapped her arms around his neck and pressed herself against him. "You know I love nothing more than a challenging battle. What about you, Keane O'Mara? Are you up to the challenge?"

His voice was a low moan of pleasure and pain. "Oh, God help us, Briana. God help us both. For I've no strength left to deny what I want."

"What we both want," she whispered against his mouth.

For the space of several heartbeats, he merely stared down at her, his fingers digging into the delicate flesh of her upper arms. Then he dragged her close, and his mouth crushed hers with a fierceness that left them both gasping.

"There's still time." He muttered the words inside her mouth as he devoured her with kisses.

She knew he meant it as a warning. But for her there was no turning back. Instead, she offered her lips to him, opening herself to all that was to come.

The sweetness, the generosity of her gesture, had him feasting like a man who had been starving for the taste of her.

His kiss seemed to drain her, then fill her, as he kissed her with a savageness that surprised them. At last, struggling for breath, he lifted his head and framed her face with his hands, staring deeply into her eyes. For the space of several moments he studied her with an intensity that stopped her heart. Then he slowly lowered his head and kissed her again, with a slowness, a thoroughness that made her head swim.

With his mouth on hers he drove her back against the railing of the balcony and wrapped her legs around him.

Briana gave a gasp of surprise. She'd been prepared for sweet, tender loving. For soft sighs and whispered promises. She hadn't been prepared for this. This all-consuming hunger. This urgent mating.

What he wanted, what he demanded, was her complete and total abandonment.

He'd called it a battle. It was, she realized, a war. Unlike any she'd ever experienced. And she had been thrust into it without any knowledge of the rules, or even what part she should be playing.

His mouth was avid, eager, searching out every sweet, hidden taste. His tongue probed all the secret recesses of her mouth, challenging hers to do the same. But just as she sighed in enjoyment, his mouth suddenly left hers to roam her face, her neck, her throat. When she arched her neck to give him easier access, he gave a hiss of impatience and tore aside the neckline of her nightshift. As his lips closed over one erect nipple, she cried out with exquisite pleasure and clutched his head. He gave her no time to recover before he moved to the other breast, to nibble and suckle until she moaned and writhed with need.

Feelings unlike any Briana had ever known seemed

to take possession of her. Her body felt more alive than at any time she could recall. Alive with sensations that had completely taken over her mind, her will. With a sigh she gave herself up to the pleasure. She knew not what lay ahead. She knew only that she wanted him to go on like this forever, touching, tasting, arousing.

With a muttered oath he pushed aside the billowing skirt of her nightshift and found her, hot and moist and ready. He covered her mouth in a savage kiss, swallowing her gasp of shock.

He was touching her in a way that no man ever had. And yet those battle-roughened fingers were bringing her the most incredible pleasure. Pleasure that bordered on pain. Before she could even form a protest, he brought her to the first peak, leaving her dazed and breathless. But while her head was still swimming, he took her on an even faster ride, until she felt herself spinning out of control.

"Keane. Wait." She pressed a palm to his chest, hoping for a moment of calm.

"It's too late, Briana." The words were torn from his lips.

She looked into his eyes, glazed with passion, and realized that this thing they had set into motion was only beginning. And she knew, in that moment, that she wanted to experience more of it. All of it. Now. This minute. With this man.

"Changed your mind?" He caught her by the chin, forcing her head up so that he could see her eyes.

Instead of an answer, she merely laughed.

His hand fisted in her hair, and he dragged her head back to feast on her neck, her throat, her shoulder. With a sigh of impatience he tore away her nightshift, feeling buttons pop and seams rip in his haste. Next he shrugged out of his breeches and kicked them aside.

He dropped to his knees, dragging her with him. They faced each other, their breathing ragged, their heartbeats labored, their bodies glistening with sheen.

The world beyond no longer mattered. The footsteps of servants along the darkened hallway went unheard. The threat of the English invaders was forgotten. For now, the only thing they knew was the dark, musky heat of passion that clogged their lungs, and the sweet, seductive need that clouded their vision until they were half-mad with it.

Keane wanted desperately to slow the madness. To give her time to savor the moment. But he could feel himself slipping ever closer to the edge. One more touch. One taste, and he would lose all control, taking them both over the brink.

"Briana. Briana." He whispered her name like a prayer, as his mouth moved over her temple, her cheek, her ear.

She had never before thought her name beautiful, until she heard it from his lips, in this growl of pleasure against her ear. She caught his face between her hands and brought her mouth to his.

"Do you know how long I've wanted you?" His words were issued on a groan as he took the kiss deeper.

"How long?" She could barely manage the words over the hunger that was driving her. A hunger that had her wrapping herself around him, opening herself to him, eager to give and take. To feed. To feast. Until they were both sated.

Instead of a reply, he dragged her down until they were both lying on the floor, cushioned only by their discarded clothes. As he levered himself above her, she saw his eyes. Hot and fierce. Dark and dangerous. And filled with such need, it took her breath away.

She knew that she would give him anything, as long as she could always see that look. In Keane's eyes she felt beautiful. She felt loved. She felt...safe.

"Dear heaven, Briana. I want you. I need you."

"And I need you, Keane. Oh, I love you so."

Love. The word pierced his heart, shattering all his control. It was more than he'd ever hoped for. All that he'd ever dreamed of. And it was his. She was his. This incredible, magnificent woman owned him. Heart and soul.

He took her with the force of a warrior in the heat of combat. He heard her cry of surprise. Felt her stiffen. Knew that he was hurting her and hated himself for it. Sweet heaven, she was a maiden. An innocent. And he was taking her like a barbarian.

He went very still, struggling to hold to a last tenuous thread of sanity. His voice was a strangled whisper. "Briana, I'm such a brute. I'm sorry...."

"Shhh." She touched a finger to his mouth to silence his protest.

He stared down into her eyes and was shocked by the intensity of passion he could see in them. An intensity that matched his own.

"Don't stop, Keane. Just love me."

He felt the last of his fears vanish. "Ah, Briana. I do, I will. Now and for all time."

He covered her mouth with his and began to move with her and she with him. Moving with a strength neither of them had known they possessed. Faster, then faster still, until they felt themselves soaring, shattering, drifting. It was the most incredible journey of their lives.

Chapter Sixteen

"**S**weet God in heaven." Still joined, Keane rested his forehead against Briana's and sucked in deep draughts of cool night air to fill his starving lungs.

She lay very still, grateful for the calm after the storm. She had feared for a few moments, that her heart would leap clear out of her chest. Even now, as she felt her racing pulse slowly return to normal, she marveled at what they had just shared. "That was..." She struggled for words. "...truly amazing. I never expected...I had no idea..."

Much to her embarrassment, she found herself suddenly weeping. For no reason.

Seeing it, Keane felt his heart stop. "Ah, Briana. Now look what I've done." Alarmed, he shifted himself above her and started to roll aside. "Forgive me, my lady. I'm so sorry...."

"Nay. That isn't why I'm weeping." She laid a hand on his cheek. "It isn't you. It's us. And this wonderful thing we did."

"You think it...was wonderful?" The vise that had begun to crush his chest disappeared. He felt his heart begin to beat once more.

She nodded. "It's like nothing I've ever known. It was…breathtaking. Is it always that way between a man and woman?"

"Not always. But it can be so beautiful, when there's love between them." He pressed a kiss to her forehead, her cheek, the tip of her nose, before rolling to one side and drawing her into the curve of his arms.

As she snuggled close, he thought how perfectly she fit. As though made for him alone.

She touched a hand to the mat of dark hair at his chest. "When were you going to admit your feelings for me?"

He frowned, shivering at the feelings that pulsed through him at her simple touch. "Never."

"Never?" She sat up, brushing aside the tumble of red curls that spilled over into her eyes. "But you just told me that you'd long wanted me."

"Aye. It's the truth." He reached up, letting his hand play with her hair. It was deceptively soft. Like her. "But I felt honor-bound to keep my feelings secret."

"How long have you wanted me?"

Though he kept a straight face, his voice was tinged with laughter. "The truth?"

She nodded.

He tugged on a curl, then wrapped it around his finger. "Since that first night, when I watched you fighting for every breath. I knew you were a brave little scrapper, Briana. And though at the time I thought you were a woman pledged to the church, I can't deny it. I wanted you."

She seemed clearly delighted with his admission. "The jaded, worldly lord of the manor wanted a sheltered woman of the church. You probably hated yourself for your thoughts.''

''Aye.'' He seemed distracted by the silken texture of her hair as his fingers played with the strands. ''It seemed just one more in the long list of sins for which I'll probably do penance for eternity. But this was one temptation I was not about to give in to.''

''Then I'm glad I told that little lie.'' As the words slipped out, she clapped a hand over her mouth. But it was too late.

His hand stilled its movements. ''What little lie?''

When she didn't respond, he caught her by the chin and forced her to look at him. ''What little lie, Briana?''

''About…the vow you made.'' She licked her lips. ''That bargain with heaven.''

He nodded. ''What about it?''

She hesitated, then squared her shoulders. ''I told you that Mother Superior said a vow wasn't really binding unless it was made in church in front of witnesses.''

His eyes narrowed. ''And that was a lie?''

''Aye.'' She bobbed her head. ''The truth of it is, Mother Superior never mentioned vows. Those made in church or otherwise. I just thought that using her name would carry more weight with you.''

At his long look she ducked her head. ''I'm sorry. I know I should always tell the truth. But you were so determined not to touch me. And I was desperate to find a way to change your mind.''

''Briana O'Neil. What a devious little vixen you are.'' A laugh bubbled up from deep inside him, then rumbled free. He threw back his head and roared. Oh, it felt so good. His heart hadn't felt this light, this free, in years. And all because of this amazing little female.

She smiled, feeling such relief at his reaction. "You're not angry with me?"

"Oh, Briana." He pulled her close and kissed her squarely on the mouth. "How could I possibly be angry when you're such a delightful surprise? Although, I suppose I should be suffering from at least a little guilt for breaking my vow."

She pulled back a little, studying him closely. "Are you? Suffering guilt?"

He laughed again. "Not a bit of it. The happiness I'm feeling at this moment can't be spoiled by guilt."

"Ah." She sighed, clearly relieved. "Then you're not sorry?"

"The only thing I'm sorry about is the fact that I was so rough with you." With his finger he traced the outline of her mouth and felt the sudden tightening in his loins. "But I wanted you so desperately. And I'd waited so long."

"I didn't mind. Though…" She paused, loving the feel of his rough fingers against her lips. "…if we're going to make love again, we might want to think about using your big bed."

He looked up at her. "Are you saying you'd rather not spend the night on my floor?"

"That would depend on how you're planning to spend the rest of the night, my lord."

The look he gave her was so smoldering, she felt her heartbeat quicken. "I thought I might show you that loving doesn't always have to be so…ferocious. It can also be slow and gentle and tender." As if to prove his point, his fingers traced the curve of her cheek, the slope of her jaw.

She moved against him like a kitten. Her smile grew. "Could we? Now? So soon? Is such a thing possible?"

His laughter was quick. And though it seemed incredible, he was already thoroughly aroused again. "I'm starting to believe, my sweet Briana, that with you anything is possible." He pulled her down against his chest and began nibbling kisses along her throat, across her collarbone to the swell of her breast.

Against the softness of her flesh he muttered, "Are you certain you aren't a witch?"

"My mother's family were Celts. It's said there were many witches among them."

"Ah." He dipped his head lower, and heard her little gasp. "That's it then. I've been bewitched. I only pray this spell is never broken."

"Aye. I'll add my prayers to yours. If ever there was a spell that I welcomed, it's this one." She sat up and traced the long, thin scar that ran from his hip to his ankle. "What is this?"

"An old wound. It's nothing."

"Nothing? From the looks of it, it's a wonder you can walk." She pressed her lips to his thigh. "I hate to think how much pain you must have suffered from this. Oh, how I wish I could erase all your pain."

Her concern for him touched him so deeply, he could hardly speak. When he could manage, he drew her up and whispered against her mouth, "You already have, Briana. Your love is all I need to erase all my scars."

"Let me kiss them all away."

As she moved over him, pressing her lips along his chest, his stomach, the length of his scar, he felt desire rise like a tide until he thought he would go mad.

"Are you doing that just to see how much I can take before I lose my senses?"

She levered herself on her elbows and stared down at those dark, narrowed eyes. How had she ever thought him cold and cruel? All she could see now was warmth. And need. And seething, burning passion.

"Tell me, my lord. Just how much can you take?"

He moved so quickly, she had no time to react, as he rolled over and kissed her with a thoroughness that had her gasping.

And then there were no more words between them, as his touch gentled and his kisses softened. His warm breath whispered over her face. He drew out each kiss like thick, sweet honey, trickling lazily over her forehead, her cheek, her jaw.

This, she realized, was another side to Keane O'Mara. A tender side he kept hidden from the world. He kissed her, touched her, as though they had all the time in the world. For indeed, they did. Now that the storm of first passion had blown over, they were free to taste, to touch to their hearts' content.

Their sighs mingled, as did their breath, as they lost themselves in the wondrous pleasures of slow, easy love.

"What are you doing?" Briana looked up to see Keane leaning up on one elbow, staring at her face as though memorizing every line and curve.

Sometime during the night he had carried her to bed, where they lay among the tangled bed linens. Their lovemaking had been at times all heat and light and speed. Rough with need. Demanding. At other times it had been as slow, as easy, as if they had known each other for a lifetime. All long, lingering kisses and soft, gentle sighs.

"I'm watching you. Do you know how lovely you are?"

"Nay." She gave him a lazy, satisfied smile. "Why don't you tell me?"

"There's this." He traced the outline of her mouth with his finger. "Some might say your lips are too full."

"And what would you say, my lord?"

"That they're perfectly formed for my kisses." He kissed her mouth lightly. "And your nose." He pressed a quick kiss to the tip of her nose. "For something so small, you manage to lift it in the air with great disdain when you're angry."

"Which isn't often, praise heaven."

"Often enough." He ignored her little snort of disagreement. "And those eyes." He kissed one lid, then the other. "I've never seen eyes like yours, Briana. One look from them can melt my heart. Or just as easily shoot sparks that would singe it until it was nothing but a charred cinder."

She pressed a finger to his lips to silence him. "Never your heart, my lord. Only the heart of my enemies."

He caught her hand and pressed a kiss to the palm. "And then there's this skin. So soft. And covered with all these fascinating freckles."

"I hate them."

"Never say that. I love them. In fact…" He began to press soft moist kisses along the parade of freckles that trailed from her shoulder to her hip. "I may have to kiss each and every one of them."

She chuckled and began to wriggle under the assault. "Stop, Keane. That tickles."

A moment later her laughter turned into a moan of pleasure, as his lips moved lower, then lower still.

"Oh, sweet heaven." Dazed at what he was doing to her with that clever mouth, all the breath seemed to leave her lungs.

He glanced up. "Oh. Did you wish me to stop, my lady?"

She saw the gleam of teasing laughter in his eyes. "If you do, my lord, I'll have to retrieve your sword and force you, under threat of death, to continue."

His words were warm with laughter. "Now that I know just how skilled you are with that sword, I'd be a fool to tempt you, wouldn't I? So, to save my life, let's see where I was. Oh yes. I recall. I was following the trail of freckles."

As the night air was filled with her giggles and sighs of pleasure, he muttered, "Ever your obedient servant, my lady."

"Look. Over there." Briana pointed to the hazy outline of the moon, which was quickly fading into the dawn sky.

The two lovers were huddled on the balcony beneath a blanket, watching as the stars began to disappear one by one. In their place were ribbons of gold and pink and mauve, and clouds gilded by a rising sun.

"I used to lie in the damp grass of the meadow with Innis and watch the sun rise over Croagh Patrick."

"I hope you were a bit more modestly attired with Innis than you are right now."

She turned her head and looked down her nose at

him. "And why would I have to be modest with Innis? He was practically my brother."

He burned a trail of kisses across her back that made her shiver. "I'd prefer not to think of you naked with any man but me, my love."

"Spoken just like a man. You make love with a woman and think you own her."

"I don't want to own you, Briana. Just your heart." He wrapped his arms around her with a possessiveness that had her breath hitching in her throat.

She turned to face him. "And does that mean that I own your heart as well?" She pressed her lips to his throat and heard his quick intake of breath.

"Aye, my love. You own me completely. Body and mind. Heart and soul."

He uttered the words with such intensity, she felt tears spring to her eyes and had to blink them away.

"Tears?" He tipped up her chin. "Over me, lass?"

"Oh, Keane. I do love you so. I still can't believe you love me, too."

One tear welled up and slid down her cheek. He kissed it away with such tenderness, she felt her heart swell with love.

And then, without a word he scooped her up and carried her across the room to the bed, where he showed her, in the only way he could, the depth of his love.

"My lord."

At a loud knock on the door, and the sound of Vinson's muffled voice from the hallway, Keane opened his eyes.

Briana awoke beside him, shoving hair from her eyes.

"My lord." The door was thrust open. Vinson, carrying a tray, crossed the room and, as he always did, deposited it on the night table. "The servant Cora is in quite a state over our lass. She's missing from her chambers and…" The old man's voice trailed off at the sight that greeted him.

The lord was lying in a tangle of sheets, his face a mask of surprise. A figure beside him gave a groan of dismay and pulled the bed covers up, leaving only a cap of red curls visible.

"I…Forgive me, my lord. I wasn't…I didn't…" Vinson stood so straight, it looked as though he'd swallowed a poker. Then, stiffening his spine, he spun away from the bed. Over his shoulder he managed to ask, "Will you or the lass be requiring anything, my lord?"

"Nay, Vinson. Nothing at the moment." Keane's voice was warm with unspoken laughter. "But you may want to close the door on your way out."

"Of course, my lord." The old man beat a hasty retreat.

When the door closed, Keane watched as Briana timidly sat up.

"Are you blushing?" He tipped up her face for his inspection.

She slapped his hand away. "Of course I am."

"You mean you're ashamed of what we did?"

"Of course not. But I didn't expect to have that dear old man walking in while we were…while I was…" She stopped, then said with exasperation, "How did he know I was in your bed?"

"It may have been that lump he spotted beside me. The one with all these…" He caught a handful of her hair. "…red curls sticking out of the bed covers."

''Oh, no.'' She brought her hands to her burning cheeks. ''Oh, Keane. Why didn't you pull the blankets higher?''

''It would have been too little, too late, my love.'' Then he was unable to hold back the laughter any longer. When he finally could control himself he added, ''I thought poor old Vinson's eyes were going to fall out when he realized you were here.''

''Oh, Keane.'' Despite the fact that she was blushing, Briana couldn't help giggling. ''The poor old dear. How will I ever face him?''

''The same way you're going to face the rest of the household.''

She gave him a look of shock.

He couldn't help laughing as he drew her close and pressed a kiss to the top of her head. ''By now, half the household knows you spent the night in my bed. And within the hour, half the village of Carrick will know, as well.''

When he heard her little sigh of dismay, he merely grinned. ''I did warn you, love.''

''Aye. You did.''

He brought his lips to her temple, and nibbled and nuzzled a path to her ear. ''I know of one way we could avoid seeing anyone.''

''You do?''

''Uh-huh.'' He brought his mouth lower, to the sensitive hollow between her neck and shoulder.

She shivered, and he drew her down among the tangled sheets. And as he began to explore all the now-familiar places of her body, he muttered, ''In fact, if you're feeling strong enough, we could hide away here all day.''

* * *

"They're coming."

The word was passed from scullery maid to cook, from serving wench to Mistress Malloy, who stood at the base of the staircase.

Lord Alcott, looking handsome in black breeches and riding jacket, led Briana, wearing a new riding outfit of russet velvet, down the stairs.

"Good morrow, my lord. My lady. Will you be wanting to break your fast before you leave?"

"Nay, Mistress Malloy. Briana and I have decided to ride first. We will want something when we return though."

"Aye, my lord. I'll see to it."

"Thank you." He glanced toward the front door, where Vinson stood staring straight ahead. "Good morrow, Vinson."

"My lord." The old man softened his tone. "My lady."

"Vinson." It was the first that Briana had spoken, and the word sounded breathy to her ears.

She'd noted that neither the housekeeper nor the butler had looked at her. Nor did the many servants they passed on their way to the stables.

"Good morrow, my lord," the stable master called as he led two horses, saddled and ready, from their stalls.

"Good morrow, Monroe. I see you've saddled Eden for Miss O'Neil. A good choice."

"Thank you, my lord. I thought, seeing the way our lass handled Peregrine, she'd be wanting a mount with a bit of fire."

"Aye."

While the old man held the horse's bridle, Keane

helped Briana into the saddle.

As Monroe handed her the reins he gave her a wide, gap-toothed smile and tipped his hat. "If you don't mind my saying, you've a good bit of fire yourself, my lady."

Keane saw the slight flush that touched her cheeks as she ducked her head and followed his lead toward the distant meadow. As soon as they had left Carrick House behind, he slowed his mount and caught her hand, lifting it to his lips.

"You see? That wasn't so bad, was it?"

"Nay." She took a deep breath. "I suppose it will get easier as the days pass."

Keane squeezed her hand and continued holding it as their horses cut a slow, steady path through the lush grass of the meadow. The thought of the days and weeks and months of loving that lay ahead warmed his heart as nothing ever had before.

As they crested a hill, he turned and glanced back at the roof of Carrick House, gleaming in the sunlight.

His voice was hushed with the enormity of his discovery. He turned to her, loving the softness in her eyes. "Do you know that this is the first time since I've returned to Ireland, that I feel as if I've truly come home. And it's all because of you, Briana O'Neil."

Chapter Seventeen

"What are we to do?" Mistress Malloy twisted her apron between her hands as she prowled the library, pausing to wipe at imaginary spots of dust.

When she heard no response from the butler, she turned.

He was staring out the window at the lovers, who were enjoying tea in the garden. "You said you could keep an eye on the master, and prevent this from going too far. And now look."

"Aye." The old man watched as Keane fed a brandied cake to Briana. "But I've never seen him happier."

"That isn't the point. What about our lass? What will happen to her when she learns the truth?"

Vinson shrugged. "Perhaps she loves him enough to forgive."

"Love. Ha." The old woman spun away and began rubbing at the desk top. "Right now, she's caught up in some romantic spell. And it's been fine for all of us here in Carrick. Just as we'd hoped, we have the arms we need to defend ourselves against the English invaders. And as long as we keep our lass dangling in front of the lord, he'll not forsake us for a more peaceful refuge. But what happens when the lass learns his secrets? I tell you, Vinson, no woman's going to forgive the sins that man has committed. What will happen when her love turns to hate, and she flees Carrick to seek refuge in her own home?''

The old man kept his attention riveted on the lovers. ''I wish I knew.''

Mistress Malloy momentarily brightened. ''Do you think he could keep it a secret from her for a lifetime?''

Vinson shook his head. ''It's not likely. Especially now that he's come back from the dead.''

''Why do you say that?''

''Because.'' The old man turned, headed toward the door. ''With this new life, he's bound to rediscover his conscience. And when that happens, he'll feel that he has no choice but to tell her everything.''

''We'll take our dinner in the library tonight, Mistress Malloy.''

''Aye, my lord. I'll alert the servants.''

''I want no servants around. Briana and I would prefer our privacy tonight.''

The old woman hesitated. ''But who'll serve the table, my lord?''

''You may do it yourself. With Vinson's help. Send the others off to bed.''

''Aye, my lord.''

Mistress Malloy hurried away, to see to the change in plans. And all the while she fretted. Tea in the garden. Intimate dinners in the library. It was all they'd hoped for and more. Except that she worried about their lass. Briana O'Neil might have a fiery nature, but it was obvious to everyone that she had a tender heart. A heart that was bound to be broken, now that she'd lost it to the lord of Carrick.

"My lord." Vinson stood beside the bed, a robe hastily thrown on over his nightshirt, his hair sticking out at odd angles.

Keane was instantly awake. He released his hold on Briana and sat up, knowing the stern old man would never violate his privacy unless it was of the utmost importance. "What is it, Vinson?"

Beside him, Briana stirred.

"A messenger came from the village. English soldiers were spotted heading through the woods."

"Have the villagers put our plan into action?"

"Aye, my lord." Vinson averted his gaze when Briana sat up, shoving hair out of her eyes before modestly drawing the blanket up to her chin. "Half a dozen men have been dispatched to the fields, to pretend to be laboring. The rest of the men have secreted themselves in the nearby woods, with the weapons you provided, awaiting the attack."

"Very good." Keane slipped out of bed and began to dress.

For the sake of modesty, Briana wrapped the blanket around herself before stepping out of bed. When she headed toward the door, Keane called, "Where are you going?"

"To my chambers. I can be dressed in minutes."

"First, my love, a kiss for luck."

She shot him a puzzled glance before crossing to him and offering her lips. It seemed odd that Keane would kiss her in front of Vinson.

Instead of the quick kiss she'd anticipated, he

dragged her roughly against him and covered her mouth with his. She felt the rush of heat, the knife-edge of excitement, and blamed it on the coming battle.

Then, just as quickly, Keane lifted his head and drew away. Briana touched a hand to his cheek, then walked away.

When the door closed behind her, Keane sat on the edge of the bed, pulling on his boots. After buttoning his tunic, he tucked a knife in his boot and picked up his sword.

"Follow me, Vinson."

Keeping his silence, the old man followed him down the hallway, where Keane paused outside Briana's chambers. As promised, she opened the door within minutes. She was dressed in the garb of a stable lad and holding a sword that was nearly as big as she.

"I'm ready," she called.

"Aye, my lady. I can see that." Keane pulled her close and pressed another kiss to her lips. "Forgive me, love. I truly regret what I must do."

With Vinson watching in openmouthed amazement, Keane gave her a gentle shove backward, then slammed the door shut and threw a brace over it.

Briana's voice was a shriek of fury as she pounded on the door. "What are you doing, Keane? I don't understand. Open this door at once."

"Nay, lass. I love you too much to see you engaged in battle with these monsters." He turned to Vinson. "You're to see that this latch is not removed until I return. Is that understood?"

"Aye, my lord." The old man's lips twitched slightly as the door was struck with such fury, the entire wall seemed to shudder. "That sounded like a chair, my lord."

"Aye." Keane grinned. "The lass has a bit of a temper, Vinson. But you'll see to her?"

"I will, my lord. You can trust me to see she's kept safely under lock until the siege is over."

"I thank you, old man."

As Keane strode away, the door was struck with a series of blows, and the tip of a sword could be seen breaking through the splintered wood.

Vinson found himself praying for a mercifully quick end to the battle. Else Carrick House might not survive the lass's fury.

Keane crouched in the woods with the men from the village. It pleased him to see that every man was armed with either sword or bow. And though they would be outnumbered by the English soldiers, at least they had a fighting chance.

Thanks to Briana.

Keane found himself smiling as he thought about how fiercely she had pleaded the cause of these villagers. It was hard to believe that he had, only weeks ago, been so adamantly opposed to arming his own people. But, in his guilt and confusion, he had convinced himself that they were better off accepting defeat, rather than risking the pain and chaos and destruction of battle.

It was one more thing for which he would always be grateful to Briana. His fierce little scrapper had helped him to see clearly what he had to do. By fighting alongside his people, he could atone for the sins of his father. And, if the fates were kind, he might even get his chance to exact retribution from the one called Halsey. He clenched his teeth. That would give him the greatest satisfaction of his life.

Early morning sunlight glinted off the swords of the first English horsemen as they started across the meadow toward the villagers in the field who were acting as decoys. Keane felt the quick rush of anticipation he'd always experienced at the start of a battle.

"Now, my lord?" Hugh McCann glanced over at him, and Keane shook his head.

"Nay. It's too soon. Our only hope for success is the element of surprise, Hugh. The English are expecting us to be as before—helpless, unarmed and terrified. They'll not be expecting a militia of trained swordsmen."

He noted that, despite the early morning chill, Hugh and the others were sweating. And why not? They were no doubt thinking about the wives and children they might never see again.

As for himself, he felt a strange sense of calm. He had no fear of death. Until he had discovered Briana's love, he would have welcomed it. And even now, thinking about the one he would leave behind, death held no power over him. It was for this he felt he had been born and bred. This was what he had trained for all of his life. He only wished he could fight these English bastards alone, to ensure that none of the innocent villagers would have to face danger this day.

His eyes narrowed as the line of horsemen drew nearer to the cluster of villagers pretending to till the soil.

"Steady, lads. Another moment." He unsheathed his sword, lifted it high over his head, then nodded. "Now, lads."

The men and boys of the village came swarming

out of the woods, wailing like banshees, brandishing their weapons. The English soldiers, hearing the shrieks, wheeled their mounts in confusion.

Keane led the way, rushing forward to engage the first soldier. Before the man could even unsheath his sword, Keane had run him through. As the soldier slipped from the saddle, Keane caught the horse's reins and shouted for a villager to mount. A big, burly lad pulled himself into the saddle and sped off, quickly overtaking several of the English who were attempting to retreat.

That first small success seemed to inspire the other villagers. Their fears were forgotten as they were thrust into the thick of battle. The air was filled with screams and shouts, and the clang of metal against metal. The earth was churned beneath the hooves of terrified horses.

"Watch your back, Hugh." Keane's warning caused Hugh McCann to turn, narrowly missing a soldier's thrust. Moments later Hugh ran the soldier through with his sword, then turned to give assistance to three lads who were holding off several mounted soldiers.

Seeing their dilemma, Keane leaped on the back of one of the horses and wrapped his arm around the soldier's throat. In desperation the soldier pulled a knife from his waist, but before he could use it, Keane caught his hand and forced it upward until it pierced the soldier's own throat. The man's shriek of surprise ended in a gurgle of pain. He was dead before he dropped to the ground.

Seeing a cluster of soldiers up ahead, Keane urged the horse forward. As he fought his way through the crowd, he heard a tight angry cry from a soldier on a distant hillside.

"Death to all the Irish."

The horseman had grabbed up a thin-armed lad of perhaps ten and two, and was holding a knife to his throat while shouting, "We're not leaving here lads until every one of these bastards is bathed in his own blood. If any man tries to retreat, he'll taste my sword. Do you hear?"

Keane felt a rush of heat and knew, even before he drew closer, what he would see.

The English soldier wore a ragged tunic over frayed breeches. His face bore the scars of multiple battles. His nose was flattened, obviously broken. Though his dark hair was long and scraggly, it couldn't hide the fact that his left ear was missing. All that remained was a white, puckered scar.

"Halsey." Keane lifted his sword and nudged his horse forward.

Seeing him, the soldier tightened his grasp on the lad. "Advance and the lad dies."

Keane's reaction was strictly instinctive. Without giving the soldier time to think, he charged. His first thrust caught Halsey's arm, causing him to drop the lad.

"Run, lad," Keane shouted. "Go back and join the others."

Enraged, Halsey wheeled his mount and charged this bold horseman who had dared to thwart his fun. His sword tip pierced Keane's shoulder.

Seeing blood spurt from the wound, Halsey threw back his head and gave a hoarse laugh. "I never met an Irishman yet who could best me in battle." He wheeled his mount yet again and charged. But this time, instead of aiming at his enemy, Halsey carefully, calculatingly, ran his sword through the neck of Keane's mount.

With a whinny of pain, the animal fell. It was only Keane's skill as a horseman that kept him from being crushed. He managed to jump to safety moments before the animal dropped to the ground in a heap. But as Keane leapt free, his sword slipped from his fingers. Before he could retrieve it, Halsey was racing his mount toward him.

"Now Irishman, let's see you evade my sword again."

As Keane danced aside, he heard the whistle of the blade and felt the spatter of dirt from the horse's hooves.

Out of the corner of his eye he could see Halsey turning his mount for another charge. He felt the thrill of anticipation. This time there would be no room for error. He would win. Or he would die.

At that moment he caught a glimpse of blurred movement coming over the hill. He glanced up to see a vision running toward him. He blinked. It couldn't be. He had given Vinson orders to keep her locked in her chambers. But there was no mistaking the figure racing toward him. It was Briana. Dressed in the garb of a stable lad and holding aloft her sword. Sweet heaven. She couldn't possibly know that she was about to confront her worst nightmare.

"Briana. No. Go back." Even as he shouted the warning, he knew it was a futile attempt. She was too far away to hear. His warning fell away, a mere whisper on the wind.

The slight distraction was just enough to cause him to lose his edge. As he stumbled toward his fallen

sword, he felt the thundering of hooves, and knew that
this time, Halsey wouldn't miss.

He heard the sound of fierce laughter. And Halsey's
voice, like a shriek of victory. "Prepare to die, Irishman."

Keane looked up as Halsey's horse reared, its front
hooves pawing the air. And then those hooves came
crashing down, beating Keane to the earth.

Pain enveloped him in waves. Pain so hot and
fierce, it robbed him of speech. Even the cry that escaped his lips was suddenly cut off. He struggled to
see, but his vision began to fade, as a great black cloud
seemed to close over him.

And then, with Halsey's laughter breaking through
the wall of silence, he felt himself swallowed up in
darkness.

At the scene before her, Briana stood, frozen in horror. She had seen Keane's momentary distraction
when he'd caught sight of her. Had watched as the
English horseman had used that moment to his advantage.

Her fault. Her fault. The thought played through her
mind like a litany.

Now, she realized the enormity of the situation. The
fighting was too far away for any of the villagers to
see or hear them. It was up to her to save Keane and
herself. She raised her sword and raced to Keane's
side.

Dropping to one knee beside him she touched a
hand to his throat and felt for a pulse. For a moment
she felt her heart stop. But then, as she located the
steady beating of his heart, she gave a sigh of relief.

He may be wounded, but he was alive. Alive. It was all that mattered.

"Keane," she called. "Can you hear my voice, my love?"

Instead of a reply she heard the sound of laughter. Laughter that scraped over her already raw nerves, starting a series of tremors that had palms sweating, her knees going weak.

She looked up to see the man who had left her for dead. Whose face and voice had tormented her in her dreams every night since that terrible attack. The sight of him left her numb and frozen.

"Halsey." She knew her voice wavered as she struggled to her feet and stood trembling as she faced the man on horseback.

"So. You know me."

"Aye." She swallowed and prayed for courage. "You once plunged your sword through my chest."

He laughed. "Forgive me if I don't recall. My sword has tasted so much Irish flesh, it's a wonder it hasn't rotted from the stink."

"It was in this very field. You didn't like the fact that I was besting you with your own sword. And like the coward you are, you had your men hold me. That way you could assure that you would win."

"I remember you, lad." His eyes narrowed. "No man bests Ian Halsey." He slid from the saddle and advanced on her, wielding his sword. "Especially one who smells of the stables."

Briana dodged his first thrust and brought her sword tip upward, catching him in the arm. He gave a yelp of pain and charged at her, his sword swinging wildly. Nimbly, Briana danced to one side, then spun and lashed out, slicing his thigh. At once his breeches were drenched in blood, and he swore as he lunged at her.

She avoided his blade, but his hand reached out, catching her roughly by the shoulder. When she tried to break free he dragged her firmly against him and wrapped his arm around her throat, pressing until he felt her go limp.

Briana struggled against the arm that imprisoned her, but it was impossible to loosen his grasp. As she struggled for breath, her vision began to fade. Black spots danced in front of her eyes. Halsey's laughter seemed to ebb and flow, and she knew that she was losing consciousness.

Her sword dropped from her fingers as she scratched and clawed at the iron band that continued to tighten around her throat. And then she could no longer stand.

Halsey gave her a rough shove and laughed as she dropped to the ground beside Keane. As she fell, the cap slipped from her head, revealing the tousled red curls.

"What's this?" Halsey's jaw dropped, and for a moment he couldn't believe his eyes. Then, grasping her roughly by the arm, he hauled her to her feet.

His gaze raked her, and she felt soiled by the look in his eyes. He lifted his hands to her tunic and in one swift motion tore it away. As the fabric shredded, his eyes narrowed on the pale chemise that barely covered her breasts.

"A female?" He gave a high, shrill laugh. "Now I've seen everything. An Irish wench who thinks she can best an English soldier."

He glanced toward Keane, who was struggling to

sit up. "Is he the reason you're here? Did you think you'd save his miserable life?"

She lifted her chin. "Nay. I thought to end yours."

"Hold your tongue, wench." He slapped her so hard her head snapped to one side. "Or I'll cut it out of that lovely mouth." He gave another laugh and dragged her into his arms. "But only after I've sampled it myself."

His sour breath filled her lungs as he covered her mouth with his. His hands groped her breasts through the thin fabric of her chemise.

Suddenly he released her as his head snapped up, and his body was jerked violently backward.

Briana watched in stunned amazement as Keane's fist connected with Halsey's nose, sending a geyser of blood spilling down the front of his tunic.

"That was for the lady. And this one is for all the people who have suffered at your hands." Keane slammed his fist into Halsey's midsection, sending the soldier to his knees.

Enraged, Halsey tossed a handful of dirt in Keane's eyes. Keane rubbed his fists over his eyes, hoping to clear his vision. As Halsey struggled to his feet, Keane struck out blindly and connected with Halsey's chin, sending him sprawling. Struggling for breath, Keane stood over the soldier, waiting for some sign of fight left in him.

"Come on, Halsey. Don't give up yet. I haven't even started."

"Nor have I." Halsey kept his back to him as he got to his knees. But when he finally stood, he turned to reveal a knife in his hands. He slashed out, slicing across Keane's chest, leaving his tunic soaked with blood. His second slash caught Keane's hand. Within moments the dirt at their feet ran red with blood.

Seeing Keane's pallor and knowing that he was hanging on by a bare thread, Halsey caught him by the front of his tunic and lifted the knife so that the sunlight glinted off the razor-sharp blade. "Now, Irishman, I'm going to carve up that handsome face. And when I'm through, I'm going to have my sport with the woman." His laughter was the high, shrill sound of madness. "And when I'm through with her, she'll know once and for all time that no man bests Ian Halsey."

As he lowered the knife to Keane's face, his smile froze. His body stiffened. The hand holding Keane dropped to his side. Then, as if in slow motion, his legs failed him and he slumped to the ground.

Keane knelt beside him and felt for a pulse. Finding none, he touched a hand to the hilt of a knife protruding from Halsey's back. Then he looked up to see Briana standing over him.

"Perhaps no man could best him." Despite her pallor, her voice was strong. "But this woman did."

Keane started to get to his feet, but the world was beginning to spin. He sank to his knees and struggled to make sense of his jumbled thoughts. "...ordered Vinson...keep you locked in your chambers."

"Aye. That was wrong of you, Keane O'Mara. But I used the bed linens to climb out the balcony. Vinson is probably still guarding my door, with no clue that I've gone."

"...not surprised, my fiery little vix..." He rested a moment, gathering his strength. "What of the battle?"

She peered off into the distance and could hear the

roar from the villagers. Briana could see their wives and children racing across the fields to share the moment. "I'd say the villagers are already celebrating their victory."

"…won?"

"Aye. And why not? They had excellent teachers." Seeing his eyes close, she clutched him with a fury born of desperation.

All the fight had gone out of her. She was, in that instant, a terrified woman in love.

"Oh, Keane. Oh, my love. Don't leave me now. I couldn't bear it."

The last thing Keane remembered was the taste of Briana's tears upon his lips, and the sound of her voice, soft and breathless, begging him to stay with her as she half dragged, half shoved him toward Halsey's horse.

Chapter Eighteen

"There are no broken bones. None of the wounds appear to be serious." Mistress Malloy smiled down at the man in the bed. "Thanks, I'm told, to our lass."

Keane glanced at Briana and squeezed her hand. She was seated beside the bed, still dressed in the filthy, bloodstained garb of the stable lad. "Aye. A more docile lass might have given up and remained in her chambers. But not Briana O'Neil. Praise heaven she isn't like other women."

Briana merely smiled, content to let the others talk while she basked in the knowledge that the man she loved was safe.

"Tell me, Vinson." Keane turned to his butler. "Did you never guess that the lass's chambers were empty?"

"Nay, my lord." The old man looked slightly red-faced. "When it grew too quiet, I thought she was probably weeping. Or sulking. It's what most females would do."

"But not our lass." Mistress Malloy's tone was filled with pride. She started toward the door. "I'll let the villagers know that the lord of Carrick is in no danger.''

"Wait." Keane sat up and carefully swung his legs to the floor. Despite the fact that his entire body was a mass of pain and bruises, he refused to give in to the weariness that tugged at him. The people were waiting. People he had begun to care about very deeply. "I'll tell them myself. Come, Briana. Let me lean on you.''

With his arm around her shoulder, Keane made his way to the balcony. The moment the crowd below caught sight of him, they let out a roar of approval.

"Ye're alive then, my lord,'' one of the men shouted.

"Aye. Are there any dead among us?''

"None, my lord. But a score of wounded.''

"Anything serious?''

"None more serious than a few broken bones.''

"That greatly relieves my mind." Keane grasped the balcony for support and lifted Briana's hand in the air. "Know this. Were it not for the courage of this lovely lady, none of this would have transpired. Without your training and weapons, the battle would have been over before it began, with many Irish lives lost. And without her aid, I surely wouldn't be here now. For it was her weapon that brought down the soldier who has been the cause of so much pain and suffering in our land. Ian Halsey is dead, thanks to Briana.''

"Three cheers for the lady, Briana,'' one of the crowd shouted.

A deafening cheer went up, as Keane lifted Briana's hand to his lips and stared deeply into her eyes.

She felt her heart leap at the love she could read in those depths.

"Now," he called to those below, "go back to your homes. And give thanks that we've been delivered, at least for now, from the scourge of the English."

"If more soldiers come, my lord, we'll be ready for them," someone shouted.

"Aye," came the roar from the crowd.

Keane and Briana remained on the balcony, watching as the long line of villagers began to slowly wind its way across the meadow. The tavern would soon be filled with revelers. As would the village green. And this night, many a father would hug his children a little tighter. And many a wife would give thanks for the safe delivery of her man.

Hours later, when Keane and Briana had bathed away the dirt and blood of battle, they took a quiet meal in Keane's chambers. And afterward, as they lay together in his bed, staring into the flames of the fire, they felt humbled by what they had accomplished. And overwhelmed by what they had almost lost.

The midnight sky was a curtain of black velvet. A path of liquid golden moonlight spilled across the bed, bathing the two people who lay side by side.

Briana found it impossible to sleep. The feelings swirling inside her were too new, too exciting, to permit sleep. And so she lay, watching the steady rise and fall of Keane's chest.

How had she lived without him for all these years? What strange fate had brought her to Carrick, to this man, and the wonderful love he had unlocked in her heart?

She smiled dreamily as she brushed a lock of hair from his eyes. Then her smile turned to a frown of concern as she noted that his breathing had become shallow. It was obvious that he was in the throes of a dream. Not a pleasant one, she realized. For he turned his head from side to side, as if to avoid something.

"…Alana."

At the sound of his voice whispering a woman's name, her heart stopped. Not some*thing*. Some*one*.

He moaned in his sleep and touched a hand to his thigh. Briana studied the raised white scar that ran the length of his left leg, from thigh to ankle. He had once shrugged it off as simply an old wound. And she'd been willing to accept that. But there was nothing simple about it. It must have nearly cost him his life.

He muttered something unintelligible, and sat straight up in bed. His eyes snapped open. He caught sight of Briana beside him, watching him.

"You had a bad dream."

"Aye." He pressed an arm to his forehead. He was bathed in sweat.

"Your leg pains you."

"Sometimes." He took several deep breaths to calm his ragged breathing. He hated the demons. They always caught him unawares, when he was asleep and most vulnerable. Since his love for Briana had blossomed, he'd been free of them. But now, perhaps because he was weakened by the wounds of battle, they were back, haunting him.

"You mentioned a name. Alana." Briana felt him stiffen. At once she was repentant. "Forgive me, Keane." She turned away. "I had no right to pry."

When he said nothing she slipped out of bed. "I'll fetch you some water. Or would you prefer ale?"

"Ale." His tone was flat.

He waited while she poured a tumbler and handed it to him, drinking it down in one long swallow. As the ale burned a path of fire down his throat, he took a deep breath.

Then, climbing from bed, he began to pace while Briana stood across the room, watching him in silence. At last he paused, turned. "I've kept the truth from you long enough. It's time I told you everything."

"There's no need."

"Aye. There is. I'm tired of living a lie."

At the harshness of his tone Briana waited, afraid to speak, afraid of what she was about to hear.

He scrubbed his hands over his face. "But where to begin?" Agitated, he began pacing like a caged animal.

When his pacing stopped, he stared out the balcony window and spoke in a tone devoid of all emotion. "When my grandfather was alive, the name O'Mara was a noble one, commanding respect from all who knew us. He was a man who loved this land and the people who lived here. After he died, the respect seemed to die with him."

Keane stalked to the fireplace to toss a log on the grate. He stood a moment, watching as the hot coals ignited the bark, starting a thin flame along its length.

Keeping his back to her he said, "It was common knowledge that my father was a wastrel. He had no time for his son, his land, his people. It wasn't enough that he squandered a fortune on every vice known to man, but he turned his back on his home as well, choosing to live in England, where he aligned himself with the king. He even accepted a title in return for a betrayal of his own countrymen. Which is why, to this day, I detest the title Lord Alcott." His tone lowered. "You wondered why I didn't want to involve myself in instructing the men of Carrick in the use of arms.

It was my father who saw to it that these people were left helpless and unarmed. He and his friends in England agreed it would be far easier to conquer men who were without weapons.''

Though Briana was shocked at the depth of his father's betrayal, she gave no reaction, for fear of silencing the anger that had been festering so long inside him.

He took in a deep breath. ''By the time I'd finished my education abroad, I was so disgusted and disillusioned with my father, I seemed destined to follow in his footsteps, just to seek revenge. In fact, I did my best to imitate him, though I told myself it was only to hurt him.''

He turned, and Briana could read the misery in his eyes. ''After one particularly decadent period in my life, I was approached by…one of Ireland's most influential leaders. A man highly regarded by all who knew him. A man I greatly respected. He suggested that if it were revenge against my father that I was seeking, he knew of a better way than the one I was pursuing. When he presented me with his scheme, I rejected it out of hand. Even I, as low as I had sunk, considered his plan unconscionable. But he continued to press until he managed to convince me that I would not only avenge my father's misdeeds, but would restore the O'Mara family name in the bargain.''

''How would you accomplish all this, Keane?''

''By joining my father and his English friends in their pursuit of pleasure. Something I had become very good at. And when they trusted me enough to let down their guard, I would be privy to all their secrets, which I would then relay to known Irish patriots.''

For the space of several seconds she went silent, as the truth dawned. "You were a spy?"

He gave a dry, mirthless laugh. "Some might call it that. I was a drunk and a cheat. I used everybody, including my own father. I sank so low, I even used my father's mistress."

He heard the gasp of surprise and turned away, not wanting to see her face. With his arms crossed over his chest he paced to the window, where he stared out at the night-shrouded land.

"Her name was Lady Victoria Cranmer, and she was considered one of the great beauties of England, with pale yellow hair and skin like milk."

"Victoria?" This made no sense. The name he had spoken in his sleep had been Alana.

"Aye. And with hardly any coaxing at all, she betrayed my father and came to my bed. After that it was a simple matter to make her my wife."

At that, Briana felt all her breath leave her lungs. She couldn't bear the pain. Her heart contracted. She had to close her eyes and grip the edge of the table to keep from being sick. Her mind simply refused to make sense of this. "You wed?"

"Aye." His voice was harsh. Bitter.

"Did you...love her?"

"Not at first. Perhaps I never really loved her. But I used her badly. And I discovered that, beneath the face she showed to others beat a kind and gentle heart. That discovery was when all my carefully laid plans began to unravel. Victoria, whose health had always been fragile, announced that she was with child."

"Child?" Briana could barely get the word out. This was becoming a nightmare. The man she loved. The man in whom she had placed her trust. The man she had begun to spin her dreams around. With a wife and child. It was all too much.

"Aye. A wee lass. Born too soon, leaving her small and fragile. Though I would never be certain if she was my child or my father's, I claimed her as my own. It was then my father chose to take his own life."

"Oh, dear heaven." Briana moaned aloud. The horror of this was growing, layer upon layer, with every word from his lips. She couldn't even find any words of consolation for the death of his father. And so she remained silent.

"We named the child Alana."

Briana blinked. At last, there was the name she had heard. Not his wife. His daughter.

"When last seen, she was a beautiful little infant, with her mother's lovely, perfect features, and the dark hair that was so much a part of the O'Mara heritage." He picked up the framed miniature from his night table. In a blur of pain, Briana studied it.

"When last seen?" Her head came up sharply. "Does her mother not intend to return to Carrick House with her?"

"Her mother is dead." He said the words with absolutely no emotion.

Dead. Briana thought about the sadness she had sensed in Keane. And the pain she could see in his eyes when he thought no one was looking. No wonder he hadn't spoken about himself and his past. It would be far too painful for words. His father. His wife. Both gone.

As if determined to purge himself of every darkness, he continued in that same controlled manner. "The child lives with her mother's family on a grand estate outside London."

"But why?"

"I gave her to them."

"Gave? You don't mean you simply…gave away your only child?"

He turned then, and she could see that his eyes had gone as blank as his tone. "As Victoria's parents reminded me, I was the one who took away their child. It seemed only fair that I should give them mine in return. And I agreed."

"You…killed Victoria?"

"It was my…involvement in Irish politics that caused her death, as well as this wound, which will pain me to my grave. I was found relaying secrets to…my Irish connection. A battle ensued. Victoria was in the carriage, awaiting my return from the boat docked at shore. My attackers killed her, then lay in wait for me. I wasn't as lucky as Victoria. I lived."

"You wanted to die?"

"Aye. I hated my life. Hated everything it stood for. I would have embraced death. It was why I was so good at what I did. A man who welcomes death is a dangerous opponent and an excellent spy. That was why I was recruited in the first place."

She licked her lips, afraid to ask the question, but needing to hear the answer. "Do you still wish to die?"

For long moments he didn't answer. He merely stared out over the silvery landscape. At last he said, "Nay. I've finally found a reason to live. But I know I don't deserve it. I don't deserve you."

"Is that why you're telling me all this? Because you think you don't deserve me?"

"Aye." He walked closer and stared down at her, seeing in her eyes all the pain and confusion and doubt his words had caused. "You're the finest woman I've ever known, Briana. Far too fine for a monster like me. I should have told you all this so long ago."

"Why didn't you?"

"Add coward to the many other things I am. I didn't want to see in your eyes what I'm seeing now."

Her tone was as bleak as her heart. This was all too much to take in at one time. "And now that I know, what do you expect me to do about it?"

"I expect you'll want to leave for your home." He picked up the decanter of ale and headed toward the door. He intended, in the few hours left before dawn, to get roaring drunk. In the doorway he turned. "I'll arrange it first thing on the morrow."

The door closed behind him. Leaving Briana alone with thoughts that were as distressing, as desolate, as the sky outside the window.

Briana stood on the balcony in the predawn chill. For hours she had paced, much the same way Keane had when he'd relayed his painful tale of horrors.

She would have given anything if he had never told her about his past. She much preferred ignorance to this pain that gripped her heart in its chilling vise. The pain was almost more than she could endure. A pain she feared might never end.

A wife, she thought, clenching her hands into fists. Not just a wife. A wife who had once been his father's mistress. What sort of man could betray his own father that way?

The answer came at once. One who had been so badly hurt as a child, he'd had no room in his heart for forgiveness. A man who had lost everyone he'd ever loved. She thought of her own family. Loud and impatient and wildly outrageous. But always loving. What would it be like to be all alone, with no one to care or to care about? The mere thought of it brought a lump to her throat that threatened to choke her.

Nay, she would not give in to such maudlin thoughts. Keane O'Mara was a man who had not only stolen his father's mistress and made her his wife, but had abandoned his own child, as well. How could he do that, after having been abandoned himself?

Again, she felt the answer in the stillness of her heart. Keane O'Mara was a man who believed he didn't even deserve the love of his own child.

And now, he fully intended to drive Briana away, as well. Not because he didn't love her, but because he felt unworthy of her love. Of any love.

He was a man who didn't fear death. A man, in fact, who embraced it. Because he believed, in the deepest recesses of his soul, that he didn't deserve to live a life of ease and contentment.

The dismal bleakness of his existence touched her as nothing else ever had.

She lifted her head, watching as the first thin strands of light began to chase the darkness. Seeing it, she was reminded of something she had read in the Book of Prayers.

As surely as light follows darkness, goodness will always prevail over evil. But only so long as good men are willing to risk whatever necessary to that end.

The words continued playing through her mind, resonating with hope. Suddenly she turned from the balcony and raced from the room.

She found Keane in the library. Except for the red glow of coals on the grate, the room was dark and cold. Keane was merely a shadowy figure, standing unsteadily by the window, a glass in his hand.

When he caught sight of her he snarled, "Go away, Briana. I'm not fit company."

Instead of a reply, she merely tossed a log on the fire and stood watching as flames began to lick along the dry bark.

"I said go away." He weaved slightly as he turned his back on her.

"Have you told me everything now, Keane?"

He refused to turn around. "Are you hoping for a few more scandals? A grisly murder perhaps? A few mutilated corpses? Haven't I said enough to shock your delicate sensibilities?"

"I just want to be certain there isn't anything else."

He lifted a hand, let it drop. "I've told you everything, Briana. And I give you my word, I'll make arrangements for you to return to Ballinarin on the morrow."

"It isn't Ballinarin I wish to go to."

He turned his head to look at her. "Where then?"

She took a deep breath. "If you truly believe that you are a monster, a scoundrel, a wastrel like your father, why don't you take steps to change your life for the better?"

He gave a dry laugh. "And how would you suggest I do that now?"

She thought a moment. "You spoke of the child. Alana. Do you love her?"

"Aye. It wasn't her fault that her father was a liar and a cheat, and that her mother was a…" He rubbed a hand over his eyes. "Forgive me. I'll not speak ill of the dead. Victoria's sins are buried with her now. My own are far worse."

"Do you believe that we can atone for past sins?"

He sighed. "I once thought so. Now, I'm not so sure."

"Tell me, Keane. How do you feel now that you've armed the villagers and taught them to defend themselves? Do you think it somehow atones for the sins of your father?"

"I hope so. Indeed, it's one of the reasons why I allowed you to persuade me of it. I wanted to restore respect for the O'Mara name once more."

"Then, what would it take to atone for the sin of giving away your child?"

He studied her for long, silent moments. "Are you thinking that I should take her back?" Seeing her smile, he shook his head. "It isn't that simple, Briana. Her grandparents are her fierce protectors. They employ an army of soldiers to guard the grounds of their estate, just to see that I never change my mind and try to take her from them."

"Will they allow you to visit her?"

He shrugged. "I haven't seen her since I left England more than three months ago. They made it plain that they didn't want me to return."

"How did Alana react when you left?"

He winced, hating the memory. The very thought of it had him tipping up his glass and draining it. "She's only an infant. She couldn't understand why her father was abandoning her. But she wept bitter tears and was weeping still as I drove off in my carriage. The sound of her cries tears constantly at my heart."

Briana thought of little Daniel McCann, his chubby fingers tugging on her hair, his sunny smile touching her heart. She knew now that her decision was the right one.

As she started toward the door Keane called, "Where are you going?"

"To tell Cora to pack a trunk with clothes suitable for a journey to England."

Chapter Nineteen

The fine carriage rolled through the streets of London. Briana, seated beside Keane, looked like any other English beauty, her gown of emerald satin with matching bonnet the height of fashion. Across from them sat Mistress Malloy. In the driver's seat was Vinson. The housekeeper and butler wore matching dazed expressions.

And no wonder. There had been no time to consider the magnitude of this undertaking. There had been the trunks to pack, the long carriage ride to Dublin, where they had boarded the ship that brought them to London. And now, within hours of departing the boat, they were on their way to Greyhall, the Cranmer estate outside London.

It was only now, as she glanced at the green parks with children playing under the watchful eye of their nurses, and she heard the voices, so different from the soft brogue she'd always known, that Briana realized the enormity of what she'd done.

She shivered and Keane reached over to catch her hand. "Cold?"

He would never know if it had been the ale that had

caused him to go along with this charade, or if he had simply wanted this all along. Whatever the reason, he had permitted himself, like his butler and housekeeper, to be caught up in Briana's elaborate plans. But now that he was back on English soil, his old instincts took over. He wanted, needed, to make amends for the life he'd lived here. Especially for the sake of little Alana.

"A little." While he warmed her fingers between his big hands, Briana muttered, "I must stop this. The lies come much too easily to my lips these days." She took a deep breath. "The truth is, I'm not cold. I'm afraid."

"Good." He grinned. Winked. "That means you're human after all. I was beginning to think you were some sort of angel."

"If you'd ask my family, they'd tell you a devil is closer to the truth."

"Even better. I'm much more comfortable with devils than angels." He straightened as the high gates of Greyhall came into view. "Now you must listen to me, Briana." He stared down into her eyes. "You musn't get your hopes up too much. I agreed to this only because I could come up with nothing better." And because he couldn't bear the thought of letting her go. As long as she was plotting and scheming, she wasn't thinking about leaving him and returning to Ballinarin. "But I know Lord and Lady Cranmer. They'll never consent to letting Alana go. Not without a fight."

"Still, Keane, we have to try."

"Aye." He gave her a smile of encouragement. "We'll try. And if necessary, we'll be gracious in defeat."

She lifted her chin a fraction as Vinson announced them and the gate swung wide to admit their carriage.

The road leading to the manor house wound through sumptuous acres of manicured hedges and carefully tended gardens. Here and there servants could be seen, pruning trees, cleaning fountains.

When at last they came to a halt in the courtyard, Keane climbed down, then assisted Briana and Mistress Malloy from the carriage.

"You'll wait here," he said to Vinson. "I doubt we'll be long. Our hosts won't be inclined to invite us to stay and sup with them."

The old man nodded.

With Briana at his side, and Mistress Malloy trailing behind, Keane started toward the entrance, where a butler stood at attention.

"Good day, Farley."

The old man looked down his nose. "My lord."

"I sent word that I was coming. Lord and Lady Cranmer are expecting me."

"Aye, my lord." The butler stood aside as they entered, then led the way along a hallway toward the parlor.

After announcing them, he held the door, then discreetly stood to one side, awaiting his orders.

"Lord Alcott." A gray-haired man in blue satin coat and breeches stepped forward and offered his hand.

Keane returned the stiff handshake, then said, "May I present Briana O'Neil. Briana, Lord and Lady Cranmer."

Lord Cranmer bowed over Briana's hand. "Miss O'Neil."

His wife, as wide as she was tall, was wearing a

gown of pale pink satin, with a neckline that revealed
ropes of pearls that all but disappeared in mounds of
pasty flesh. She had apparently donned as much jew-
elry as she could manage, in order to remind her guests
of her extreme wealth. She gave a barely perceptible
nod of her head in greeting.

"My wife and I are surprised by your visit."

"I don't know why you should be." Keane was
careful to keep the anger from his voice. "I came to
see my daughter."

"It isn't convenient." Lady Cranmer's tone was
pure ice. "The child is with her nurse. There are
schedules to see to. When to eat. When to sleep. I
don't believe in veering from such schedules."

"And when does she play?" Keane demanded.

"Play?" The woman's eyes flashed. "Babies don't
need to play, Lord Alcott. What they need is a firm
hand. And a nurse trained in the discipline of child
rearing."

"Is this the same nurse who raised Victoria?" As
Keane's temper went up a notch, so did his voice.

The older woman flushed at the reminder of what
her daughter had become. A mistress to one Irishman,
and wife to another. "I'll not tolerate that tone in my
house."

Briana, seeing the temper flare in Keane's eyes,
stepped between them. "I'm sure you won't object if
we just go up and have a nice visit with Alana and
her nurse?"

"But I do object." Lady Cranmer looked to her
husband for support. "The child has forgotten you,
Lord Alcott. You'll only stir her up again."

"The child?" Keane clenched a fist at his side. "Do

you ever call her by name? Her name is Alana. Do you ever hold Alana? Kiss her? Cuddle her?''

At the dark look in his eye, Lady Cranmer took a step back and lifted her head. ''Now you see why we must forbid you from seeing the child. If she has inherited that temper, Lord Alcott, it is up to us to see that it is eliminated before she grows to be a bold, defiant young woman.''

''What will you do? Beat it out of her?''

''We shall see that it is eliminated. By whatever means necessary.''

Seeing that Keane and Lady Cranmer had reached an impasse, Briana turned to Lord Cranmer, giving him her brightest, most persuasive smile.

''I don't believe that Lord Alcott has explained my presence here.''

''Nay, my lady.'' Ever the gentleman, Lord Cranmer seemed as determined as Briana to remain civil throughout this awkward ordeal.

''Lord Alcott and I are to be wed.'' She saw the way Keane's head swiveled and chose to ignore him. ''And I thought, before the wedding, I would present his child with a few gifts.''

''How very sweet, my dear.'' The older man actually managed a smile. ''Did you bring these gifts with you?''

''Aye.'' Briana nodded toward Mistress Malloy, who fumbled in her satchel and removed a soft, hide-covered ball, much like the one she had presented to Daniel McCann. Then she unwrapped the animal-shaped cakes which Cook had baked and carefully wrapped in linen squares.

''Perhaps, while Lord Alcott visits with you here,

our housekeeper and I might be allowed to have a glimpse of Alana.''

The older man glanced toward his wife for approval. When she gave a grudging nod of her head, he turned to the butler. ''Will you show the ladies the way, Farley?''

''Aye, my lord.''

''And see that one of our soldiers accompanies them as well,'' Lady Cranmer said through gritted teeth. She was leaving nothing to chance.

The butler left and returned minutes later with a swordsman. Briana and Mistress Malloy followed them up the stairs to a second-story suite. Inside, a dour-faced nursemaid rocked in a chair by the fire, while a dark-haired infant sat in a small enclosure made by lining up several chaises to form a barricade along one side of the room.

''Maida,'' the butler called. ''Lady Cranmer has sent these ladies to have a visit with the child.''

The nursemaid didn't bother to get up. ''Have your visit then. But don't be long. It'll soon be time for her rest.''

Briana managed her most charming smile as she turned to the butler. ''Thank you, Farley. I'm sure the two of you would be more comfortable waiting in the hall. I noticed a bench that looked most inviting.''

The soldier and butler glanced at each other, then nodded.

''We would indeed, my lady,'' Farley muttered.

As the door was closing, Briana could see the two men walking toward the bench, which was only steps away from the nursery.

She crossed to the little girl and reached out her

hands. "Oh, look at you. Aren't you the prettiest little thing in the whole world."

And she was indeed. With eyes that would rival the bluest summer sky, and glossy dark curls framing the face of a cherub.

At the sound of Briana's lilting voice, the child smiled and lifted her arms.

Briana picked her up, cradling her against her chest. "Would you like to see what I've brought you?"

When she held out the ball, the little girl did exactly what baby Daniel had done, tasting it, chewing it and cooing with delight.

Briana sat her down in the middle of the room and began rolling the ball toward her. Excited at the prospect of playing, Alana clapped her hands and snatched up the ball, chewing and drooling.

"Look what else we have, luv." Mistress Malloy, getting into the spirit of the game, reached into her satchel and brought out one of the little animal cakes. Breaking off a small piece, she handed it to Alana, who stuffed it into her mouth and waited for more.

"Here now." The nurse came out of her chair with a vengeance and advanced on them. "The child isn't allowed to eat sweets."

"I don't think a little taste will hurt her." Briana winked at the housekeeper. "What do you say, Mistress Malloy?"

"I quite agree." The older woman sniffed. "Why, when Lord Alcott was a lad, Cook always used to sneak him bits of sweets. She thought it helped make up for his loneliness."

"Well, such frivolous things aren't permitted here at Greyhall. I'll take that." The nursemaid reached down and took the cake from the housekeeper's hand.

Then, to assure that it wouldn't be given to the child, she stuffed it into her own mouth before returning to her chair by the fire.

"Oh, that wasn't very nice of you." Mistress Malloy showed a flash of temper, quickly unwrapping a second cake and feeding a small piece to Alana.

But Briana surprised the housekeeper by shaking her head.

"You're quite right, Maida. Maybe you'd care for another cake."

The nursemaid nodded. "I would indeed. I've a taste for sweets."

"Mistress Malloy, see if you can find more cakes in that satchel," Briana said.

The old woman rummaged through her bag and came up with a third, and even a fourth cake, which she dutifully handed over to the nurse.

"And perhaps, while you're eating it, Maida, you'd be willing to show us the rest of the nursery." Briana scooped up the infant, eager to take her as far away from the men outside the door as possible.

"There's not much." Almost sluggishly the nurse heaved herself out of the chair and led the way to the sleeping chamber. Inside was a bed for the baby, and another for the nurse. Beside the bed was a night table. Positioned in front of the fire was a chaise. On the far wall was a wardrobe.

Briana's gaze moved to the wardrobe, assessing its size, before motioning to the housekeeper. "Oh, look at the lovely view from that balcony."

"The view?" Mistress Malloy looked slightly confused. But when Briana arched a brow, she turned. "Ah. Yes. The view. It's lovely."

"Wouldn't you like to enjoy it? Just for a few moments?" Briana urged.

"Aye. I suppose I would."

"Here, Mistress Malloy." Briana thrust the baby into her arms. "Perhaps Alana would like a bit of fresh air as well."

As the housekeeper carried the baby to the balcony, the nursemaid sat down on the edge of the bed and yawned.

"You might want to keep an eye on your little charge," Briana admonished her.

"Aye. Of course. I'm not supposed to let her out of my sight." Struggling to stifle another yawn, the nursemaid walked slowly to the balcony.

Alone in the room, Briana snatched up a shawl and a blanket, then made her way to the two women.

"Here now. What've you got there?" The nursemaid's tone was challenging.

"Just something to ward off the breeze." Briana casually handed the shawl to Mistress Malloy, saying, "You might want to cover Alana so she doesn't take a chill."

She then opened the blanket and smiled. The nursemaid arched a brow. "Is that for me?"

"Aye. Since you've been in these stuffy chambers, you might want to wrap it around you." Briana draped it around the woman's shoulders, leaving the rest dangling to the floor.

While Mistress Malloy watched in amazement, the nursemaid's eyes began to close. For a moment she clung to the edge of the balcony for support. Then she fell backward as though in a faint. The blanket cushioned her fall and she landed with a soft thud.

"What...whatever has happened to her? Here now,

lass, what are you doing?'' Mistress Malloy demanded as Briana began to haul the blanket and its burden toward the wardrobe.

''Just seeing to it that she's made comfortable for a while.''

''I don't under—''

''Hush, Mistress Malloy. There's no time for explanations.'' Briana rolled and shoved until the nursemaid was safely tucked into the wardrobe, with the blanket wrapped so firmly around her, she couldn't move her arms or legs. Then she forced the door closed and motioned for the housekeeper to follow her to the other room.

''Oh, what have you done?'' Mistress Malloy moaned. ''What in the world is going on here?''

''I've disposed of one problem.'' Briana pointed to the child, sleeping peacefully in Mistress Malloy's arms. The housekeeper seemed amazed that the child had fallen asleep so quickly.

Briana draped the shawl around the housekeeper's shoulders, then allowed the ends to dangle loosely in front, completely hiding the fact that the child was in her arms. ''Now, in order to see this to its conclusion, you must do exactly as I tell you. And, for heaven's sake, act as though nothing is amiss.''

''Act as though...'' The housekeeper's face had turned the color of raw dough. Her voice was edging toward hysteria. ''Act as though...''

''Hush now. Not a word.'' Briana touched a finger to her lips.

At that precise moment the door was thrown open. Farley stepped inside and glanced around, the swordsman behind him. ''Where is Maida?''

Thinking quickly, Briana kept her fingers on her

lips. "Shh. She's putting Alana down for her rest. She asked that we not disturb her."

The soldier drew his sword and stepped around the butler. "I was told to see that no harm should come to the nursemaid and the babe. I'll just have a look for myself."

Terrified, Mistress Malloy opened her mouth to speak. But all that came out was a squeak.

"Aye, I suppose that's best." Briana gave a shaky laugh. "Though I do hope you don't place too much value on your life. Maida threatened us with mayhem if we disturbed the child's sleep."

"Aye." The butler, aware of the nursemaid's temper, nodded in agreement. "I've tasted the back of her hand a time or two. As has the child."

Briana sucked in a breath of anger.

The soldier, prodded by the butler's words, seemed to think better of it and turned away. "I'll just keep my vigil out in the hall, until the child awakes."

Farley nodded and held the door. When they exited, he said stiffly, "You will follow me back to the parlor."

Briana held back, placing a hand beneath the housekeeper's elbow. The old woman was trembling so violently, even her hair was shaking.

"I believe this journey has been too much for you, Mistress Malloy." Briana didn't need to pretend concern for the old woman. She feared at any moment the poor old thing might just keel over.

When they reached the foot of the stairs Briana said, "I think you should wait in the carriage with Vinson."

"Aye." The housekeeper's voice was a croak of alarm.

"I'll help her," the butler said as he opened the front door.

"Nay. Lord Alcott's manservant is just outside." Briana stepped out the door and motioned for Vinson, who hurried over. "See that Mistress Malloy is made comfortable in the carriage. Lord Alcott and I will be joining you shortly." Under her breath she whispered, "Hold tightly to her, Vinson. She may yet faint."

"Aye, my lady."

Briana took a deep breath, then followed Farley to the parlor, where Keane and the Cranmers sat glowering at one another.

"Here you are." Feeling slightly breathless, Briana crossed the room and caught Keane's hand. "I think it's time we left."

"Not until I am permitted to see my daughter."

Briana's head snapped up. "What? When did you decide this?"

"Now. I've not come all the way to England just to be turned away at her door. I have no intention of leaving here until I'm allowed a visit."

"But..." Briana hadn't counted on this. She chewed her lip. She had to get him out of here. And quickly. Before the nursemaid awoke and managed to free herself and shout a warning to the soldier outside her door. The opiates she'd put in the cakes were the smallest dose possible, because she'd expected to use them only on the baby. Even now, Maida could be coming round. It was only a matter of minutes before this whole scheme would begin to unravel, and they would be facing a score of armed soldiers.

"Alana is sleeping, Keane. If you should wake her, you'll only make her cry."

He turned on her with a look of pain and disbelief.

"I never expected this of you, Briana. Of all people, I thought you would stand with me in this."

"I do, Keane. Truly I do. But you must believe me. It is best for everyone if we go. Now." She tugged on his hand, desperate to flee.

Lady Cranmer narrowed a look on her husband, and he shot to his feet. "Farley, ask the captain of my guard to accompany Lord Alcott and his party from Greyhall. Immediately."

"Aye, my lord." The butler left, returning minutes later to announce, "The captain of the guard and his men have taken up their positions alongside Lord Alcott's carriage, my lord."

"Come, Lord Alcott." Lord Cranmer offered his arm to his wife. The two led the way to the front door, with Keane and Briana trailing slowly behind.

Briana saw Keane glance toward the stairway. Under his breath he muttered, "I'm a fool to go without seeing her. To have come so far, and to be denied my only chance."

"There will be other chances, Keane. Many other chances to see your daughter. You must believe me."

But his eyes were bleak as he paused at the foot of the stairs. "I'd fight a hundred men. A thousand, for one chance to free her from this hellish prison."

Briana closed her eyes. She had to get him out the door and into that carriage. It was their only hope.

"Come, Keane. Please, I beg of you."

When he merely stared at her she whispered frantically, "Trust me, love. And trust that I would never ask this of you unless I had a very good reason."

His eyes narrowed. He seemed about to offer resistance, but in the end he stepped out the door.

There were no civil handshakes as he took his leave.

He merely helped Briana into the carriage, then climbed in behind her. Without so much as a glance at the Cranmers he said stiffly, "Drive, Vinson."

"Aye, my lord."

The carriage jolted forward, with a line of soldiers on either side. As they followed the curving ribbon of road toward the high gate in the distance, Keane looked at the housekeeper.

"Mistress Malloy. You look as though you're feeling sick. Was Alana's treatment so bad then?"

The housekeeper couldn't manage a response. Her lower lip quivered, and she had to struggle to keep from crying.

The slow procession seemed to go on forever. And when at last they passed through the gate, and started back toward London, Keane leaned back and pressed a hand to his eyes. "What a fool I've been. All this," he muttered. "For nothing."

"Nothing?" At the sound of Briana's lilting laughter, he opened his eyes.

"Go ahead, Mistress Malloy," Briana said. "Give Keane his surprise."

"It was as much a surprise to me as it will be to you, my lord. Our lass confided her plans to no one."

"Only because I knew you'd have spoiled everything by fainting, Mistress Malloy. As it is, I feared you wouldn't make it out the door with our secret."

"What secret?" Keane demanded. "What is this all about?"

With trembling fingers, Mistress Malloy handed him her bulky shawl.

He arched a brow at Briana, then opened the shawl and stared at the baby, sleeping as peacefully as an angel.

"But how can this be? How did you…?"

She shook her head. "All in good time, my lord. For now, I think you'd better order Vinson to get us to the docks as quickly as possible. For any minute now, the Cranmers will discover what we've done. And I hardly think our two swords will be enough to stop their private army."

Chapter Twenty

"**P**raise heaven we're finally back on Irish soil." Mistress Malloy would have kissed the ground, if she hadn't felt so weak.

The journey across the Channel had been a nightmare of fears. All night, as they'd battled storms and wind and waves, they could see far behind them the lights of a ship following in their wake. They had no doubt the second ship was one commissioned by the Cranmers. The only thing that kept them from being overtaken was the forces of nature.

"We must get to Carrick quickly," Keane muttered as they climbed into a waiting carriage.

"Nay." Briana put a hand on his arm. "Think, Keane. Carrick House is the first place they'll look for us. I know a better place. A place where we'll be safe for as long as we choose to remain."

Keane arched a brow. "Your home?"

She nodded. "Aye." Her voice softened as she spoke the word. "Ballinarin."

Briana glanced at Mistress Malloy, lulled into sleep by the swaying motion of the carriage. Seated across from her was Vinson, also sleeping, now that they had employed a driver for the last half of their journey so that the elderly butler could take a much-needed rest.

Beside Vinson was Keane with his little daughter asleep in his arms. He had rarely let her out of his sight since they'd been reunited. He reached across to catch Briana's hand in his. "We need to talk."

"Aye. We will. Soon. I promise." She smiled at him, then turned to watch as familiar landmarks came into view.

They had spent the night in a small cozy tavern, tucked up under the eaves, with the sound of rain falling softly on the roof, and the laughter of strangers coming from the public room below. There had been no time to say the things that were in their hearts. Briana and Mistress Malloy had shared one room with Alana, who slept in a small wooden trundle beside their bed. Keane had shared the room next door with Vinson.

In the morning, while they'd shared a simple meal of gruel and meat and biscuits, their gazes had locked for one brief moment. They'd felt the curl of heat, the tug of familiar feelings deep inside, and knew that, when at last they reached their destination, they would be able to put the past behind them and look to the future. A future that suddenly looked considerably brighter with each mile.

"Look." Briana pointed, and Keane leaned forward to stare out the window. "Croagh Patrick. Our people have lived in its shadow for hundreds of years."

As the carriage veered through a pass carved out of stone, she pointed to the sides of the hills, cloaked with stunted, twisted shrubs and trees. "When I was a little girl, I thought a giant had come through here, slashing with his sword.''

''You were a fanciful child, I see.''

''Aye.'' As they exited the pass she nodded toward the waterfall, spilling hundreds of feet from the top of the mountain into the river below. ''It's easy to be fanciful in Ballinarin. It's a place apart. Lonely and wild. Savage and yet so beautiful. As though some heavenly artist had painted this scene, intent upon using every color. See there.'' She pointed to the clumps of rhododendrons, ablaze with reds and pinks and purples.

Keane followed her direction, hearing in her voice a softness, a reverence he hadn't heard before. ''Even the clouds are different here.''

''Aye.'' He glanced heavenward. The clouds above seemed torn and shredded by the wind. Some gauzy white, others with edges tinted gold and mauve in a sky so blue it hurt to look directly at it.

''You've come home, Briana.''

''Aye. At long last. Home.'' She had to take in a deep breath to keep from weeping.

As the carriage rolled through the village, a woman herding a flock of geese stopped to stare at the passengers in the carriage. Spying Briana's fiery hair she called, ''Look. It is Briana O'Neil.''

A husband and wife, tending their garden, looked up and joined in the chorus. ''Aye. So it is. I'd know that hair anywhere. Our lady Briana has returned.''

Then a cluster of lads heard the voices and one of them leapt on the back of a pony, shouting, ''I must take word to Ballinarin at once.'' Digging in his heels, he sped off to spread the news.

"I can see that our arrival won't be a surprise," Keane said with a smile.

"Nay. In our little part of Ireland, there are few secrets."

Keane watched as her hands, held firmly in her lap, clasped and unclasped. As the grey stones of the keep loomed up before them, her eyes filled. Tears rolled unchecked down her cheeks.

The doors to the keep were thrust open and voices could be heard shouting as people began spilling out into the courtyard. By the time the carriage came to a halt, every single person in Ballinarin had assembled. Cook and housekeeper. Scullery maid and stable lad.

Standing in front was the entire O'Neil family.

Keane stepped down and assisted Briana from the carriage.

"Oh. Sweet heaven, it's true then." Moira O'Neil raced forward to embrace her daughter. Her tears mingled with Briana's. "Oh, my sweet, beautiful daughter. You're truly back with us."

"Let me at her." Rory rushed forward and picked up his baby sister, swinging her around and around, as he had when she'd been a little girl. "God in heaven, how I've missed you."

"And I've missed you, Rory. Oh, how I've missed you."

As soon as he set her on her feet Conor came forward to hug her fiercely. "We feared the worst. When you never arrived home, we sent word to the abbey. Reverend Mother assured us you'd left months ago."

"Aye." Briana clung to him, then turned to take hold of Rory's shoulder as well. "There were times I feared I'd never see my big brothers again."

"What about me?"

She turned, and for a moment couldn't believe her eyes. "Can this be little Innis?"

He laughed and swept her into his arms.

When he set her down she caught his hands and held him a little away. "How can this be? You're as tall as Rory and Conor. You've become a man while I was away."

"I should hope so. Because you've become..." He tousled her hair. "You've become almost a woman."

"Almost? Keep a civil tongue." She turned to the two young women who had walked up to stand quietly beside her brothers. "AnnaClaire. Emma." She hugged one, then the other, before catching sight of the fullness of their gowns. "Can it be that I'm about to become an aunt, not once, but twice?"

"In fact," AnnaClaire said softly, "this will be your third time." She signalled to a small, dark-haired lad who was the image of Rory. "Come Patrick. Meet your Aunt Briana."

The lad held back, too shy to greet this stranger.

Briana felt tears threaten once more. "A nephew? And I didn't even know he existed."

Suddenly the crowd fell silent as one figure stepped forward. Gavin O'Neil looked the same as when Briana had last seen him. A lion's mane of silver hair framed a craggy face that was still rugged and handsome. Though his middle had thickened, he still bore the traces of a seasoned warrior, with broad shoulders and muscled arms.

For several seconds he merely stared at her, as though he couldn't quite believe his eyes.

"So. You've come home then." His voice was the same as well. A fierce growl.

"Aye."

''Well then. Come and give me a kiss.''

She closed the distance between them and pressed her lips to his cheek.

He caught her by the shoulders and held her a little away. His eyes narrowed as he studied the woman before him. His daughter. And yet, not his daughter. Where once she had been round, almost chubby, she was now thin and angular. Her lush mane of fiery tangles had been cropped, leaving a cap of curls framing a face that, if possible, had grown even more beautiful.

She had become a stranger.

While he studied her the others gathered around them, joining hands to form an unbroken circle.

From his position by the carriage, Keane watched, feeling at that moment like an intruder. And wondering what it must be like to belong to such a large, emotional family.

The voices became a chorus of questions.

''Where have you been?''

''How have you been living all these months?''

''What about the lads who accompanied you?''

Briana held up her hand. ''All in good time. For now, you must meet some people who have become very important in my life.''

She crossed to Keane and caught his hand, pulling him toward her family.

''This is Keane O'Mara. He saved my life. And now, for a little while, he seeks sanctuary here at Ballinarin. Keane, this is my family.''

Gavin O'Neil offered a stiff handshake, while Moira clasped his hand in both of hers and said, ''Our home is yours, Keane O'Mara. For as long as you desire.''

Rory and Conor mirrored their father's wary greeting, while their wives were as enthusiastic as Moira.

Briana waved the housekeeper and butler over. "Mistress Malloy and Vinson are carrying Keane's greatest treasure of all. His daughter, Alana."

"Oh, how precious she is." Moira opened her arms to the child, and, seeing the fatigue in the eyes of the old servants, became the efficient hostess. "You must come inside at once and let us make you comfortable. How far have you journeyed?"

As the housekeeper struggled to keep up she said, "Clear across Ireland. And before that, London."

"You were in England?" Gavin's eyes narrowed.

Briana caught Keane's arm and started toward the door. "Aye. But we'll tell you everything later, Father. For now, I wish to wash away the grime of our journey. And taste Cook's salmon."

"And so you shall." Moira turned to her daughter-in-law. "AnnaClaire, will you ask Cook to see that the lads catch some fresh salmon for our evening meal?"

"Aye." The young woman hurried away.

As she stepped inside, Briana paused a moment to drink in the familiar sights and scents of her home. Memories washed over her. Fresh tears filled her eyes.

Keane laid a hand over hers. "Are you all right?"

She took in a deep breath to calm herself. "Aye. It's just so...overwhelming."

"I know." He touched a hand to her cheek.

Just then Gavin walked in, stopped, then cleared his throat. Behind him, his two sons watched in silence.

"You'll want to refresh yourself in your old room, Briana," Gavin said sternly.

"Aye. Come with me, Keane. I'll show you where I spent the first ten and five years of my life."

"He can see that later." Gavin paused, then strove

for a softer tone. "I'm sure our guest would like some ale to wash away the dust of his travels." His eyes challenged. "Wouldn't you?"

Keane nodded. "Aye." He gave Briana a gentle smile. "You go ahead upstairs. I'll see you later."

She squeezed his hands. Then, with a swirl of skirts, she turned away and raced up the stairs.

Gavin led the way to his library, with Keane walking between Rory and Conor. All four men were grim-faced.

"Oh, this is wonderful." Briana sat between her two sisters-in-law, AnnaClaire and Emma. Keane was across the table, with Rory on one side of him and Conor on the other. As always, Gavin O'Neil sat at the head of the table, with his wife at the opposite end. Friar Malone sat on the right hand of Gavin, with Innis on his left.

"I must tell Cook that this salmon is even better than I'd remembered."

"I'll have her cook it every day now that you're home," Moira said. "We need to see that you eat more. You've grown very thin, Briana."

Briana laughed. "Now you're beginning to sound like Keane. He wondered if they'd ever fed me in the convent."

"How did you two become acquainted?" Friar Malone asked as he helped himself to a second portion. Ordinarily he curbed his appetite, as an act of self-denial. But this, he consoled himself, was a special occasion.

"Keane found me lying in a field, more dead than alive. He took me to his home, Carrick House, and nursed me back to life. If it weren't for him, I wouldn't be here now.''

"We are forever in your debt, my lord." Moira's eyes filled and she looked down, embarrassed that her emotions were so close to the surface. But it would have to be forgiven, for her youngest child was home with her. And her heart was so full, she thought it would surely burst.

"Tomorrow I'd like to visit the families of the lads who accompanied me." Briana pushed aside her plate. Suddenly her appetite had fled just thinking about the sad news she would have to relay.

"Why?" Gavin's voice boomed out the single word. It was the first time he'd spoken since the festive meal had begun.

"They need to know that their sons all died as heroes. They gave their lives to save mine."

"I'll tell them," he said firmly. "There's no need for you to speak of something so painful when you've just come back to Ballinarin."

"Aye. There is." Briana's voice was just as firm. "I was there. I saw what happened. Their families need to hear it from my lips. I'll be the one to tell them."

Gavin's eyes narrowed. "Are you defying me this way just to test my patience?

"Patience?" Briana returned his dark, angry stare without flinching. "When did you manage to acquire such a virtue as patience?"

He picked up his goblet and drank. His fingers tightened on the stem of the goblet. "I'll overlook such impertinence, since it's your first night under my roof. Perhaps you've forgotten, since you've been living at…" He turned and fixed Keane with a scowl.

"...Carrick House." He swung his look back to his daughter. "But in this house, my word is law. Anyone who dares to disobey me..."

"I know the rest." She shoved back her chair; got to her feet. "Anyone who dares to disobey you is banished. For you and you alone are judge, jury and executioner."

As she started to flounce away he leapt up and caught her arm. "You've never forgiven me for that, have you? It will always be there between us, festering, but never healing."

"That's where you're wrong, Father. It was the only sermon that was preached to me every day for three long years at the abbey. And finally, after a flood of tears, and even more prayers and more misery than you can ever imagine, I succeeded in forgiving you."

When the words were spoken aloud, she paused, realizing she had spoken the truth. In her heart she had truly forgiven her father.

She turned and laid a hand on his cheek. "Perhaps the problem is not my forgiveness. Perhaps it's time you looked in your own heart to see if you can forgive yourself."

For a moment there was only stunned silence. All those around the table seemed to hold their collective breath at the challenge hurled at Gavin O'Neil by his impertinent daughter.

Suddenly a cry of anguish was torn from Gavin's lips. "Oh, sweet heaven. I feared I'd never live to see my youngest child, my only daughter, again. Was terrified that my punishment would be that I'd never get to hold you again. And now you've come back to me. And I don't deserve you. I don't deserve this blessing. This second chance at happiness."

And then, while the others looked on in amazement, he dragged her against him and crushed her to his chest while he wept bitter tears of remorse.

Friar Malone looked up and was heard to mutter, "Praise be. Our Briana has done what no amount of prayers and fasting could have accomplished. I do believe there will finally be peace in Ballinarin."

"You must tell us everything." Emma looked up from the blanket she was knitting. She sat on a chaise beside AnnaClaire, whose young son, Patrick, had fallen asleep in her lap.

Moira sat in front of the fire, with Briana at her feet, cuddling a sleeping Alana against her chest.

"I'm told by Keane's servants that I would have died had he not fought for me."

"How romantic," AnnaClaire said. "Do you love him?"

Emma's needles went still.

"Aye. With all my heart."

"Does he love you?" Moira held her breath.

"Aye. I'm hoping Friar Malone can marry us while we're here at Ballinarin. Then, when we return to Carrick House, we can have another service there for the benefit of the villagers of Carrick, who have a great affection for Keane."

"Have you two spoken of all this?" Moira asked softly.

Briana smiled. "There is no need, Mother. We each know what is in the other's heart."

She saw the door to her father's library open. Her father and brothers and Keane had been behind closed doors for what seemed hours. She smiled, thinking about the silly haggling over dowry and the formal betrothal, which Friar Malone would no doubt announce at tomorrow morning's Mass.

As the men began to file out, Briana turned and handed the sleeping Alana to her mother, then made her way to Keane's side. "We were just talking about you."

"Briana."

He sounded so weary, she found herself glancing up into his eyes. They were dark and shuttered. And as icy as when she'd first met him.

"What is it, Keane? What's wrong?"

He took a deep breath and looked around at the others, who were watching and listening. "I didn't want to tell you like this. Perhaps we could find a more private moment."

"Nay." She felt a flutter of fear, then banked it. "Whatever you have to say, can be said in front of my family."

"All right." He took her hand between both of his and stared at it, avoiding her eyes. "I've decided to leave on the morrow."

"Leave Ballinarin? Where will you go?"

"Home. Back to Carrick House."

"But the Cranmers' army…"

"We have our own village militia now. I doubt the Cranmers are willing to face a hundred swords and knives for the sake of a child they don't really love. After all, they were merely using Alana to hurt me. I do believe they'll give up their claim to her now that she's back in Ireland. Perhaps, in time, our lives will all return to normal."

She smiled and squeezed his hands. "I pray it's so. I do wish we could have spent more time here at Ballinarin. I was just telling the others that I'd hoped Friar

Malone could be the one to bless our marriage. But if
you think it's best to leave, I'll be packed and ready
on the morrow.''

When she started to turn away, he caught her hands,
holding her still. ''You don't understand, Briana. I'm
afraid I didn't make myself clear. I'm returning to Carrick House tomorrow without you.''

''What…? Why…?'' She stopped, tried again.
''What do you mean? Keane, why are you saying
this?''

''You're home now, Briana. In the bosom of a family who loves you.''

''And I love them. But I love you too, Keane. It's
only right that I go with you.''

''I'm afraid that isn't possible. Your life is here
now, in Ballinarin.''

''Nay.'' She shook her head, sending red curls
dancing around her cheeks. ''My life is with you.''

''Briana, I know I saved your life. But you also
saved mine. We're…even now. And you musn't confuse gratitude with love.''

''Confuse…'' She felt her eyes fill and blinked furiously. ''I'm not confused. And what I feel isn't gratitude.''

''Of course it is. I'm grateful too, for all you've
done for me.''

There was a fine, thin edge of hysteria now in her
voice. It wavered as she shouted, ''Why are you doing
this, Keane?''

His voice was as calm as hers was frantic. ''I'm
getting on with my life. And you must do the same.''

''We aren't to be wed?''

''Nay.''

He watched as her face went white and bloodless.

Then she turned and fled up the stairs, while her whole family stood as still as death.

Without another word he made his way to the guest chambers and closed himself inside. It would be better, he thought, if his heart were to bleed where no one would witness it.

Chapter Twenty-One

Keane stood on the balcony, watching the stars, and thinking about the time he and Briana had watched them together. How long ago it seemed now. A lifetime ago.

There would be no sleep for him this night. His mind was in turmoil. His soul felt bruised and battered. And his heart was surely shattered beyond repair.

He looked up at the knock on his door; gave a hiss of disgust at the intrusion. Pulling it open, he was surprised to see Moira O'Neil standing in the hallway.

"May I come inside?" she asked softly.

"Of course." He stepped aside and waited until she entered, before closing the door.

She walked to the fireplace and stood a moment, staring into the flames. Then she turned to face him. "I think I know what you're doing."

"Do you?"

"Aye." She nodded. "You've seen my daughter returned to her loving family, and you feel you have no right to take her from it."

"That may be a small part of it. But I assure you,

there's much more involved here. There are things about me you don't know, madam.''

"I'm sure there are. We all have our secrets. But my daughter loves you, Keane. And I'm not sure she'll ever be the same if you leave her.''

"She'll survive." His tone warmed, softened. "Briana's a survivor.''

"She is that. And you love her." Moira put a hand on his arm and looked up into his eyes. "If I had any doubts before, I no longer have them now.''

He nodded. "Aye. I love her. With all my heart.''

She was silent a moment. Then she said, "Though I hardly know you, I do know this. What you do, I believe you do for the noblest of reasons. I can see in your eyes that it is breaking your heart to break Briana's heart.''

"I'll survive.''

She surprised him by lifting herself on tiptoe, much as her daughter, and pressing a kiss to his cheek. "I have very powerful prayers, Keane O'Mara. And I intend to pray that you change your mind.''

"There's no chance of that. But I do thank you, anyway.''

When she was gone, Vinson, who had been in the sleeping chambers preparing the lord's bed, walked through the doorway. Without a word he filled a tumbler with ale and handed it to Keane.

"Thank you," Keane said brusquely. "Go to bed now, old man.''

"Aye, my lord.''

As Vinson backed away Keane changed his mind. His harsh tone softened. "Wait. As long as you're here, Vinson, stay a moment. Pour yourself a glass of ale.''

Surprised, and more than a little pleased, the elderly servant did as he was told.

"Have you ever been in love, Vinson?"

The old man blinked. This was the last thing he'd ever have expected to be asked. "You know I've never wed, my lord."

"Aye. But that isn't what I need to know. Have you ever been in love? Truly in love?"

The old man stood a moment, studying the young man he'd known since the day of his birth. This was not a question to be answered lightly. The fact that Keane O'Mara was pacing the floor instead of retiring to his bed after such an exhausting journey spoke volumes about the depth of his concern.

Vinson cleared his throat. "I was. Once. She was the great love of my life."

"How did you feel?"

Vinson took a long time to think it over before saying, "Wonderful. And terrible. Bold. Terrified. Miserable. And miserably happy. So proud that she would even smile at me. And so humble when I learned that she shared my feelings."

Keane nodded, feeling a kinship with this old man. He'd felt all those emotions. And more. "Why didn't you wed, if she shared your feelings?"

"Her family considered me beneath their station. I was a manservant. That meant that she would have to spend her life in servitude as well."

Keane thought of Briana's comment to him. *We are all accidents of birth.* "Did she ever marry?"

The old man nodded, then took a long drink of ale to soothe the hurt that was still able to catch him by surprise after all these years. "Aye. She was given in marriage to a farmer. I heard that she bore him three sons.''

There was a look in the old man's eyes Keane had never seen before. And that, in turn, caused him to do something he'd never done. He stepped closer and clapped a hand on Vinson's shoulder. Squeezed gently. ''Thank you, Vinson. I'm grateful that you would speak of this to me.'' He lowered his hand and turned away. ''And I'm sorry that you were denied the chance to ever have a family of your own.''

The old man cleared his throat. Keane waited, with his back to him, knowing there was something more that Vinson needed to say.

''I've never felt denied the pleasure of a family, my lord. For I've always thought of you as my son.''

The door closed softly behind him.

Keane stood for long minutes, before returning to the balcony, where he watched clouds scudding over the moon and obscuring the stars. Though now he watched through the haze of mist that had somehow clouded his eyes.

Briana knelt by the balcony and watched the preparations for the journey going on in the courtyard below.

She got to her feet slowly, as if awakening from a dream. It occurred to her that she'd been kneeling here most of the night. And though she had dozed, she'd found no comfort in sleep.

She'd forced herself to go over in her mind everything Keane had said. Every cruel word. Every cutting phrase. But all she had come up with were more questions. How had Keane gone from lover to stranger in scant hours? Something had happened to cause this change in him. Something or someone had managed to convince him that he had no right to her love. Had convinced him to leave her, even if it meant breaking her heart.

But what or who? And why?

She detested this feeling of helplessness. It was exactly what she had suffered when she'd been banished to the abbey. She'd felt then that her life had been snatched from her, and she'd been helpless to take it back.

She began to pace furiously back and forth, rubbing at her temples. Think. She had to think. There had to be an answer. And she had to find it now. Or she would have the rest of her life to live once again with the endless days and nights of emptiness. And all the regrets.

Needing to take some sort of action, she let herself out of the keep and made her way to the stables. A ride across the verdant hills around Ballinarin had always helped to clear her mind and see the right path to take.

Keane descended the stairs to find the entire O'Neil family waiting for him, as well as Friar Malone. As his gaze swept the faces, he was almost relieved to see that Briana wasn't among them. He didn't know how he'd manage to hold together if he had to see her one last time.

Hopefully this would be easier. Of course, it meant that the last image he would have of her would be of her lovely face, twisted in shock. And the sound of those heart-wrenching tears.

He carefully wiped all thought from his mind. And

kept his tone devoid of emotion. "How kind of all of you to see us off on our journey."

"You're sure you won't agree to wait a few days?" Moira stepped away from her family and paused beside him. "Your housekeeper and butler must be exhausted. I'm sure they would relish a few days to recover before starting off across the country. Not to mention your darling little daughter."

At the mention of Alana, he blanched. Mistress Malloy had told him the child had cried for Briana until, exhausted, she'd cried herself to sleep.

He bent low over her hand. "We are most grateful for your hospitality, madam. But it's time we took our leave."

He shook hands with Briana's brothers, and managed a few words to each of their wives. Then he turned and offered his hand to Gavin O'Neil, who accepted stiffly.

They stepped out into the courtyard where Vinson was just helping Mistress Malloy into the carriage.

Keane glanced at a nearby wagon, loaded with food, blankets, fine linen. There was even a cradle tucked among the supplies.

"What is all this?"

Gavin shrugged. "I wanted to see to your comfort. You've a long journey ahead of you."

Keane's tone was cool, controlled. "That isn't necessary."

"I know it isn't. But I wanted to do something."

"To salve your conscience, Father?"

At the sound of Briana's voice, everyone turned.

She sat astride her favorite stallion. From the way the animal blew and snorted, it was obvious she'd pushed him to his limits.

She slid from his back and stood, feet apart, left hand on her hip. In her right hand was a sword.

"What are you doing with that?" Gavin demanded.

"It seems symbolic, Father. This was the start of my education."

"And what is that supposed to mean?"

"When I took up the family sword, I realized the meaning of power. The power to fight men on their own level. With this sword in my hand, men must listen to me. Without it, my voice is but a whisper on the wind." She turned to Keane. "Don't you agree?"

"What's the point, Briana?" His voice sounded tired. "We've said all there is to say."

"Nay, my lord. You've had your say. Now it's my turn. And you will listen." She turned to include her family. "All of you will have to listen. Because I hold the power."

Gavin started toward her. "By God, I'll not..."

She moved so quickly, it seemed no more than a flash of light. And suddenly the buttons on his tunic fell to the paved courtyard. There was a collective gasp from those watching.

At her audacity, Gavin took a step back, eyes wide with shock, and focused, really focused, on his daughter. When had she become so fierce? Aye. Fierce and...nearly as skilled as he. It would have taken great finesse to remove the buttons from a man's tunic without inflicting so much as a scratch.

"It took me a while. Most of the night, in fact, and all this morrow. But I finally managed to piece together what has been done here." Her voice was low with anger. "The O'Neil men have decided, as always, my fate. They've decided that Keane O'Mara is not a fit mate for the virginal Briana O'Neil, lately of the

Abbey of St. Claire. And even after you'd realized that
I was no longer that virgin, you decided that you knew
what was best for me."

"God in heaven, Briana. That you would speak
such things aloud." Rory's brow was furrowed with
brotherly concern. "Have you no shame? No pride?"

"Nay. I've none left. Thanks to all of you." She
pointed the tip of her sword at his chest. "Did you
know, Rory, that you were my first hero? The Black-
hearted O'Neil. Sweeping across the land in an orgy
of killing, bent on finding and destroying the man who
wiped out an entire clan. It was so heroic. So romantic.
Thus are legends born."

She turned, pressing the tip of her sword to Conor's
chest. "And you, Conor. Studying abroad and then
thrust into the danger and intrigue of Elizabeth's
Court, while at night you became the infamous
Heaven's Avenger. I wanted to be like you. To travel
the world. To taste the adventure."

"Is that why you believe God put you on this
earth?" Gavin O'Neil's face was red with anger. "To
compete with your brothers?"

"Compete with them, Father?" She laughed. "Nay.
Had I been born a man, I'd have bested them. But I
was born a female. And in your eyes, that meant I
must learn to be...docile." Her eyes flashed. "This
docile female has finally realized the truth."

"And what is this great truth?" he demanded.

"I know that Keane O'Mara has a past of which he
is now ashamed. Some of it was his own choosing.
And some of it he did reluctantly, because he was
convinced that such things were for the good of Ireland. He actually violated his own conscience, for the

sake of others. Would that not, in your opinion, make him a hero?''

Gavin eyed her narrowly and held his silence.

''I see you still disapprove, Father. What I didn't know until now, was the name of the person who would be so persuasive with such an impressionable young man.''

Gavin glanced at Keane, then back to his daughter. ''Did he reveal this information?''

''Nay, Father. Keane would never do such a thing. I've had to come to such conclusions on my own. You're a man of great charm and charisma, Father, when it is to your advantage to be. Mother has often told us how she left her home and family, and came to you without so much as a dowry, because she was so in love with the handsome, charming, *persuasive* Gavin O'Neil.''

His chin came up, in much the same way Briana's always did when she was angry or challenged. But to his credit, he managed to hold his silence.

''Now, Father, we'll talk about your persuasiveness. Or should I call it your dishonesty?''

''How dare...'' When she lifted the sword and took a step closer he blinked in amazement and clamped his mouth shut.

''Keane told me he was approached by one of the most influential men in Ireland. A man of great wealth and power. And even when he thought the plan was unconscionable, he was finally persuaded otherwise.'' She took a step closer. ''There is only one man I know who could hold such power over another. The man who taught us all, before we could even walk, that Ireland's freedom was more important than anything else in this world, including our very lives.''

"Do you now dispute that?" Gavin demanded.

"Nay, Father. You misunderstand. I am as fiercely patriotic as you. As Rory. As Conor." Her voice lowered, softened. "As Keane. In fact, Keane O'Mara is the finest, noblest man I've ever known. What he did, he did for Ireland. His sacrifice was great. Greater than you will ever know. For he was willing to give, not only his life, but his good name as well. And because of what he gave freely, you now consider him beneath you, unworthy to become a member of your fine, upstanding family." Her voice dropped to almost a whisper. "Just so you know. Keane O'Mara did not seduce me. Nor did he use his worldly knowledge to any advantage. In fact, he behaved in a most honorable manner, doing all in his power to protect my virtue. It was I who pursued him. What I gave him, I gave freely. Because I love him."

Gavin was outraged at her bold admission. "Consider what such coarse language is doing to your mother and to your brother's wives. Not to mention the good priest."

"Ah. I see." She smiled then. A chilling smile that did nothing to ease her father's frown. "Are you telling me, Father, that you waited until the good priest blessed your union before lying with my mother?"

"God in heaven, Briana." Rory and Conor stepped forward, shocked at their sister's behavior. "You would besmirch your own mother? Where have you learned such things?"

She turned on them. "Would you have me believe, Rory, that you never touched your beloved AnnaClaire until the day you wed her here at the chapel? Will you swear that in front of the good Friar Malone?"

AnnaClaire covered her mouth, to hide her smile.

Seeing it, Rory turned toward the old priest and saw his lips twitch. He clamped his mouth shut.

"And you, Conor." Briana turned toward her middle brother. "When you were tossed into all that passion and intrigue at the Court of Elizabeth, were you and Emma unmoved by it? Did you save yourselves for marriage?"

Conor clenched a fist at his side. "Be careful, little sister. I care not what you say about me. But leave Emma's name out of this scandalous talk."

Emma surprised him by laying a hand on his arm and smiling at her sister-in-law. "What you suggest happens to be very true, Briana."

At that, Briana managed a half smile. "Thank you, Emma. Your honesty is refreshing."

She turned to Keane, who had remained silent through this exchange. Pressing the tip of her sword to his chest she said, "Now we will talk about you, my lord. You think you know what is best for me? That you can decide, without consulting me, what will make me happy?"

"I saw your tears, Briana, when you first saw your home. And I saw the love in your eyes when you were surrounded by your family. Can you deny those feelings?"

"Nay. I love Ballinarin. And all who dwell here. And will for all my life. But that doesn't change the way I feel about you. And I know that you feel the same way about me. Can you deny it?"

When he said nothing, her smile flashed in triumph. "You see? You cannot say the words, for you know them to be a lie. Without me, what would your life be like now? It was I who persuaded you to teach your villagers to defend themselves. Was I not right to do so?''

''Aye.'' He watched her, loving the way the morning sunlight turned her hair to fire and her eyes to gold.

''Was I wrong to persuade you to go to England and reclaim your daughter?''

''Nay, Briana.'' She was so magnificent, she took his breath away. ''You were not wrong.''

''Then what must I do to persuade you to admit your love for me, Keane?''

''You can begin by lowering that damnable sword.''

''Nay. It is my only power. Without it...''

He caught her by surprise, dragging her close and wrenching the weapon from her hand. He tossed it aside with a clatter, muttering, ''Woman, haven't you yet figured out your true source of power? It's this.'' He drew her firmly against him and kissed her until they were both breathless.

Oh, how long he had wanted, needed this. Just touching her had the heat rising, the blood surging through his veins.

As for Briana, she was so stunned, all she could do was cling to him. She had been so desperately afraid. Afraid that her bold confrontation would only drive him further from her.

When at last he lifted his head, he was aware that the entire household was staring at them in stunned silence.

He flashed a wicked smile. ''Well, it would seem my plans have changed again.'' In one smooth leap he pulled himself onto her stallion's back, then reached down and lifted her into his arms. ''And it would seem, Gavin, that Briana has seen through all of us. If she can forgive me all the sins of my past, as she has forgiven you, what choice have I except to do her bidding?''

"Where are you going?" Gavin demanded.

"For now, we're going to find a quiet place where we can finish this...lover's quarrel, and come to some sort of understanding."

"And then?" Gavin shouted.

"Then, I think you and the good friar had better plan a wedding. The sooner the better." He wheeled his mount. "And Gavin, I'll expect a very large dowry to take this troublesome lass off your hands."

With a clatter of hooves he urged the horse across the courtyard, then headed toward a distant meadow.

When the others were far behind, he brought the animal to a halt and slid from the saddle, still cradling Briana in his arms.

"A very large dowry to take me off my father's hands. I can't believe you really..." The words died in her throat as he covered her mouth with his.

"God in heaven, Briana," he muttered inside her mouth. "Have you no mercy? I'm starved for the touch of you, the taste of you."

"Oh, Keane. No more than I. But I need to know. Did you mean it when you spoke of a wedding? I need to know our future...."

"This is our future," he muttered against her mouth, as he took it with a savageness that made them tremble. "You are my future, Briana O'Neil. From this day on, there is no past." They came together in a firestorm of passion, unlike any they'd known before. And as he lost himself in her he whispered fiercely, "There is only tomorrow. And all the tomorrows of our lives."

Epilogue

⤜⤛⟡⤜⤛

The chapel at Ballinarin, the ancestral home of the clan O'Neil, was filled to overflowing with family and friends who had come from as far as Malahide Castle in Dublin, and Bunratty Castle in Clare. The mood was festive as they prepared to witness the union of Briana O'Neil, only daughter of Gavin and Moira, and Keane O'Mara, Lord Alcott, rumored to be one of the wealthiest men in Ireland, and one of its greatest patriots.

In a small room off the chapel, Briana, wearing a gown of white, stood quietly, head bowed, lips moving. Sunlight spilling through a high, narrow stained-glass window bathed her in a rainbow of colors.

"Praying, are you?"

At the sound of Rory's voice, she looked up, then hurried forward. "Memorizing what I want to say to Keane."

"You needn't put yourself through so much trouble, little sister."

"And why not?"

He caught her hands and held her a little away, looking her up and down with approval. "When he sees you looking this beautiful, every single thought will go out of his brain. The poor fool won't know what happened until it's too late.''

"Oh, you.'' She hugged him, and he drew her close to press a kiss to her temple.

"I still can't believe my little sister is all grown up and getting married.''

"If you tell me one more time about how you used to carry me around on your back and be my obedient horse, I may have to throttle you.''

"And ruin that lovely gown?'' He laughed. But there was a twinge of sadness in his smile. "I hope you know that if you ever need me, for any reason, you need only send me a missive and I'll be at your side.''

She pressed her forehead to his. "Still my hero, are you?''

"Aye. And ashamed of how I let you down.''

"You didn't, Rory. I know you were just looking out for me.''

He swallowed, too overcome to say more. "I'd better join AnnaClaire. She has her hands full these days with young Patrick. I'll probably have to take him out of chapel halfway through the service.'' He squeezed her hand. "Be happy, Briana.''

She nodded and watched him walk away. Minutes later she looked up to see Conor standing in the doorway, studying her in silence.

"I've just left Keane,'' he said as he walked toward her. "And if it's any consolation, he's as nervous as I was on my wedding day. Like a warrior about to taste his first battle.''

She caught his hand, and offered her cheek for his quick kiss. "That doesn't sound like Keane.''

"You don't understand what marriage does to a man. Or rather the thought of a marriage ceremony, with pomp and pageantry and all."

"Would you do it again, Conor?"

He laughed and nodded. "Aye. For Emma. For myself, I'd rather be run over by a carriage."

Brother and sister shared an easy laugh. He took both her hands in his and lifted them to his lips. "I haven't been much of a brother to you these last years, Briana."

"You had no choice. I wasn't here."

"But I immersed myself in my own life, and gave little thought to what you were going through. I hope you and Keane will visit us often. I want us to have what we once did."

"I'd like that, too." She brushed a kiss over his cheek. "Even when we're apart, we'll always have something special that binds us together."

"Aye."

They both looked up at a timid knock on the door. Seeing Innis, Conor bid goodbye, leaving his sister alone with the lad who had once been her dearest friend.

"Innis." She hurried to his side and looped her arm through his. "I'd hoped you'd come to see me before the ceremony."

"We've seen little enough of each other since you've returned."

"Aye. My fault, I'm afraid. There was so much to catch up on. And the plans for the wedding."

"And Keane."

"Aye. And Keane." She waited a moment, then took a breath. "You don't approve?"

He shrugged. "It isn't for me to say. Rory and

Conor seem to like him well enough. Even your father's come around.''

"But not you?''

"It isn't Keane. He seems a decent sort. It's…'' He disengaged his arm from hers and crossed to the table, where her veil and prayer book lay. His big, work-worn fingers played with the edge of the veil. "I'd always thought…'' He tried again. "When you went away, I thought I'd die of loneliness.''

"I know. It was the same for me. At least you had Rory and Conor and their wives. And all the lads from the village.''

He looked up. Met her direct gaze. "They weren't you.''

And then she understood.

"Oh, Innis.'' She stood where she was, afraid to go to him. Afraid to touch him. He was so grown up now. Almost a man. With a man's feelings. She knew that she had to tread carefully. "Of all the things taken from me, losing you was the worst, Innis. You were my best friend. The brother I chose, rather than the ones given me by my family. The one I always opened my heart to. We stood together, against the others. The two outcasts. Remember? You, because you were the only survivor of your clan. And I, because I wanted so desperately to have what my brothers had.''

"Aye.'' He nodded. "That's it. We always stood together. And when you were sent away, I was more alone than ever. And I used to dream of storming the abbey and rescuing you from that horrible life.'' He ducked his head. "It shames me to admit that I never even tried.''

"Shame? Oh, no, Innis.'' She did go to him then, and threw her arms around his neck, hugging him fiercely. "We'll never know what might have been, if we'd never been separated. But this is now. I'm so happy. And I want you to be happy with me."

"What's this?"

At the stern voice from the doorway they both looked up. Keane was studying them with a frown. "I leave my bride-to-be alone for a moment and find her in the arms of this handsome lad."

Even though he blushed clear to his toes, Innis felt a sense of satisfaction, that a man like Keane O'Mara would consider him a threat.

"I hope you just came in here to wish Briana luck."

"Aye." The lad leaned over and kissed her on the cheek. His big hand squeezed her shoulder and suddenly he meant every word. "Luck and love, Briana."

"Thank you, Innis. You know I wish you the same. Always."

As the lad brushed past him Keane said, "There's a lovely lass out there with pale yellow hair and dimples in each cheek, who's been asking for a certain lad she claims is the finest horseman in all of Ballinarin. Would that be you, Innis?"

His smile brightened considerably. "Lindsay. Aye. I've been teaching her to ride."

"You'd best be careful, Innis." Keane winked and offered his hand. "I've seen what a dimpled smile can do to a man's heart."

"Aye." The lad accepted his handshake, and even clapped him on the shoulder. Then, with a quick glance toward Briana, he was gone.

Keane barely noticed his exit. He was too busy staring at the vision before him. "Ah, Briana. I've never seen you looking so lovely."

"You weren't supposed to see me until I walked to the altar."

"I couldn't wait. I had to see you this minute. Or die."

With a laugh she walked closer, touched a hand to his forehead. "I believe you do have a slight fever."

"Slight? I'm burning up. And feel this?" He caught her hand, placed it over his heart.

"Oh, my. It's racing like a runaway team."

"Aye. I'm not sure I'll make it through the ceremony. I think we should sneak away right now. We could have a village priest marry us on the way back to Carrick."

"I never took you for a coward, Keane O'Mara."

"You see? This is what you'll be stuck with for a lifetime. Maybe you'd better reconsider."

She laughed and wrapped her arms around his neck. "Not on your life. I went through too much to get you here. I'm not letting you get away now."

Against her lips he muttered, "Tell me. Did Mother Superior have an uplifting sermon for such an occasion as this?"

Her cheeks turned nearly as red as her hair. "I must confess something." She was so embarrassed, she didn't notice the way his mouth curved with humor. "I hated the sound of Mother Superior's voice. She was constantly preaching. And so I learned to close my mind to her, and take myself off in memory back to Ballinarin, riding across the green meadows with Innis and Rory and Conor. I...made up most of those things I attributed to her."

He did smile then. And pressed his lips to hers as he whispered, "You're not a very good liar, Briana. I figured it out a long time ago."

"You…knew I was lying?"

He touched a finger to her mouth, and felt the heat growing. "Aye. But you were such a joy to watch, I didn't have the heart to tell you. Oh, my beautiful, clever little Briana. What a wonderful delight you are. I can see that my life is always going to be filled with sweet surprises."

A shadow fell over them and they looked up to see Gavin O'Neil standing in the doorway, glowering at them.

"Could the two of you keep your hands off each other until after the ceremony? It's about to begin. The bishop's here and a cardinal from Rome. I thought I'd bring them in to talk to the two of you about your…marital duties and such."

Briana grinned, while Keane nearly choked.

"Nay, Father. I'll not speak to the bishop or the cardinal. I've told you before. They are free to assist at the Mass. But I want Friar Malone to be the one to say the words."

"Now, about this other business…" Gavin flushed. "Your mother tells me I'll not be giving you to your husband."

"Nay, Father. I give myself. Freely. Besides, I've just decided something. I wish to walk up the aisle beside Keane, carrying Alana in my arms. We're a family now. I want the whole world to know it."

"You'll scandalize the entire congregation, Briana."

"Aye, Father. I probably will. But it will be nothing new, will it?"

Gavin glared and turned to Keane, "I should be grateful you're taking this obstinate little female off my hands."

"Aye. You should indeed." Keane caught her hand and brought it to his lips while he smiled into her eyes. "And when she fills my home with children, I'll expect their grandfather to be as generous as he was with the dowry."

"You drive a hard bargain, Keane O'Mara."

"I had a good teacher, Gavin O'Neil."

"Come along, then. Let's finish this thing you've started."

As he turned away, Briana called, "Wait, Father."

He turned. She crossed to him and wrapped her arms around his neck. "I'll miss our battles," she murmured against his cheek.

"As will I." He drew her into his arms and closed his eyes for a moment, remembering the wee lass who used to snuggle against him just this way. She would, for all time, have the ability to tug at his heart. Or break it. "Know that I love you, Briana."

"And I love you, Father."

He turned away, brushing a tear from his eye.

The sound of a harp could be heard, filling the chapel with the sweetest of music.

Mistress Malloy and Vinson paused in the doorway and watched as Keane took Briana's hand.

"Excuse me," the housekeeper said. "I've brought Alana, as you asked, to watch from my arms as her father is wed."

"Thank you, Mistress Malloy. But I've changed my mind. She won't watch from afar. She'll be part of it. As she will always be a part of our lives."

Briana took the infant from her hands and cuddled her close. At once the little girl closed her chubby fist around a red curl and made soft cooing noises.

While Keane watched, the housekeeper lifted the veil from the table and settled it over Briana's head.

"Nay, Mistress Malloy. Lift it away from my face."

"But it isn't proper to show the bride's face before the ceremony."

"I don't want to hide, Mistress Malloy. I want to see where I'm going." She shot a quick brilliant smile at Keane. "And who I'm going with."

Keane threw back his head and chuckled. "I'd expect no less from you, my love."

The housekeeper did as she was told, then watched as Keane and Briana and baby Alana walked from the room and started up the aisle.

The old woman brushed a tear from her eye and stood in the back of church beside the butler.

"You're not sorry, are you Vinson?"

"Sorry?"

"That we threw those two together, for the sake of Carrick?"

The old man cleared his throat. Just a short while ago he and Keane had taken a quiet moment, to speak of love and life and the strange twists and turns that sometimes lead to the most glorious of surprises. This day, two of the most influential families in Ireland were being joined. And two of its most fiery leaders were uniting. What sort of warriors would their union produce? Only time would tell. But if he were a betting man...

"It all worked out for the best, didn't it, Vinson?"

"Aye, Mistress." He cleared his throat, and swallowed down the lump. "All for the best."

At the altar, Friar Malone was preaching about the mysteries of life, and the joys of love shared. Of the strength of family, and the loyalty to country.

For Briana O'Neil, everything he spoke of was here, in her lover's eyes. In his quiet strength. In his noble spirit.

Home, her heart whispered. And she found herself smiling through her tears. With Keane O'Mara at her side, she had truly come home.

* * * * *

"This book is DYNAMITE!"
—Kristine Rolofson

"A riveting page turner…"
—Joan Elliott Pickart

"Enough twists and turns to keep everyone guessing… What a ride!"
—Jule McBride

See what all your favorite authors are talking about.

Coming October 1999 to a retail store near you.

HARLEQUIN®
Makes any time special ™

Silhouette®

HARLEQUIN®
*M*akes any time special ™

WIN A DREAM

In celebration of Harlequin®'s golden anniversary

Enter to win a *dream!* You could win:

- A luxurious trip for two to *The Renaissance Cottonwoods Resort* in Scottsdale, Arizona, or

- A bouquet of flowers once a week for a year from **FTD**, or

- A $500 shopping spree, or

- A fabulous bath & body gift basket, including **K-tel**'s *Candlelight and Romance* 5-CD set.

Look for **WIN A DREAM** flash on specially marked Harlequin® titles by Penny Jordan, Dallas Schulze, Anne Stuart and Kristine Rolofson in October 1999*.

FTD · RENAISSANCE. COTTONWOODS RESORT · SCOTTSDALE, ARIZONA · **K·TEL**

COMING NEXT MONTH FROM

HARLEQUIN
HISTORICALS